When [   ]wn as
Baron Rac[   ] as the
Mad Baron, though he preferred [ ] called
Phinn—first set eyes on Lady Olivia Archer
at a ball, he understood *magnetism* in a way
he never had before.

Given that he was something of an expert
in it, this was remarkable.

He knew about the materials and forces at
work, but he'd never viscerally understood
the unseen force until he couldn't tug his attention from her. He'd never felt it.

Once he saw her, looking away was a
physical impossibility.

She had been standing alone on the balcony circling the ballroom, as if she were
lonely in a crowded room. It was a feeling he
knew all too well and one he didn't expect
to share with a woman. For a moment Phinn
stood there, disengaged from the crowd,
peering up at her, and observed. She had
lovely fair hair and a pale complexion. Her
every movement—from the slight tilt of her
head to the way she traced her fingers along
the balustrade—was controlled and graceful.

In a glance, he could see she was all he
wanted in a wife.

Maya Rodale

Wallflower Gone Wild

AVON

An Imprint of HarperCollinsPublishers

AVON BOOKS
An Imprint of HarperCollins*Publishers*
10 East 53rd Street
New York, New York 10022-5299

Copyright © 2014 by Maya Rodale
Excerpt from *The Bad Boy Billionaire's Girl Gone Wild* copyright © 2014 by Maya Rodale
ISBN 978-0-06-223126-0
www.avonromance.com

First Avon Books mass market printing: April 2014

Avon Trademark Reg. U.S. Pat. Off. and in Other Countries, Marca Registrada, Hecho en U.S.A.
HarperCollins® is a registered trademark of HarperCollins Publishers.

Printed in the U.S.A.

10 9 8 7 6 5 4 3 2 1

This book is dedicated to all the good girls.
And to Penelope, who follows the rules only as
they suit her.
And to Tony. Because I said so.

Acknowledgments

MANY THANKS TO Sara Jane Stone, Amanda Kimble-Evans, and Tony Haile, for reading early drafts of this manuscript. I am also indebted to Caroline Linden for allowing me to use *50 Ways to Sin*, the naughty book her characters read in her novel *Love and Other Scandals*.

Wallflower
Gone Wild

Prologue

"Let the great husband hunt begin!"

—LADY PENELOPE, TO HER GRADUATES

Lady Olivia Archer's first season
London, 1821

IN SPITE OF extensive preparation from Lady Penelope's Finishing School for Young Ladies of Fine Families, Lady Olivia Archer was a failure on the marriage mart. The season had scarcely begun when it was abundantly clear her education would be useless for attracting suitors.

"I daresay gentlemen don't care to hear about embroidery," Olivia remarked to her friends—and fellow wallflowers—Lady Emma Avery and Miss Prudence Merryweather Payton. She had just returned from one of the three dances on her otherwise empty dance card.

"We're supposed to ask gentlemen about themselves," Emma remarked. "But what are we to do if they ask us about ourselves?"

"Exactly! 'A young lady should be seen and not heard,'" Olivia said. It was one of The Rules they had dutifully learned. "But it would be rude not to reply."

"I tried that and it was a disaster," Prudence said with a shudder. "I spent a half hour listening to Lord Gifford talk about the drainage ditches on his estate."

Nearby, Lady Katherine Abernathy—their classmate from Lady P's—burst into laughter, along with the group of young, handsome, eligible bachelors surrounding her. It was safe to say they were not discussing drainage ditches. Or embroidery.

Olivia eyed Lady Katherine with something like jealously before stifling the sort of base emotion in which ladies did not indulge. No, ladies were serene and kind. The rule breakers traveled down a dangerous path of vice, onward to ruin. Proper ladies were rewarded with good husbands and every happiness.

But it looked like Lady Katherine was having an awfully good time.

"Perhaps we should have spent less time learning how to pour tea and more time learning to flirt," Olivia murmured as she watched Lady Katherine playfully bat her eyelashes at the hordes of young men around her.

By the end of Olivia's first season, even attempting to learn how to flirt would prove impossible, for men dared not venture into the wallflower corner of the ballroom, which was where Olivia spent most of her evenings.

Lady Olivia's second season
In ballrooms

Dressed in a modestly cut gown, made of fabric in a not very flattering shade of white, Olivia made the rounds of soirees and balls with her mother *constantly* by her side, wrangling gentlemen for conversation, since Olivia had spent "far too much time wallowing with her wallflower friends" instead of seeking a husband during her previous season.

"Tell Lord Stanton about your watercolors," Lady Archer urged.

Olivia obliged and watched the gentleman's eyes glaze over. Honestly, she couldn't blame him. Was there a duller subject than a young lady's watercolors? Nevertheless she told him of painting every afternoon on Tuesdays and Thursdays. Wickedly, she considered informing him that her favorite subject to paint was the male nude.

Wickedly, the idea actually appealed to her.

But to say such things in polite company was Not Done. So instead Olivia told him about the vexations of trying to paint a kitten with a ball of yarn. The gentleman patiently listened for a moment before excusing himself to refill his glass. Or say hello to someone. Or call for his carriage.

"Tell Lord Babington about your singing," Lady Archer suggested. "Olivia has a lovely voice."

Olivia obliged and saw Lord Babington's gaze wander. Truly, she understood. Was there anything sillier than speaking about one's singing? But the alternative was to burst into song right here in the ballroom.

Ladies do not burst into song.

But wouldn't it be funny if she did? Olivia stifled a giggle as she imagined it. Her mother's sharp elbow in her ribs restored her focus.

No. She would *never.*

But she thought about it.

"Tell Mr. Parker-Jones about your embroidery, Lady Olivia."

"I spend my free hours embroidering," Olivia said with a distinct lack of enthusiasm.

"How interesting," the gentleman murmured, when really it was the very definition of tedium. Meanwhile his attention was obviously drawn to Lady Katherine, who laughed at men's witty jokes all whilst leaning forward to display her bosom to an advantage.

Olivia had a very small bosom, which was always covered.

Ladies do not flaunt themselves.

"You mustn't speak so much of yourself, Olivia," her mother admonished and Olivia restrained an exasperated sigh.

Young ladies do not sigh exasperatedly.

"Gentlemen don't care to hear about the trials of ladies," her mother carried on, contradicting all the conversations she'd just foisted upon Olivia and unsuspecting men. "You must ask him about himself. It is every man's favorite subject."

Lord Pendleton did not disprove her mother.

Believing he had found an interested audience in Olivia, he expounded at length about his hunting dogs, his disgruntled tenants, and the vexations of a countryman in a big city like London.

Because ladies smiled prettily even if they were dying inside, Olivia did just that. But her gaze did stray to her fellow wallflower friends, laughing amongst themselves.

She couldn't help but notice all the handsome young gentlemen who flirted with the other girls who didn't have such overbearing mothers. Or a nickname like Prissy Missy because of their exceedingly proper manners and conversation.

Which was funny because deep down she didn't think of herself as a Prissy Missy. She was a girl who liked to sing and dance, who wished to flirt with rakes and be kissed improperly. Unfortunately, the circumstances were never quite right for her to be that girl. She was too busy being A Lady.

"Is that punch, Olivia? Ladies ought to have lemonade only." Olivia simply handed the glass to a passing footman. Never mind that a gentleman had offered it to her and her mother would have cautioned that A Lady wouldn't refuse.

Lady Olivia's **third** *season*
Lord Archer's library

At the beginning of her third season Olivia's parents requested her presence in the library for an interview about her marital prospects. Or distinct lack thereof. Truly, she was just as vexed by her single state. She wanted to be married. She wanted romance. She wanted a family of her own. But what could she do? She'd done everything *right*. She wore modest gowns, perfected ladylike habits and bit her tongue from impolite or forward comments. Still, the good husband and happiness she'd been promised eluded her.

Olivia perched upon a settee. Her parents sat opposite. The room was hardly used; Lord Archer spent most of his time at his club, avoiding his wife and daughter, except for when Grave Matters intruded.

"Olivia, now that you have finished your second season—" her mother began.

"Without making a match," her father grumbled, needlessly pointing out the painfully obvious. "After the investment we have made in your education."

"We must do better during your *third* season. I have made a list of prospects for you," her mother said, handing Olivia a sheet of paper. "We shall spend particular effort to further our acquaintance with these gentlemen whom your father and I find to be eminently suitable candidates."

With each name she read, Olivia felt queasier and queasier. If these were the Good Husbands she'd been promised, then she'd been tremendously deceived. If these were the husbands her parents thought her capable of snaring, then she was horrified.

"Lord Eccles?" Olivia questioned, looking up from the paper. "But he is positively ancient! I'm certain he predates the flood!"

"Young lady—" her father warned. One could discern the severity of his mood by the color of his face. At the moment, Olivia likened it to a rosé wine.

"Yes, but you'll be a viscountess and a well-off widow within a few years," her mother pointed out.

Olivia thought she might be sick on the carpet. Even though young ladies did not cast up their accounts in the library.

"And Lord Derby does not keep his hands to himself," Olivia said, shuddering. "Every young lady knows to steer clear of him."

"He also has six thousand a year and a plot of land adjoining one of our estates," her father replied as if that were all that mattered. As if her hopes and dreams were insignificant. As if her days and—shudder—nights with this man were beside the point. Not to her they weren't!

In the end the Horrid List mattered not one whit. While Olivia had at least learned not to talk about watercolors, embroidery, or her musical endeavors with gentlemen, the knowledge had come too late.

Finding herself in conversation with *any* gentleman—even candidates on the Horrid List—proved to be an impossibility. Her reputation preceded her: men lowered their gazes or turned away as she strolled through the ballroom fighting to keep her head held high and a smile on her face.

She thought about calling for their attention and making a speech: *Gentlemen, let me assure you that I have no interest in speaking of hair ribbons either. In fact, I'd be much obliged if one of you young handsome bucks were to kiss me instead.*

Obviously, she did no such thing. But imagining it kept a smile on her lips and her eyes dry.

Sometimes, that wasn't enough. When her mother was by her side, the aversion was even more obvious. At Lady Farnsworth's garden party, Mr. Middleton actually launched himself into a hedge to avoid the Archer women.

There were many people Olivia would have launched herself into a hedge to avoid. Like Lady Katherine Abernathy, Lord Derby, or Lord Eccles. But young ladies smiled and made polite conversation. They did not seek refuge in the shrubbery. And yet, she admired Mr. Middleton for doing as he wished, hang propriety.

As the calling hours and evening soirees ticked by, Olivia discovered that being a young lady was not all it was cracked up to be. But everyone said if she behaved and followed the rules, happiness would be hers. Lady Penelope had impressed this upon her students. Olivia's mother drilled it into her daughter. All the conduct books and purse-lipped dowagers only confirmed it.

Mr. Middleton and the hedge wasn't the worst. Not by a long shot.

She'd been named London's Least Likely to Cause a Scandal. Olivia had the distinct displeasure of learning this by overhearing a conversation between a group of young bucks, just down from Oxford. She'd eyed them longingly. They were the sort of men that made a girl's pulse race with nervous anticipation. She was no exception. Mustering her nerve, she forced herself to step closer, perhaps in their line of vision. Perhaps where one might notice her and ask her to dance.

She straightened her spine and tugged down her bodice as low as possible (admittedly not very far). Lingering nearby, she adopted Lady Katherine's pout, which men seemed to find irresistible.

The gents hardly noticed; they were in the throes of a lively conversation.

"After all, when could she cause a scandal? She's too busy with her hair ribbons and embroidery," said a tall, dark-haired stranger. Lud, he was handsome. Olivia inched closer, prepared to laugh at the silly girls who only bothered with hair ribbons and embroidery.

But then a ginger-haired fellow said, "Don't forget her watercolors and singing."

Olivia froze, afraid they were talking about her. Slowly, she started to inch backward, ashamed for thinking one of them would want to dance with her.

"Even if Prissy Missy were so inclined," another one said—and she knew they were speaking of her—"with that mother of hers constantly by her side, how could she even attempt anything scandalous?" The lot of them groaned at the mention of her mother.

"Lord save us all from the Archer ladies," another one said, and the others heartily agreed.

Olivia slinked away, heartbroken and horrified. Perhaps happily-ever-after was not for her.

Chapter 1

Lord Castleton, who embarked on his ritual grand tour and extended it by quite a few years, has sent word that he will soon return to England.

—"FASHIONABLE INTELLIGENCE"
BY A LADY OF DISTINCTION
THE LONDON WEEKLY

Lady Olivia's fourth season

As OLIVIA STOOD along the perimeter of the ballroom, amongst the wallflowers, she was achingly aware of the minutes ticking by. Minutes in which her prospects for marriage grew dimmer. She tried to calculate how many minutes were remaining before Lady Penelope's Ball commemorating the hundredth anniversary of the school, and thus how many minutes remained before she was a confirmed spinster, a failure on the marriage mart, and an utterly hopeless case.

No graduate in the history of the school had failed to make a match within four seasons. Except, perhaps, for Olivia. They might as well call her London's Least Likely to Marry.

"Is everything alright?" Prudence asked just

when Olivia was trying to divide forty-four days by the number of minutes in a day. "You look ill."

"I'm trying to do maths," Olivia explained, before giving up. She was terrible with numbers.

"It's not a good look for you," Prudence told her in the way that only a dearest friend would.

"What do you think of taking a turn about the ballroom?" Olivia asked. She was impatient just standing there. Waiting. Always, waiting.

"Yes, let's. How diverting," Prudence murmured. Arm in arm they ventured from the wallflower corner into the rest of the ballroom where, all around them, men and women flirted and conversed and arranged for marriages or assignations. They found their way to the balcony that lined the upper portion of the ballroom.

"There you both are!" Emma exclaimed. "I want to introduce you to some friends of Blake's."

Both Olivia and Prudence frowned. Blake was the Duke of Ashbrooke, and until he married Emma, had been a notorious libertine. His friends were not interested in the likes of London's Least Likely.

"I think that perhaps . . ." Olivia began. There was something about being foisted on uninterested gentlemen that her confidence couldn't quite take this evening. Much as she wanted to fall in love and marry, she was just exhausted with the constant failure of trying. It was time to consider what she might do instead. Perhaps she and Prudence could share a house and be spinsters together.

Emma was having none of that, though.

"Oh, do come!" she exclaimed before practically dragging Prudence with her.

"I'll be right there," Olivia said. "I just need a moment."

Slowly, she paced along the balcony, allowing her fingers to trail upon the balustrade. Gazing down, she watched the surge and pull of the crowd, enjoying the view of the dancers spinning in circles from high above . . . but *oh* how she wished to be among them. She was so tired of standing by, waiting.

And then she saw him.

Rather, she saw how the crowd moved around him. They seemed to step aside as if he were Someone of Great Importance. Like every other man in the room, he wore a suit of evening clothes. But the similarities seemed to end there. This man was taller, his shoulders broader. The way he moved suggested he was a man of determination and action. His hair was cut short but tussled, as if he'd pushed his fingers through it rakishly or . . . as if he'd wickedly come from a woman's bed.

One could easily imagine him as a rogue or a pirate. In fact, one did.

Intrigued, Olivia strolled slowly along the balcony, keeping pace with this man as he walked through the ballroom. *Who was he?* She didn't recognize him from previous parties. Perhaps he was the Lord Castleton mentioned in the newspapers—the one who was expected to return to town after an extended period abroad. Olivia didn't care: whoever he was, he was new and thus he didn't know that she was Prissy Missy or one of London's Least Likely. Her heart started beating in triple time at the possibilities.

And then, inexplicably, he turned and looked directly at her.

Her heartbeat stopped.

Her breath caught in her throat.

He was beautiful. And he was gazing intently at her. Until this moment, Olivia had no idea that one could *feel* another person's gaze from across the ballroom. She had never been hit by lightning, but she could imagine it might have felt something like this. She couldn't move. She couldn't breathe. She felt the spark of intrigue, the spark of lust, the spark of possibility.

She watched as he murmured something to a nearby friend before he started walking toward the stairs leading up to the balcony.

She had to meet him. Immediately.

Olivia walked quickly to the stairs leading down to the ballroom. Was this the moment she met the love of her life? All had seemed lost—was this the moment her lucked changed and her life truly began?

The handsome stranger was waiting for her at the bottom of the stairs. As Olivia made her way down, step by step, she thought how Lady Penelope's education had prepared her for this moment: after hours of walking up and down stairs with books on her head, she was now able to hold his gaze as she descended the stairs.

"Hello," he said. His voice was everything a man's ought to be: low and strong, and somehow the sound of it made her feel warm from the inside out.

Ladies did not converse with gentlemen to whom they were not introduced. She heard her mother's voice in her head, reminding her of the rules. But what was she to do—run off and find someone to introduce them? The spell would be broken. Even though it went against everything she'd been taught, she fought her instincts and whispered, "Hello."

The handsome stranger reached for her hand, which she gracefully extended. His fingers closed around hers. He pressed a kiss upon her hand. It was a perfectly proper gesture and yet it felt . . . wicked. She had never felt wicked before. Why had no one told her how thrilling it was?

For a moment they just gazed at each other.

And then, not having much practice speaking with gentlemen, she blurted out the first thing that came to mind: "Your eyes are very green."

Indeed they were: green, and shadowed by dark lashes, and when he smiled—as he did now—his eyes crinkled slightly at the corners. It was then that she noticed the scar. It was a thin slash stretching from his temple to his cheek-bone.

Who was this man? Where had he been these past four seasons?

He took a step closer to her and gazed down at her mouth. Her lips parted. Was this the moment of her first kiss? Olivia's every nerve tingled. It was those sparks again.

Stupid thoughts intruded, this time in the voice of Lady Penelope herself: *Ladies did not engage in unchaperoned interludes with gentlemen, acquainted or not.*

If she kissed him now, he might think she was That Sort of Girl. According to everything she'd been told, men did not marry That Sort of Girl. And given the almost palpable attraction between her and this stranger, she didn't think one kiss would be enough. Given that her sole aim in life was to marry, and immediately . . .

Olivia sighed, with wanting to be wicked and yet feeling so reined in by the rules.

Just as she started to consider throwing caution to the wind, wrapping her arms around this handsome stranger, and pressing her lips against his, the sharp and cruel voice of Lady Katherine intruded. Worse, she was accompanied by her coven of shrewish friends, including the Ladies Crawford, Mulberry, Falmouth, and Montague.

"Lady Olivia, is that you? *With a gentleman?*" Lady Katherine's incredulousness was all too clear. Olivia bit her lip in annoyance. Of course she would have to ruin this moment by intruding and informing this handsome stranger that he was with one of London's Least Likely. "I never thought I'd see the day."

The gentleman lifted his brow questioningly. Olivia wanted to die. Or perhaps flee. However, both the gentleman and the vicious pack of ladies blocked her path back to the ballroom.

She turned to glare at Lady Katherine as she passed by on the stairs. But Katherine just gave a cruel smile before pushing Olivia into the man's arms with a sudden nudge of her elbow.

He caught her, of course. Olivia gasped as she hit the firm wall of his chest. His arms closed around her for one precious, maddening second. Breathing deeply, she found herself intoxicated by his scent. For just a moment, she closed her eyes, wanting all the rules to vanish, along with Lady Katherine and the rest of the haute ton who called her Prissy Missy and London's Least Likely. She just wanted to *be* and she wanted to just be with this man, whoever he was.

Young ladies do not amorously embrace gentlemen to whom they are not married.

Her mother's voice intruded upon her thoughts with yet another rule, although . . .

"Oh my God," Olivia muttered. That *was* her mother's voice she heard nearby, inquiring if anyone had seen her daughter. Fearing her mother would discover her thusly—and ruin *everything* by having a hysterical fit or worse, telling

her to enlighten this man about her embroidery—
Olivia scrambled out of his embrace and fled into
the safety of the crowded ballroom, where her
mother found her and demanded they return
home directly because Lady Archer was feeling
unwell.

Olivia went to sleep dreaming of that handsome stranger and how they might meet again.

Chapter 2

Lady Penelope requests the attendance of her graduates and their husbands at a ball celebrating the one hundredth anniversary of the school.

—AN INVITATION

Lord Archer's library
The following day

OLIVIA RELUCTANTLY JOINED her parents in the study for what was likely to be another dreadful interview about her marital status. For approximately ten minutes the previous evening she thought there might be hope for her yet. If only she could see that handsome stranger again . . .

"Splendid news, Olivia!" her mother exclaimed with a bright smile upon her face.

"Oh?" Olivia said cautiously, having long ago learned they had very different ideas of splendid. "What is it?"

"Your father has an excellent prospect for your hand in marriage."

"Who is it?" The hair on the back of Olivia's neck stood up in warning. Her parents had, in their previous efforts, shown a deplorable definition of what made a gentleman excellent. She didn't dare entertain the possibility the handsome man from the night before had tracked her down and asked to wed her already.

"It's a good match!" Lady Archer said brightly. Perhaps even too brightly. Olivia's eyes narrowed. "His lordship has an income of ten thousand a year and . . . well, he is titled. He has asked to court you and has expressed an interest in marriage already!"

A formal agreement of courtship was tantamount to a betrothal, especially once the news hit the ton.

"Yes, but who is it?" Olivia asked impatiently. Was it that man with the green eyes? She hadn't any suitors, just a few gentlemen who asked for the occasional waltz or politely conversed with her when they found themselves idling in a ballroom. Not one of whom seemed to possess anything resembling an ardent passion for her, or even a remote inclination toward matrimony . . . or a title and ten thousand a year.

Her mother smiled. Her father cleared his throat.

" 'Tis Lord Radcliffe."

Olivia gave a startled cry as she leapt to her feet. *"The Mad Baron?* You cannot be serious!"

Every girl in London was familiar with the Mad Baron, who served as a cautionary tale of the perils of what lurked on the marriage mart. His first wife died under his roof—and under mysterious circumstances—after they had fought bitterly. Some say she'd been poisoned, others said she'd been strangled. What was agreed upon was that the circumstances were highly suspicious and not natural.

He never ventured into society, for who would receive him?

Every girl feared finding herself betrothed to the likes of him—a vile, reclusive, murderous seducer.

"You want to marry me off to the Mad Baron who reportedly killed his previous wife?" Olivia choked out the words and tears stung her eyes.

"He was never charged," her father remarked. A strangled sob escaped Olivia.

"Really, there is no need for hysterics," her mother said briskly. "It's just gossip. Ladies do not gossip."

"I do not want to be courted by him and I absolutely do not want marry him!" Olivia protested, finding it very difficult to modulate the tone of her voice.

"Nonsense! You don't even know him," her mother cried.

"Which is one of the reasons I would not like to be married to him," Olivia replied. She carried on, even though her father's face was pink and darkening into angry shades of scarlet. "We are strangers. What kind of man inquires about marrying a woman he's never met?"

The kind who was so reprehensible no woman would have him unless he resorted to such secretive and manipulative measures. Had they been properly introduced at a ball, she might have rebuffed him. But no, he'd now enlisted her parents in a formal courtship, which left her little recourse.

"He has seen you. And made inquiries about you," her father said. "Told me that he had come to London to find a wife and learned you were the kind of girl that didn't make trouble, which was exactly what he was looking for. I told him you were a docile, biddable girl who would make him a fine wife, and he was pleased to hear it."

"See, Olivia!" her mother said with glee. "All of our efforts have come to fruition. You are the perfect lady and shall make the perfect wife for this gentleman."

Olivia fell silent. She'd prepared her whole life to be the perfect lady and perfect wife for a perfect gentleman. Not a Mad Baron. Not a man who cared so little for her heart or mind or feelings that he wouldn't even arrange an informal meeting before a formal courtship. Not a man who *murdered his wife.*

She'd never been disobedient in her life. Even last night, when she'd had every temptation to act recklessly, she hadn't because good girls made good matches. The slow burn of regret started to smolder in her belly. If only she had done things differently in the beginning . . . or at least kissed that man last night. If only . . . if only . . .

It was too late for all that.

Or was it?

"I won't do it," Olivia said firmly. "Tell him that I said no."

"Olivia!" her mother shrieked. Even though ladies did not shriek.

"You must marry!" her father thundered. "Young ladies marry! That is what they do."

She knew it was pointless to explain that she *wanted* to marry. She just didn't want to marry *the Mad Baron*.

"No, thank you. I am ever so flattered by his attentions," she said with a nod toward politeness. "But the answer is no."

Her mother and father exchanged the sort of concerned glances that spoke volumes. There was a sinking feeling in her stomach and she wasn't quite sure she could breathe. This couldn't be happening. Not him. Not her. She'd been so good.

She did not deserve this.

"Well you see, daughter, the matter is all but settled," her father said gravely. "I have given my permission to the marriage. The contracts have been drawn up. All that awaits is a perfunctory courtship and your acceptance. Do you recall our conversation last season?"

"How could I forget?" Olivia asked bitterly.

"The fact of the matter is that you need to marry and you have shown that you require assistance in the endeavor," her father said. "We have made a suitable match for you. Lord Radcliffe has a title and a good income."

"His estate isn't too far from our country seat, so we can come make frequent visits," her mother said encouragingly.

Worse and worse! A vision of her future life as the Mad Baroness appeared before her eyes: long stretches of solitude punctured only by visits from her parents. That is, if she wasn't murdered on her wedding night.

She'd be bound irrevocably to a man who valued her for her docile, biddable nature. She'd never fall in love, or have a man fall in love with her.

"But what of my wishes?" Olivia whispered. "What of love or—"

"Olivia, it is high time you set aside such foolish notions," her mother said. "We'd like to have the banns read on Sunday."

In other words, she was to meet him. He was to propose. She was to say yes.

This was the moment where she ought to nod and thank her parents for sorting out the pesky business of who would own her for the rest of her life. A dutiful daughter would do it. A good girl would be grateful for the attention to her welfare. A better person would appeal to their emotions or care for her happiness.

Olivia had always been a dutiful daughter, a good girl, and a good person. And all it had landed her was a vile and violent fiancé. So she didn't thank them or wordlessly accept her fate. She appealed not to their emotion or reason. She simply refused.

"I won't do it." Her voice sounded foreign to

her ears—there was an edge and depth to it she'd never heard before.

"You will marry him, Olivia Elizabeth Catherine Archer—" her mother threatened.

"If I have to drag you down the aisle myself," Lord Archer finished, his face now the color of port.

To which Olivia uncharacteristically replied in a steely voice, "We shall see about that."

Duchess of Ashbrooke's sitting room

"It so happens that there are worse fates than remaining unwed for Lady Penelope's Ball," Olivia declared. Catching a glimpse of herself in a mirror, she saw that her eyes were bright with anger and her cheeks uncharacteristically flushed.

Emma (once a Wallflower and now a duchess) and Prudence (still London's Least Likely to Be Caught in a Compromising Position) fell silent, sipped their tea and considered the possibilities of what could possibly be worse than the worst thing in the world.

Meanwhile, Olivia seethed. A portion of her anger was reserved for her parents, of course, for making such an unconscionable match without consulting her. She seethed because the world was unfair to young ladies who had such little say in their fate.

Oh, she didn't *have* to marry the Mad Baron. But as soon as word got out, it was highly unlikely that she would attract any competing suitors. Except for the handsome stranger from the other night—from whom she foolishly fled—no one was interested in her.

Olivia burned as she recalled all those *years* in which she had simply watched and waited and hoped, to no avail. She'd followed all the rules and now—this. A fate worse than remaining unwed for Lady Penelope's Ball. A fate worse than eternal spinsterhood. Once she was wed to this cruel, murderous baron there would be no chance of falling in love. She could kiss happily ever after goodbye.

"Very well, I can't imagine anything worse," Emma said, breaking the silence and Olivia's raging sulk.

Then she told them. The words tumbled out. Enraged, her tongue tripped over the sentences as she described her misfortune. Her voice was decidedly not in the moderate, dulcet tones she'd been cultivating her whole life. She was raw. Scared. Angry.

"The Mad Baron?" Her friends had the expected reaction: a startled cry of shock and fear.

Prudence and Emma shared matching looks of horror, combined with pity and a dash of concern. Olivia took some satisfaction that they shared her distress at the news, but on the whole it felt much, much worse. Her fears were not unfounded. Her anger was not an overreaction. This was not a bad dream from which she would awaken.

It was real and it was awful.

"Is he as horrid as I'm imagining?" Emma asked. "Keep in mind that I have a very active imagination and a taste for gothic novels."

"I have yet to make his acquaintance," Olivia answered bitterly. "Which has not stopped my parents from giving him permission to court me and marry me. Thus, I have no idea how horrid he is, but I suspect given his reputation and devious methods of courtship, he is quite horrid indeed."

"Let us not forget that he killed his first wife," Prudence unnecessarily pointed out. One could hardly forget that gruesome detail.

"Allegedly, according to my father," Olivia muttered. "He has not come to town since he 'allegedly' murdered his wife. But why would he? No one would receive him, *except for my parents*."

Had they such little care for her? Such little faith in her prospects? There was no denying she wasn't a success on the marriage mart. But courtship from the Mad Baron would be a new, unfathomable low.

From every angle, this situation made Olivia feel utterly worthless. The only person who wanted her did so for all the most heartbreaking reasons: because she was biddable. And docile. And a good little girl. As if she were nothing more than a conduct book personified. As if she weren't a woman who wanted to be loved.

"At least you won't be a spinster for Lady Penelope's Anniversary Ball," Prudence pointed out.

"Which will take place in forty-three days. Not that anyone is counting."

"But is it a fate worse than death?" Emma mused.

"Your perspective is soothing my nerves immeasurably," Olivia replied dryly. "My choices are to be the only unwed girl in the history of Lady Penelope's Finishing School for Young Ladies of Fine Families or to marry the Mad Baron and then suffer an untimely demise."

"I'll probably be unwed as well," Prudence added, affectionately patting Olivia on the hand. "We can suffer together."

"Both of you, enough!" Emma cried. "You will be find good husbands in time. I am sure of it."

"Words to live by. From the starry-eyed, deeply-in-love duchess," Prudence remarked dryly. She and Olivia shared A Look. Ever since Emma had fallen in love and wed her handsome, charming, and utterly besotted duke, she'd been insufferably optimistic in all things. She'd even begun to play matchmaker, introducing Olivia and Prue to the duke's eligible friends at every opportunity. Unfortunately it was all the more apparent that they just didn't quite take. Their reputations as London's Least Likely preceded them, and none of the rakes, rogues, or bachelors of the ton were inclined to forget it, as much as the Duchess of Ashbrooke might encourage them to.

Honestly, it was embarrassing. It was almost worse than the wallflower corner.

"Lady Penelope's Ball is but one night of torture, but this marriage will be for the rest of my life," Olivia said.

"Which probably won't be long," Prudence said. "If you do marry the Mad Baron."

"Prudence!" Emma exclaimed, horrified.

"Well that is some consolation," Olivia said darkly. It also made her think.

If she didn't have long to live ... what would she do?

She wouldn't marry the Mad Baron, for one thing. She wouldn't paint another flower arrangement or stitch another sampler. She'd devote herself to what mattered: a delicious first kiss that made her weak in the knees, waltzes with handsome gentlemen who held her far closer than was proper, somehow finding the love of a reformed rogue, and above all, discovering what *she* liked and who she was when she wasn't delicately walking the straight and narrow with the promise of a reward on some far off day. She would find that handsome stranger and kiss him until she was weak in the knees.

She would live *now*.

"I have been the perfect lady," Olivia said slowly, stating the obvious. "We were led to believe that ladylike behavior would be rewarded with good husbands and happily-ever-after. We were gravely misled."

"You're right," Prudence agreed. "All our lives we were told to stand up straighter, smile when we didn't feel like it, never refuse an invitation to waltz, always be kind and obliging under every circumstance. How well has it worked out for us?"

The three girls fell silent. It hadn't worked out very well for them at all. Two were practically confirmed spinsters and about to become the matrimonial failures of Lady Penelope's Finishing School.

But one of them had landed a duke.

"Well, it worked out for Emma," Olivia said finally. She was truly happy for her friend. Deeply and truly happy. Just weeks ago they'd all had such dismal prospects. But it wasn't fair that Emma should have the magical experience of falling in love and Olivia should be forcibly betrothed to the Mad and Murderous Baron.

"My luck didn't change until *we* very improperly and wickedly and falsely announced my engagement to the duke," Emma said. "And by 'we' I mean you two."

"You're welcome," Prudence said kindly.

"Interesting point from London's Least Likely to Misbehave," Olivia said, referring to Emma's old nickname. "We've all been far too good for far too long."

"So it logically follows that we ought to misbehave," Prudence stated. "Especially you, Olivia."

"Do go on," Olivia murmured. Her heart started thudding because Prue had that mischievous look in her eye that foretold mischief, possibly trouble, potentially disaster.

Prudence explained: "If perfect ladylike behavior has gotten you practically betrothed against your will to a man who desires you for precisely that quality, then it logically follows that unlady-like behavior will get you out of it."

"She has a point," Emma said with a growing enthusiasm. "Your parents will never let you out of the match, but he might. Especially if the biddable bride he wanted turns out to be a hysterical, troublesome shrew who constantly plagues him with scandals."

"They will pressure me into accepting," Olivia said, seeing the potential of Prue's plan. "But they cannot force him to wed me if he decides we don't suit."

It went without saying she would do everything in her power to prove to him that they did not suit. Her life and future happiness depended upon it.

"You must break all those ladylike rules of your mother's," Prudence confirmed.

Young ladies do not break the rules.

Olivia smiled mischievously. *They do now.*

"And then he'll break the betrothal!" Emma exclaimed. "Oh, this shall be fun!"

"What shall Olivia do that will shock the ton and repel the Mad Baron?" Prudence wondered.

The girls fell silent. Brows furrowed thoughtfully. Heartfelt sighs were heaved.

"Well if I'm not going to be a perfect lady, then I'm going to have a second pastry," Olivia said, helping herself to one. And then another. She thought about telling her friends about the stranger, but it was all too sad now. Besides, she didn't want to interrupt their scheming.

Then their furrowed brows and frowns turned into wicked grins as outrageous acts of impropriety occurred to them.

"You must wear different gowns, for one thing," Emma said, and they all glanced at Olivia's plain and modest day dress of ivory and blue striped muslin. "Something that says Woman of Mystery rather than Virginal Spinster."

"You could appear drunk at a ball," Prudence suggested. "That would horrify all the dowagers and marriage-minded mamas. And the stuffier gentlemen, including the Mad Baron."

"And then you ought to smoke a cheroot on the terrace in the company of rogues," Emma added. "The gentlemen will be terribly awkward from the shock of a lady intruding upon their boring conversation about horses and whatnot."

"And when I'm at a ball, drunk and stinking of smoke, I'll speak my mind instead of always saying the polite thing," Olivia said, thinking of all the times she bit her tongue.

"No more polite conversations on the weather!" Emma said. "I think we should all join Olivia on her quest."

"You ought to stroll into White's," Prudence started. "And then sit down, put your feet on the table—and do let your ankles show—and then order a brandy."

Olivia wrinkled her nose. "Do I have to drink it?"

"Yes," Prudence said. "In one swallow and then slam the glass down on the tabletop for emphasis."

"Then I shall demand they bring me the betting book and I shall cross out our names as London's Least Likely," Olivia said, grinning. Her stomach turned somersaults at the thought. She would *never*, of course. But what if she dared?

"You must have an unchaperoned encounter with a gentleman, preferably a scandalous one," Emma added.

"But then you must be seen by a gossiping busybody," Prudence said. "Otherwise it doesn't count."

"After all, if you are alone with a rogue and no one saw it, did it really happen?" Emma punctuated this philosophical question with a lift of her brow.

"A deep, philosophical question from a duchess," Prudence remarked.

"In general, you must spend as much time as possible in the company of rogues and women with scandalous reputations," Prudence added matter-of-factly. As if gentlemen hadn't been known to launch themselves into hedges to avoid Olivia. That would have to change immediately.

"Perhaps you'll even fall in love with one," Emma said.

"And he'll whisk you off to Gretna Green before the Mad Baron knows what hit him," Prudence concluded.

"You know all the rules, Olivia," Emma said. "You just have to break them, one by one, as you encounter them."

Chapter 3

A violently rouged woman is one of the most disgusting objects to the eye.

—*The Mirror of Graces*, a Regency conduct
book given to Olivia on the occasion of
her twelfth birthday

Archer House
The following day

OLIVIA SAT BEFORE the mirror whilst her maid, Mary, forced her pale blond hair to curl. Lord Radcliffe was coming to tea and Lady Archer had given strict orders that Olivia was to appear at her very best, which meant she'd endure the hot iron and have her hair tangled up in an arrangement with strings of pearls and hair ribbons. She'd don one of her prim white day dresses and conduct herself with the utmost delicacy and care to avoid dirtying the gown. Young ladies must always be impeccably turned out and above reproach.

There was no other option.

Or was there?

Break the rules, one by one, as you encounter them.

Having spent her whole life dutifully obeying

every order, it was a strange and curious thought to consider deliberately doing the opposite. Oh, she had entertained thoughts of, say, putting Lady Katherine in her place with a cutting remark, or playing bawdy songs on the pianoforte at a musicale, or forsaking conduct books in favor of the romantic novels Emma was always reading (and Olivia discretely borrowed because *ladies did not read such rubbish*). She'd like to lift her skirts and run through Hyde Park instead of strolling. Wear lip paint and diaphanous gowns. Flirt with a rake and perhaps be the subject of a rumor.

Olivia always thought *one day* . . . one day she'd get to do all of these things when she left her parents' house and married the sort of dashing man who unlocked this side of her and encouraged high-spirited behavior.

She had nurtured her vision of this perfect happily-ever-after. Her husband would be handsome, charming, and always know what to say. He'd look at her with a gaze that sparkled lovingly and would always try to steal a kiss. They'd live in a large house with a pack of noisy children and she would *never* yell at them if they got jam on their skirts or broke a vase. In beautiful dresses and on the arm of this perfect husband, everyone would forget they'd ever called her Prissy Missy and that Mr. Middleton had jumped into a hedge to avoid her.

But if she married the Mad Baron, who selected for her *because* she was Prissy Missy London's

Least Likely to Cause a Scandal, then she'd be condemning herself to a short life of the utmost propriety. The very thought made her want to jump into a hedge to avoid him.

It was a dreadful fate, one sorely lacking in kisses, waltzes, and adventures of all kinds. She'd never fall in love. Or be deeply loved and passionately desired. Instead, she'd manage servants and embroider in solitude until her fingers bled.

"You're awfully quiet today, Lady Olivia," said Mary, while she took care not to burn her with the iron. "Are you nervous about meeting your intended?"

"Wouldn't you be? Especially given his reputation as a murderer?" Olivia replied. But she was more nervous about what she was going to do.

Something scandalous.

Something unladylike.

The sooner she made it clear she was *not* the woman he expected, the sooner she could . . . return to being a wallflower. Or do something outrageous to land a loving husband, as Emma had done.

"I suppose," Mary agreed. "But it could just be gossip. He's here already, you know. He came with his solicitor. They're both meeting with your father right now."

There was only one reason a solicitor would be here: to draw up marriage contracts. It was absurd that they'd progress with such alacrity when she'd never even met the man! They must think her so docile, obliging, and desperate to be wed that she'd agree to any proposal. It seemed she would have to show they were gravely mistaken. She was finished being the Dutiful Daughter.

"Have you seen him?" Olivia asked.

"I have," Mary said, not quite meeting Olivia's eye in the mirror.

"And?"

"His solicitor is more handsome," Mary ventured. And that said it all, really.

"I suppose he is wretched. Tell me, is he old and fat with beady eyes and a malevolent air?" If she learned anything from novels, it was that villains always possessed beady eyes and a malevolent air.

"Time to tighten your corset and put your gown on," Mary said brightly, thus confirming that the Mad Baron was the most repulsive, loathsome man in Christendom and that she must do whatever it took to get out of this match.

If only she had kissed that stranger!

"Mary, I think I seem a bit pale," Olivia said as an idea occurred to her.

"That's your complexion," Mary said. "Lovely and fair, like porcelain."

Indeed, everything about her was pale and fair and angelic and forgettable. She wasn't colorful or wild or desirable.

"But perhaps I could use a spot of color on my lips," Olivia said. "And perhaps some kohl for my eyes. Do you have any?"

"This is an unusual request, Lady Olivia," Mary said uneasily. She glanced toward the bed-chamber door. "I fear your mother . . ."

Proper Ladies did not wear lip paint or otherwise adorn their face. Only a certain kind of woman did that, and men in search of docile, biddable wives were not interested in Those Women.

"I'll take care of my mother if you fetch me some lip paint. Please, Mary. My future happiness depends on it."

WHEN OLIVIA DESCENDED the marble steps to greet her parents and the Mad Baron in the foyer, she was perfectly poised and the very picture of a Perfect Lady. From the neck down.

Thanks to a heavy-handed application of lip paint and rouge, she looked like a trollop. A drunk trollop. A drunk trollop who had applied makeup while standing on one foot on a ship at sea during a storm. Her lips—and a bit beyond—were a fierce shade of crimson. Her cheeks were pink, perhaps even fuchsia. As if she were her father in one of his rages, or as if she were burn-ing up with embarrassment. Her eyes had been lined with enough kohl for her to be mistaken for a raccoon.

Olivia felt absolutely ridiculous, but completely resolved in her rebellion.

She thought she looked tremendously unap-pealing.

Now if only the Mad Baron would think so as well.

Her mother shrieked before clamping her gloved hand over her mouth and muffling her sobs with one of her handkerchiefs. Her father, clearly mortified, reddened considerably. His jaw clenched and his eyes bulged under the strain of withholding an enormous bellow of rage.

Olivia *never* made her parents angry. In fact, this was the first time she was the subject of anything other than praise. She felt her stomach twist. It took every ounce of her determination not to run upstairs, scrub her face, and return with her sincerest apologies. Any such instinct vanished when she set eyes on the loathsome man himself.

The Mad Baron—who was indeed a corpulent elderly man with a dark scowl of disapproval—loudly cleared his throat of phlegm. Olivia did not conceal her shudder of revulsion. The thought of sharing a bed with this man strengthened her resolve immeasurably.

She would *not* marry the loathsome man who looked so dismissively at her. She would not have him touch her. Honestly, she should have drenched a bottle of perfume on herself as well.

The other man—his solicitor, presumably—stepped forward and provided more of a heart-stopping shock.

She recognized his captivating green eyes and his mouth, which she had almost kissed.

The scar she had noted in the candlelight was far more foreboding in the daylight.

The handsome stranger merely lifted one brow.

Olivia thought his lips might have quirked up at the corners—dear God, he was laughing at her! Dear God, this was more mortifying than she had expected.

Perhaps the solicitor was amenable to bribery—and if so, she'd just need to fetch her pin money in exchange for him burning the marriage documents. Then she hoped never to see him or the Mad Baron again.

"Olivia! Go upstairs immediately," her mother hissed.

"Whatever for?" she inquired, as if she had no idea, honestly.

"What impertinence!" her mother gasped. Olivia felt an odd thrill. She'd never been impertinent in her life.

"Never mind that, wife. Let's get on with the introductions and this bloody tea party," Lord Archer said with a *furious* look at his daughter. His cheeks reddened to the color of a soldier's red jacket. Olivia hadn't seen that shade since she had unwittingly used his smuggled French brandy during a tea party with her dolls. "Lord Radcliffe, may I present my daughter Lady Olivia," Lord Archer ground out. "I have no idea what has gotten into her. Or on her face."

But it wasn't the corpulent old man with the beady eyes who stepped forward. For a second Olivia felt relief. That is, before the truth of it dawned upon her.

Lord Radcliffe—the man she'd presumed to

be the solicitor, the man who was her handsome stranger—fixed his gaze on her raccoon eyes and bowed slightly. A tremor of fear rocketed up her spine.

She had nearly kissed a murderer! Thank God she hadn't.

"It is an honor to make your acquaintance, Lady Olivia." It was the Mad Baron himself, bending over her outstretched hand. He wasn't what she had expected, but he terrified her all the same. His gaze fixed on her was unnerving, as if he were memorizing her to think of later.

The scar, she noted, stretched from his temple to his sharply slanting cheekbone, just below his eye. Was it the work of his late wife, acting violently in self-defense? Olivia assumed so.

His mouth was full. Sensual. It was the kind of mouth she might have imagined kissing if it weren't curved into a faintly bemused smile. He thought her ridiculous. *Good.*

Olivia merely stared at him in horror. The kohl made her eyes twitch. Her lips tasted like bitter paint. She ought to say, *It is a pleasure to make your acquaintance, my lord*, but the words stuck in her throat.

Her wits struggled to function, save for one thought: she should have added more paint. Or fled already. Her knees weakened as she took note of his towering height and broad shoulders. He could overpower her in an instant if he so chose.

Her every instinct told her to run. But instead

Olivia fixated upon what seemed to be her only course of action: behave so abominably that a man who sought her out for her biddable, ladylike qualities, would run screaming back to whatever shire he'd come from.

"Olivia." Her mother nudged her in the ribs. She was supposed to reply to the Mad Baron.

Olivia had spent an inordinate number of hours perfecting a curtsy that highlighted the grace of her movements and conveyed her regal bearing yet deferential temperament. Today she gave a short perfunctory bob, the sort a servant might give when asked to forgo their afternoon off and empty chamber pots instead.

"Terribly sorry, my lord," her mother begged his pardon. He merely nodded. She anxiously clutched at one of her embroidered handkerchiefs. "Olivia does excel at the curtsy. Olivia, do try again. Endeavor not to embarrass us. "

Seething inwardly, Olivia sank into the lowest most obsequious bow imaginable, exaggerating each movement from the extra deep bend in her knees to the pompously raised pinky fingers holding her gown aloft.

"Very nice," Lord Radcliffe remarked, glancing from mother to daughter. Olivia refused to acknowledge his gaze. She just couldn't.

She was introduced to the solicitor next, a Mr. Morris, who left with the finalized marriage contracts in his hands after bidding them good day. His parting words: "They only need to be signed."

"Tea. Let's do have some tea," her mother said, bustling ahead and urging everyone to take their seats on the settees near the fireplace. "Olivia, why don't you pour?"

"Of course, Mother," Olivia said with an exaggerated sweetness, because that was expected of her. "I should be delighted to pour the tea for our esteemed guest."

No one knew the etiquette of serving tea better than Olivia (practiced daily at three o'clock), which was how she was now so deftly able to violate every small point of etiquette. She gripped the handle with her fist and clasped the spout as well. She did not inquire if the Mad Baron preferred one lump of sugar or two, or if he took milk, or enjoyed it plain and bitter.

The only thing preventing Lady Archer from exploding into a furious tirade was the rule that Ladies Do Not Explode in Furious Tirades, especially when they had company.

But when Olivia overpoured the tea so that it spilled into the saucer, it was purely an accident due to the unnerving way Lord Radcliffe fixed his green eyes upon her.

She became all too aware of the ridiculous paint on her face and her outrageously poor manners. She remembered the heat she'd felt from his gaze the other night. The powerful connection she'd felt with him was still lodged in her memory. Worst of all, she still viscerally recalled the hope she felt when their gazes locked.

And now she was embarrassed and terrified.

In handing a cup of tea to the Mad Baron, she saw the mean-looking scars on his hands and almost dropped the cup.

"Thank you," he said.

"You're welcome," she replied.

They had officially spoken almost five words to each other. Next, the wedding night.

Olivia reached out for one of the ginger biscuits on the tray. Her mother said a lady only ever ate one, to be polite, and no more, lest she be thought to have insatiable appetites.

"How are you finding London, Lord Radcliffe?" Lord Archer inquired.

"It's incredibly busy and intriguing, isn't it?" he replied, with a smile that Olivia might have conceded made him handsome if she were so inclined, which she obviously was not. "I'm enjoying the taste of city life, though I do prefer my home in Yorkshire. I have a large, rambling estate with much privacy."

Olivia did not like the sound of that. *Rambling* meant vast distances between his and the next. *Privacy* meant no one would see if she were in trouble. She helped herself to another biscuit. So much for her fantasy of living in a house with neighbors close by for frequent visits.

"How large is your house?" her mother inquired.

"Five stories, including the attics and basements," he answered, with a glance at Olivia, who frowned.

Did he have to mention attics and basements? Everyone knew that if one were to keep maidens captive, or conduct any sort of nefarious activity, one didn't do it in the drawing room, but in dusty attics and damp basement dungeons. He had said dungeons, hadn't he?

Olivia availed herself of another biscuit.

"The estate itself is lovely," he continued, with an uneasy glance her way. "Very quiet, and remote. There is a lot of dense forest."

Underneath all of her face paint, Olivia paled. *Remote* meant there would be no one to hear her scream. Not that ladies ever screamed. Unless their lives were in danger. Which hers would be. *Oh dear God.*

She sharply set down her teacup and it clattered loudly against the saucer. Her mother frowned. Olivia felt a surge of anger: how could they think of marrying her to this man?

"There's not much society," he added with a faint smile. Was it a regretful smile, or one that promised evil mischief? She stole another glance. Definitely the latter.

She would be left alone, utterly alone, with this man! Olivia blinked back tears, which made her eyes burn when they mixed with the kohl. She dabbed at them with one of her embroidered handkerchiefs, ruining it forever.

"And how fares your scientific endeavors?" her father inquired, ascertaining that a subject change was in order.

"They keep me occupied from morning to

night, really," Radcliffe answered. "Some find the work dangerous, but I think it's fascinating and enjoy the challenge."

Dangerous work? Dear God, what did this man do? Gentlemen were supposed to play cards, write poetry to ladies, drink port, and little else. At their clubs. In London.

If the two of them were to marry—which they most certainly would not do—she faced a wretched solitude, without even Emma or Prudence to provide solace in her decades of exile. She would lose her wits entirely. She'd stroll the halls in her ghost-like, virginal dresses mumbling to herself ("I won't marry him, I won't!") and carrying on conversations with imaginary friends. She would be known in all the London papers as the Mad Baroness.

"One reason I have come to town is to work with the Duke of Ashbrooke on the Difference Engine," Radcliffe explained, and *that* caught Olivia's attention.

Emma's husband was involved in this? Olivia would have Words with her friend. Perhaps she'd ask Emma to implore the duke to send this Mad Baron away and leave her in peace. In the battle for her freedom and future happiness, Olivia resolved that all possible avenues be explored.

"I do believe that wasn't the only reason you came to town, Lord Radcliffe," her mother added, almost *flirtatiously*. Olivia rolled her eyes because ladies did not roll their eyes. She'd always wanted to try it.

"I did come with the intention of taking a wife," Radcliffe said, gazing at her intently. Her pulse started racing with pure terror. "It's time for me to try again."

Again. There it was: the cold fact of his previous wife. Whom he murdered. Allegedly.

"And you have done just that! Isn't that so, Olivia," mother said, turning toward her. "He came just for you."

She ought to murmur *How lovely* or something obliging like that. Instead, Olivia replied: "I don't think I had much to do with the matter at all."

Her mother pursed her lips. Her father started turning pink again. The Mad Baron quirked his brow.

"Have you given any thought to the wedding, Lord Radcliffe?" Lady Archer asked, even though there had been no proposal. Olivia quite feared the words "marry me" would be the next ones out of his mouth.

Instead he said, "If it comes to that, I shall allow you both to make the plans. I'll be busy with my work on the engine. I also understand that ladies delight over matters like these and it's best if men stay out of their way." The Mad Baron added, "Whatever you wish, Lady Olivia."

"You say that *now*," she drolled.

"Olivia!" Her father shouted.

"I beg your pardon?" Radcliffe asked. Poor man was quite confused. Was he daft as well as mad? How could he not know that she—or any other woman in London—would not wish to marry him? Just because she almost kissed him in a dimly lit corridor didn't mean she wished to marry him now that she knew who he was and the violence he was capable of.

"It doesn't signify," Lady Archer snapped with a sharp look to her daughter.

"Truly, it doesn't," Olivia said earnestly, in spite of the furious glares of her parents. Oh, she was going to have an earful later. Better that than a lifetime with this scarred man with his dangerous occupation and violent past, who potentially seduced maidens in dimly lit corners of the ballroom.

"Perhaps you could tell me about yourself, Lady Olivia. What do you like to do?" the Mad Baron asked.

Olivia opened her mouth to give a snarky reply, but nothing came to mind other than the tragic truth that she did not know what she liked to do. It would probably break her mother's heart to learn her daughter didn't absolutely *delight* in floral arrangements or practicing the pianoforte or any of her other hobbies.

"Olivia likes to watercolor," Lady Archer said before Olivia could utter a word. "Embroidery is one of her pastimes; she is excellent with a needle. Floral arranging is another of her talents. She will be an excellent household manager."

"Just what I need," Lord Radcliffe said with a smile that might have been handsome were he not condemning her to a short life managing the linens and planning menus with the chef.

Just what I do not want to be.

Any hopes for love and companionship in a marriage would be lost if she did find herself reluctantly walking down the aisle with this man. He thought her a silly female who would be content to manage his servants and languish in utter solitude. The scars did nothing to assuage her fears. Neither did the way he looked at her. The makeup had not been enough. She would have to be worse.

Chapter 4

WHEN PHINNEAS COLE—FORMALLY known as
Baron Radcliffe, and popularly known as the Mad
Baron, though he preferred to be called Phinn—
first set eyes on Lady Olivia Archer at a ball, he
understood *magnetism* in a way he never had
before.

Given that he was something of an expert in it,
this was remarkable.

He knew about the materials and forces at work,
but he'd never viscerally understood the unseen
force until he couldn't tug his attention from her.
He'd never felt it. Once he saw her, looking away
was a physical impossibility.

She had been standing alone on the balcony
circling the ballroom, as if she were lonely in a
crowded room. It was a feeling he knew all too
well and one he didn't expect to share with a
woman. For a moment Phinn stood there, dis-

engaged from the crowd, peering up at her, and observed. She had lovely fair hair and a pale complexion. Her every movement—from the slight tilt of her head to the way she traced her fingers along the balustrade—was controlled and graceful.

In a glance, he could see she was the opposite of Nadia, which was all he wanted in a wife.

Phinn walked purposefully through the crowds until he met her at the bottom of the stairs in that darkened corridor. For his second wife, he meant to do everything right, from the first introduction to the proposal.

Meeting like this—having not been introduced, and being without a chaperone—was awfully roguish. But he couldn't leave. When she was knocked into his arms, he had a hard time letting go. Phinn wanted her, wanted to lose himself in her.

He couldn't blame her for panicking and fleeing, but he wished she had stayed. He wanted to know her. He would know her.

Later, he inquired about her to his friend, Lord Rogan.

"That chit? Lady Olivia Archer. Better known as Prissy Missy. And she's one of London's Least Likely, but I can't recall if she's one least likely to misbehave or be caught in a scandal."

That was all Phinn needed to hear. He'd come to town to help build the Duke of Ashbrooke's Difference Engine to debut at the Great Exhibition, and to marry a woman who would keep his house, warm his bed, and otherwise wouldn't cause him any trouble or distract him from his work.

It seemed he found her on his first night in London. When he found the perfect woman, upon whom he was transfixed, why wait to make her his wife?

He hadn't managed an introduction that night, but obtaining permission to court her had been the matter of a quick interview with her father. Phinn was glad; he had feared the business of finding a wife would drag on, eating up time better spent on his work.

Yet once he properly met Lady Olivia Archer, Phinn's worst fears—another disastrous match to a wildly unpredictable wife—were confirmed.

After a disastrous meeting at the Archer home, he returned to the home of his friend, Lord Rogan, with whom he was staying whilst in London.

They'd attended Oxford together and struck up a genuine if unlikely friendship when it was discovered that their different personalities served each other well. Rogan's sociability kept Phinn from becoming a complete recluse, devoted only to his studies. Phinn had ensured that Rogan didn't fail out of school and he was the one person Rogan could rely on when, say, he required bailing out from the local magistrate, which had happened regularly.

Phinn collapsed into a chair in Rogan's study.

"Well that was not what I had expected," he said, pushing his fingers through his hair, as he did when he was frustrated. Unfortunately, it didn't exactly help dispel rumors about his mad behavior. But then again, he'd never given a damn about what society thought.

"What *did* you expect from tea with your blushing, virginal bride and her doting parents?" Rogan inquired.

"Doting is one way of describing Lady Archer," Phinn remarked dryly. She was a tall, fair, and stern woman. Everything about her was perfectly done.

"Do the words 'overbearing harridan' get more to the point?" Rogan asked with a cheeky grin.

Phinn ignored his friend. He couldn't *agree* to such coarse terms for a woman who might be his future mother-in-law. But he couldn't deny them either. Lady Archer's constant admonishments about her daughter's behavior were notable. Then again, her daughter's behavior had been deplorable.

There had been no sign of the graceful, elegant girl he happened to fall for at first glimpse. He still looked for her, under all the rogue, scowls, lip paint, and rude behavior. Where had she gone?

"And if by blushing you mean she had an inordinate amount of paint upon her cheeks?" Phinn asked. He knew all there was to know about physics, but nothing on the matter of women's fashion. "And what of the black stuff around her eyes and the red stain upon her lips? Is that the fashion in London these days?"

"Among a certain kind, perhaps," Rogan replied with a wink and an emphasis on *certain kind* that left no doubt to his meaning.

"But not demure, saintly, innocent ladies," Phinn clarified.

"Not women nicknamed Prissy Missy, no," Rogan confirmed.

"She wore excesses of it," Phinn said with a frown. "Excesses."

"I should have liked to see that," Rogan said, chuckling.

"She looked comical," Phinn admitted. It was so badly done, it had to be deliberate, though he didn't like what that suggested about her feelings toward him. He was surprised to discover how much he cared. "I wanted very badly to laugh at the reaction of her parents. I thought they were going to have an apoplexy right there in the foyer. But I feared the wrath of Lady Archer."

"Lady Archer is a terrifying creature. London gents learned long ago to avoid her at all costs. Ask Middleton about it sometime," Rogan said. "Perhaps your lovely fiancée did it in a misguided effort to impress you."

"One might be inclined to think that, were it not for the rest of her manners," Phinn mused. "But then again, my expertise is on machinery, not the minutia of tea time etiquette. I am not sure if she despises me, is simply odd, or if I am giving the matter too much consideration."

"Knowing you, I'd say you're giving the matter too much consideration," Rogan said. "Then again, I think most thinking is too much. Say, did you take my advice and tell her about how large your estate was?"

"Yes. And I don't think she cared in the slightest," Phinn said, remembering how she paled when he mentioned the vast lands attached to his country house. "In fact, the more I told her about it, the more horrified she seemed."

"You probably should have told her the size of your bank account or the size of your—"

"Really?" Phinn asked, leveling his friend with a stare.

"I digress," Rogan amended.

"This bride business is exactly as I expected," Phinn said, frowning. "And precisely what I had hoped to avoid."

"Suffocating, claustrophobic, depressing," Rogan supplied.

"Confusing. Confounding. Governed by unknown forces that adhere to no logic and following laws I am not aware of," Phinn corrected. Couldn't it be simple: man meets woman, marry, develop affection?

But then he thought of that strange pull he felt to Olivia.

He thought things would be easy with her. After all, he'd learned she was known as London's Least Likely to Cause a Scandal and that she was on her fourth season and was thus presumably eager to wed. Her father was all but ready to call in the Archbishop when he approached him.

When were things ever simple?

Any other man might have been repelled by Lady Olivia's behavior. But given that it was so at odds with her reputation as a Prissy Missy, he found himself rather intrigued. Like mathematical problems that didn't add up, Phinn had a hankering to resolve the discrepancy.

"Regretting all the time spent with your experiments rather than with wagers and women?" Rogan asked.

"Yes," Phinn conceded. "Somewhat."

"Perhaps you ought to have spent more time studying the complexities of female behavior instead of all those machines and mad experiments of yours," Rogan suggested. What remained unspoken: perhaps his first marriage wouldn't have been such a wreck. "This may be your opportunity. Consider it an experiment."

"You have a point," Phinn agreed.

"Excellent," Rogan said with a grin. "I'll ring for our hats and coats. We can start at Madame Scarlett's."

"A brothel? I'm practically betrothed, Rogan," Phinn protested. "Also, it is only four o'clock in the afternoon. Also, I'm due to meet with the duke regarding our project."

"You want to be prepared for your wedding night, do you not?" Rogan asked, still angling to visit the brothel. At four o'clock. In the afternoon.

"I've been married before, Rogan," Phinn said dryly. He wasn't a novice. Nadia's passionate tem-

perament wasn't *always* a problem—just outside
of the bedroom.

"And how did that work out for you?" Rogan
asked with a daring lift of his brow, knowing full
well the answer. This wasn't the first time his
friend tried to dissuade him from the matrimonial
state. A circle of hell, Rogan had once likened it to.
With Nadia as his wife, Phinn hadn't disagreed.

"My marriage was an unmitigated disaster and
never-ending nightmare," Phinn replied. "Everyone knows it."

"And yet you are trying again," Rogan said.

"Well they don't call me the Mad Baron for
nothing," Phinn remarked dryly. Oh, he knew
what the gossips used to say of him. But honestly,
he couldn't really be bothered. Out in Yorkshire,
there was really no point. Besides, it had been
years since Those Events, and he presumed everyone had forgotten about it by now. "What am I
going to do, Rogan?"

"About what?" Rogan asked, and Phinn re-
pressed a sigh of exasperation over his friend's
deplorable attention span.

"Lady Olivia. She's not quite the woman I
thought she'd be."

Phinn had expected her to be sweet and lovely.
Given the powerful connection they shared the
other night, he didn't think she'd be so contrary
when they met properly. It was puzzling—and
puzzles did always intrigue him.

"Look, Phinn, it's a sad fact that women don't

just throw themselves at men—unless you're one of those rakes like Ashbrooke, Gerard, or Beaumont. Damn blokes have all the luck," Rogan grumbled. "So you have to woo her. Make her like you."

"I'd hoped to avoid wooing," Phinn said.

"I'm given to understand it's a necessary step toward matrimony, which you seem to have your heart set on."

"My heart isn't set on anything. I just need a wife."

"Just make her like you," Rogan said ever so simply. "Here's what you have to do: You have to impress her. Show her that you're one hell of a strong, dashing rogue. Women love strong men." To punctuate his point, Rogan flexed his arms, purportedly to reveal his biceps. But Rogan's main activities were drinking and reckless living, not, say, laboring under the sun. The demonstration was not impressive, though his point was taken.

"Are you suggesting I demonstrate feats of strength?"

"Show her how strong and virile you are. And muscular. Women are always going on about men with the figures of Greek gods."

"Are they?" Phinn was not aware that women "went on" about such things. Then again, like any sensible man, when he saw a pack of women deep in discussion, he marched in the opposite direction.

"Do you not see them in the British Museum, pretending to be all interested in Greek and Roman statues? Is there anything duller than old hunks of stone? No. They're really just ogling all the muscles and trying to discern what is under the fig leaf."

"I am not in the habit of watching young women ogle statues," Phinn replied.

"You really need to get out of your study more," Rogan said matter-of-factly and probably not incorrectly.

"I really want this to work, Rogan." His housekeeper had been nagging him to take a wife—"a nice one this time"—and the thought of a woman to share meals and his bed did hold a certain appeal. Especially if this wife wouldn't cause trouble or distract him from his work. And then there was the matter of the strange force that drew him to Olivia. But he couldn't say such rubbish, and especially not to Rogan, who would never let him live it down. Instead, he said, "I'd hate to have to start at the beginning."

"Feats of strength, I tell you," Rogan said confidently. "Or at the very least, you must get her away from her mother. In fact, see if you can steal a moment alone with her at a ball. Women love stolen moments in dark, secluded places with gents. They're not supposed to, but they do. Trust me."

Chapter 5

*This week in unexpected couplings: there are rumors
that Lady Olivia Archer, better known as London's Least
Likely to Cause a Scandal, is being courted by none
other Lord Radcliffe, better known as the Mad Baron by
trembling young maidens.*

—"FASHIONABLE INTELLIGENCE"
BY A LADY OF DISTINCTION,
THE LONDON WEEKLY

UPON OLIVIA'S ARRIVAL at a ball, three things always happened. First, she contrived to lose her mother in the crowd. Then she made her way through the throng of guests with her head held high, pretending that she didn't see all the men who subsequently made themselves scarce as soon as they became aware of her approach.

Finally, she found Emma and Prudence standing near the lemonade table. It was likely that Olivia and Prudence would remain there, off to the side, for the duration of the ball, save for the occasional trip to the ladies' retiring room just to liven things up.

But tonight was different.

Olivia was distinctly aware that instead of

averting their gazes, people gave her looks that could only be described as pitying. The women offered half smiles—before turning to whisper to their companions. The men still looked away, but without their usual alacrity.

Olivia concluded the obvious: the ton was aware that the Mad Baron was courting London's Least Likely to Cause a Scandal. Her throat constricted at the thought.

She had spotted Emma and Prue just ten paces away when Lord Dudley, of all the people in England, stepped in front of her.

She stepped to the right, intending to walk around him, for that bounder couldn't possibly mean to speak to *her*. But Dudley also stepped to the right, blocking her path.

She stepped to the left. So did Dudley.

Lady Olivia's polite vocabulary lacked the words to describe him, other than to say that he was universally disdained because of his cruel wit and hotheaded behavior. And yet the scoundrel was invited everywhere due to his father's influence.

Thus when Dudley stepped before Olivia, obviously intent on speaking to her, a knot formed in the pit of her stomach. This could not be good.

Other people nearby were of the same mind, for they turned to stare in expectation of a scene. The constantly tormenting Lady Katherine was smirking. For the first time in four seasons, Olivia found herself the center of attention.

"Lady Olivia," Dudley said, bowing deeply. "I understand congratulations are soon to be in order."

Olivia didn't reply because she didn't have anything to say—though not for lack of want or effort. Tomorrow at breakfast she would think of a devastating retort. For now . . . nothing.

"I have something you may find interesting," Dudley said with a smirk.

"I rather doubt it," she replied. Nearby, someone chuckled.

Dudley was not dissuaded. He handed her a broadside. With just a glance she could read the title, printed in large letters: *The Mad Baron: The Gruesome Story of an Innocent Maiden's Tragic Love and Untimely Death. A True Story.*

It had published six years ago—shortly after the Murderous Incident. Olivia knew this because a fellow student at Lady Penelope's School for Young Ladies had procured a copy. All the girls had eagerly passed it around, relishing in all the gory details of the sordid story and praying they'd never, ever have to marry *him.*

"Go on, take it," Dudley said with a smirk. "You'll want to know what you're in for on your wedding night."

"I have already read it," Olivia told him, hoping she sounded bored and not terrified. But Dudley shook the leaflet at her, leaving her no choice but to take it. Then, with her lip quivering from the cruel reminder that she was to possibly wed the worst man in the world, she walked past Dudley toward the wallflowers. She let the broadside fall to the ground, to be trampled on by the hordes of satin slippers.

"What was that all about?" Emma asked. Even though she was a duchess now, she still spent a fair portion of every ball with Prue and Olivia.

"Dudley is the worst," Prudence said vehemently. The other girls agreed.

"He wished to give me a copy of the broadside about *the Mad Baron*."

"Remember reading that at Lady Penelope's?" Prudence asked. "I had nightmares for weeks. Truly terrifying stuff."

"Prudence!" Emma exclaimed. Prue ignored her.

"Remember the part where he had his brother killed so he could seduce his intended?" Prudence asked with gruesome relish.

"Only to eventually kill her, too," Olivia said. "Oh, I remember."

"Your mother is bearing down toward us at a furious pace," Emma remarked.

The girls turned to look. Lady Archer meant well. Her sole task in life was the suitable marriage of her daughter, and Lord help anyone who stood in her way. If only she might spend more time embroidering or painting or doing charitable works and less time trying to find a husband for her daughter.

"And she has the Mad Baron for company," Olivia muttered when she spied him with her mother. If she didn't know better, she might have thought he looked dashing in his evening clothes. But she did. So she didn't.

"You didn't say he was handsome, Olivia!" Emma exclaimed, tapping her on the shoulder with her fan. Honestly, her friend had gone soft. Romance had wrecked her. The Duke of Ashbrooke had made a muddle of her brains.

"Handsome in a terrifying sort of way," Prudence murmured.

The Mad Baron stood in stark contrast to the other gents. He was taller, broader in the shoulders. Everyone else wore brightly colored waistcoats; his was dark gray.

Looking at him through the eyes of her friends, Olivia noted his strong chiseled features, which would have been softened by a smile. Or a lack of that dramatic slash of a scar. He wasn't handsome. He was dangerously beautiful, but fear clouded her vision so much that she could only see *dangerous*.

"Good looks don't signify when he's a murderer," Olivia lectured. "I'll hardly care that he has nice green eyes when his hands are closing around my neck."

"I want to meet him," Emma said, glancing curiously in his direction.

"I as well," Prudence added. "I've never met a murderer before. That I know of."

"And I need to visit the ladies' retiring room," Olivia said. Her heart was pounding furiously, like a poor gazelle aware of a lion stealthily advancing toward it. "Urgently."

They expertly maneuvered through the crowd in the ballroom and along the corridor. With the door locked, Olivia exhaled a sigh of relief and lay down on the settee.

"Are you just going to avoid him all night?" Prudence asked.

"Yes. That is precisely what I intend to do," Olivia replied. "He can't possibly propose if he can't speak to me. If he doesn't propose, then I needn't marry him."

"I confess that I want to meet him," Emma said. Again.

"Have your husband introduce you," Olivia suggested. "I cannot believe he hasn't already. In fact, I cannot believe you didn't mention that your husband was involved in this disaster."

"Honestly, I had no idea!" Emma protested. "He mentioned an acquaintance coming down from Yorkshire to help with the engine, but I didn't put two and two together. Apparently, in addition to terrifying young ladies, the Mad Baron is also an expert in machines. They are constructing the engine at a warehouse that had been converted from stables on Devonshire Street. Blake hasn't had him come 'round to the house. At least not while I was at home."

"Even Blake thinks he is a danger to young women everywhere," Olivia muttered.

"And he is at large in this ballroom," Prudence

said in a hushed whisper, purposely designed to make the hair on Olivia's neck stand up.

"You may succeed in avoiding his company this evening," Emma said. "But what about the rest of your life?"

"What do you mean?" Olivia asked. "My plan to avoid him is perfect. I don't know why I didn't think of it sooner."

"You know your parents will put you two together at every opportunity," Emma said practically.

"You must repel him by breaking the rules, remember?" Prudence said. "If only because it will be so much more entertaining for the rest of us."

"It's too bad we didn't bring the sherry," Emma said. "We could get Olivia ragingly drunk."

"We should prepare better next time," Prudence concurred. "Though it's a pity to waste the opportunity this evening."

"What else was on the list?" Olivia asked.

Prudence rummaged through her reticule, pulling out a folded sheet of paper.

"You brought it with you?" Olivia asked, mildly appalled.

"I thought we might need it," Prudence said with a smirk because she was right.

Emma snatched the list from her hand and read, " 'Keep the company of known rakehells and scoundrels.' "

"Well one can't swing a cat in this ballroom without hitting one," Prudence said.

"Yes, but speaking to one will be another matter entirely," Olivia said with a sigh, remembering the vision of Mr. Middleton *launching* himself into a shrubbery to avoid her and her mother. For the remainder of the party he was pulling twigs and leaves from his hair.

"We'll just have to get crafty with our methods," Prudence declared with what could only be described as an evil grin. "I daresay, this party just got interesting. We have not one but two missions: avoid the Mad Baron at all costs whilst keeping the company of rakes and rogues. Let's hope your mother brought her smelling salts this evening."

ROGAN HAD PERSUADED Phinn to attend the ball, as it would afford him the opportunity to steal a moment alone with Lady Olivia. Or possibly make the acquaintance of another woman who wouldn't mind marriage to a notorious man with a dark past.

Very quickly it became clear that both were daunting prospects. Young ladies glanced at him appraisingly—and when they caught glimpse of the scar or realized who he was—they turned away. Finding this tremendously irritating, Phinn scowled mightily, which probably didn't help matters.

Lady Archer proved to be another obstacle to his plans. In her clutches, he was introduced to at least half of the ton—all of whom acted as if the scandal with Nadia had happened last week instead of six years earlier. He noted the nervous glances, as if they expected him to commit some violent act right here in the ballroom.

Phinn was reminded why he'd avoided coming down to London. The machinery in his workshop in Yorkshire—once he'd rebuilt it after the fire— didn't give a damn about his reputation or bother him with inane conversation.

If he were not so fixated upon finding Olivia, it might have tried his temper. His legendary Radcliffe temper. *That* would give them something to talk about.

He had spotted her earlier in the evening with her friends. By the time he and Lady Archer managed their way through the crowds, they were gone. *Fled*, if he wanted to be precise about it, which, being scientifically inclined, he couldn't help but do.

Things had been different when they first met. Before she knew who he was, they had shared a connection that was too strong for him to give up on after one disastrous meeting. Being a science-minded man, he wasn't about to quit his court-ship and begin anew after one failed experiment. He'd make another attempt to discern if they were truly incompatible or if they'd just gotten off to a rocky start.

If only he could do so without Lady Archer.

"Do you see Olivia?" she asked, fanning herself and craning her neck trying to peer through the crowds.

"I do not," he lied. She was standing in a crowd around the lemonade table. He recognized an opportunity. Turning to his future mother-in-law, he asked, "Perhaps you'd like to find a seat and I shall bring you a lemonade?"

Lady Archer thought that would be lovely.

Phinn made his way toward Olivia, his gaze fixed on her. She looked beautiful tonight. Her hair was in some arrangement with tendrils that emphasized her slender neck. She looked as she did the night he first set eyes upon her—simply lovely and innocent.

Nadia had been dark and wicked. In comparison, Olivia looked like sunshine and happiness.

A shorter, rounder girl with reddish hair stood beside her. He watched them whisper furiously to each other in the terrifying way only women could. What were they discussing? Phinn wasn't sure he wanted to know.

"Radcliffe!"

Phinn turned and saw the Duke of Ashbrooke. The duke had earned a reputation as quite the rake—before falling in love with his wife, Emma. What was less known was the duke's mathematical genius. He'd conceived of the Difference Engine and how it would work. Through the Royal Society, he'd reached out to Phinn about drafting the plans and building the engine.

Hence, Phinn's trip to London.

"Good to see you out, Radcliffe," the duke said. "I wanted to introduce you to my wife, Lady Emma."

Lady Emma was a petite brunette who gave him a slightly crooked smile.

"How do you do?" he asked, stealing a glance at Olivia.

"Very well, thank you," Lady Emma replied. "I am quite keen to make your acquaintance, especially since you are courting one of my dearest friends."

That caught Phinn's attention.

"Small world, isn't it?" Blake—the duke—mused.

"She's really a lovely girl," Emma said.

"Yes, I think so. Beautiful, too," Phinn said. Much of women's behavior seemed to defy logic to him, but he did know that what was told to one would be made known to the others. He ought to name this phenomenon. Publish a paper on it. Or use it to his advantage.

"We were surprised at your sudden courtship," Emma said, and Phinn stored that information away. *Too much, too soon.* But what was to be gained by waiting? "We hardly know you."

"What would you like to know?" Phinn asked.

Lady Emma glanced left, then right, then leaned in close.

"Did you do it?" she asked in a low voice.

"Emma!" Blake exclaimed.

"He's intent upon marrying my best friend," she explained. "I *must* inquire."

"Women," Blake muttered, shaking his head. Phinn grinned, not daring to show his agreement any other way.

Lord Archer hadn't inquired. He'd merely said, *I trust those rumors about your previous wife are nonsense,* and then moved on to talk of Olivia's generous dowry.

"Does your house truly have a dungeon?" Emma asked, and he peered at her curiously, wondering where the devil she got an idea like that. "And after the wedding—*if* there is one— will you really lock Olivia away in your vast and remote country estate?"

Phinn was still trying to fathom what the devil she was talking about.

"Pardon my wife and her intrusive—though entertaining—questions," the duke said.

"We'll see how the courtship goes first," Phinn replied evasively.

"Yes, we shall," Emma replied in a manner that made him distinctly uneasy.

A commotion by the lemonade table caught his attention. It involved Olivia—and her hands on another man. She wasn't *his,* but Phinn still experienced a surge of possessiveness that woke his Radcliffe temper. He took a deep breath, forcing it back.

THERE WAS A mob around the lemonade table. Olivia and Prudence joined the crowd not for a drink, but to be in the vicinity of Lord Gerard, who had recently appeared in the gossip columns after suffering a carriage accident at first light, upon which it was discovered that his friend's wife was in the carriage with him. Given their lack of attire, there was little doubt as to what they had been doing together. There was a duel, of course, and it was rather remarkable for him to show his face this evening.

"You ask him," Prudence said, gently nudging Olivia, while eyeing Lord Gerard's broad shoulders, clad in a fine black wool jacket. His tawny colored hair was long, curling around the collar.

"No, you ask him," Olivia replied. He was such a tower of virile masculinity. The idea of talking to him made her feel out of sorts. She hadn't prepared for this, and in her nervousness, her palms became damp.

"You're the one who's supposed to be cavorting with disreputable gentlemen," Prudence pointed out in a whisper.

"Cavorting?" Olivia echoed. "I'm not sure I know how to cavort."

"Just think what Lady Katherine would do," Prudence advised. Olivia could just imagine it: she would probably purr and caress his arm while promising sin with her gaze. Could Olivia do that? Her heart started to pound. Nerves were certainly going to get the better of her. "I thought I just needed to be seen in the vicinity of a rake."

"You are too good for your own good," Prudence declared.

Mustering her courage, Olivia lightly pressed her gloved fingertips on Lord Gerard's sleeve, getting his attention. He turned. Slowly. And then looked down at her.

Olivia peered up at the face that launched a thousand sighs among the ton. His features were sharply defined and utterly noble. He peered down at her with a jaded expression. Lord Gerard's eyes were heavy-lidded and dark, making her wonder if he were tired or bored or hiding something.

How on earth was she supposed to speak to him? Let alone purr and caress him?

"Excuse me," she said, ever polite. "If you wouldn't mind, my lord, handing a glass to my friend and me . . ." She'd begun to stammer.

By now a few people had turned to glance at the unusual sight of Lord Gerard paying attention to one of London's Least Likely. She couldn't flee, even if she wanted to.

Good manners compelled him to honor the request of a lady. Even if he glanced nervously at the said lady, as if expecting a lecture on good manners.

"As you wish," he murmured in the most devastating way. Olivia thought she ought to have been so daring sooner. Lord Gerard was speaking to her and fetching her a drink!

He handed Olivia and Prudence a glass of lemonade.

Olivia smiled prettily up at him. That she could do. Promising sin with her smoldering gaze would have to wait until she could practice.

He warily returned her smile. Was she making

him nervous? Why did that prospect make her giddy?

She should say something witty or flirtatious. If only she could wink without contorting her face into an unappealing expression. Instead, she sipped her lemonade in what she hoped was a seductive and inviting manner. Again, something they really ought to have covered at Lady Penelope's School for Young Ladies.

"Thank you," she said.

"My pleasure," he replied. There was a faint upturn at the corners of his mouth. This was ever so slightly amusing to him. But at least he wasn't dismissing her outright.

"Are you enjoying this evening?" Olivia asked.

"Yes. And you?"

"Yes," Olivia said, a touch too breathlessly. Lord Gerard noticed, too, which made her blush.

Truly, this could be the beginning of a grand romance if she could only think of something perfect to say. Then he'd raise his brow, intrigued, as rogues were known to do—as Emma had informed them from the novels she read. Then they'd waltz and years of dancing lessons wouldn't have gone to waste after all. They'd fall in love, quickly, and he'd wickedly suggest they elope to Gretna Green and—

"Oh!" Olivia cried out as *someone*—Prudence—bumped into her, causing her to spill her lemonade all over the front of Lord Gerard's pale blue silk waistcoat. She fearfully glanced up at him; his expression was as inscrutable as ever, though that mere hint of a smile was now definitely a frown.

"I'm so sorry!" she said, also terribly sorry to have ruined their almost-moment. "You have my sincere apologies."

"It's all right," he said. But it wasn't really. He'd been doused with lemonade and would have to retire early or smell of lemons or take his waistcoat off. The thought of *that* brought a furious blush to her cheeks.

She pulled a handkerchief from her reticule (*young ladies are always prepared*) and attempted to dry off Gerard's waistcoat, which of course resulted in her hands upon him . . . and his waistcoat, which was his abdomen, really. Olivia was aware that it was firm under her touch and that this was the first time she'd had such intimate contact with a man.

Although it didn't feel intimate—not with dozens of people looking on with slightly bemused, slightly horrified expressions. Her cheeks were still hot. She was hot, all over. She straightened, awkwardly clutching the handkerchief, and looked around. For once, everyone was staring at her.

Olivia's gaze locked with the Mad Baron's even though he stood at a distance. How she managed to find him in the crowd escaped her. There was just some pull between them, she supposed, even though she knew better now.

Still . . . still . . . she could see his green eyes

fixed intently upon hers. The intensity of his gaze unnerved her. Had she made him angry? Had she embarrassed him? Was that not the point of this ridiculous exercise?

Above all, *why* did she have the urge to smooth back his hair and apologize? Prudence was right: she was too good for her own good.

PHINN SET OFF after Olivia, only to be stopped by Rogan, who had deigned to appear in the ballroom after disappearing into the card rooms upon their arrival hours ago. Phinn scanned the room to see where Olivia had gone to now.

She'd had her hands all over some fellow, which led to the inconvenient revelation that he already felt possessive of her. There was no logical reason he should feel that way. Such a sentiment also revealed that his attraction to her was not entirely based upon her lovely appearance and perfect reputation. It was deeper, more primal. He wanted her hands on *him*.

"Ah there you are," Rogan said brightly.

"How fares your wagering? Losing more than you can afford?" Phinn inquired, still scanning the room for Olivia.

"I was. Sadly," Rogan said dejectedly. "We don't all have your freakish ability to predict winning hands and to be so inscrutable about it."

"It's mathematics. Probabilities, etcetera, etcetera," Phinn explained again. "I've spent hours trying to teach you." Rogan would just prattle on about luck and the rush of the game.

"You lost me at mathematics," Rogan said jovially. And loudly. "How fares your quest to steal away with your intended?"

"Shhh," Phinn urged when a few people nearby turned with alarmed expressions. Bloody hell, now he'd read about his nefarious plans to abscond with an unwilling bride in the morning papers. "I don't want to steal her away. Just have a bloody moment alone," Phinn said, pushing his fingers through his hair. And then lowering his voice he added, "I have managed to divest myself of Lady Archer's company."

"Well that's a start," Rogan concurred.

"Then I ran into Ashbrooke and his wife," Phinn said, still unsure if he was annoyed or amused by Lady Emma. It spoke well of Olivia that her friends cared so deeply as to make the inquiries she did. But what was this talk of dungeons?

"Look at the lofty company you keep," Rogan retorted.

"Meanwhile," Phinn went on, "Olivia manhandled some gentleman by the lemonade table."

Rogan began to choke on his whiskey and Phinn thought about smacking him on his back. Hard.

"And now . . ." Phinn's voice trailed off as he caught a glimpse of Olivia's lovely blond hair. She was heading toward the terrace. If he could meet here there, it would be perfect. They'd be able to talk without the horrid crush in the ballroom interfering.

"Lady Archer! Good evening," Rogan said.

"Good evening," she replied, looking from one gentleman to the other.

"This is Lord Rogan, one of my oldest friends," Phinn said. "He was just telling me he fancied a waltz, and I do believe I heard one starting now."

"Actually, it's a quadrille," Lady Archer corrected.

"I've been spending far too much time in the country," Phinn said, adopting a dejected expression. If he had a wife like Olivia, he'd know these things. Or she would know them for him. "Perhaps you two will dance and talk about the wedding."

Lord Rogan, who usually consorted with the light-skirts of the demimonde and women of negotiable affections, had no choice but to smile and ask Lady Archer to dance. Phinn made his escape.

PRUDENCE LED OLIVIA away from Lord Gerard and his soaking waistcoat, seeking another opportunity for scandal. Olivia must cavort with rogues, plural.

"What just happened?" Olivia asked, aghast.

Prudence just smiled and explained: "What happened was that you broke at least seven rules of etiquette. You spoke to a gentleman to whom you had not been introduced. You asked for something you wanted, rather than wait prettily for someone to notice that perhaps you were parched and in need of refreshment. And then you had your hands all over Lord Gerard's abdomen!"

Prudence paused before concluding with, "You're welcome."

"I suppose you're the mysterious push that caused me to lose my balance and spill my drink," Olivia remarked.

They paused to chat near a pillar. Before them dozens of couples were dancing, including— Prue gasped—was that Lady Archer doing the quadrille with a young man? No, it couldn't be. But it was. Best not to mention it. Olivia and Prue lingered near the doors to the terrace, while Prudence explained the situation.

"You were seen cavorting with a rake instead of just standing next to one," she said. "Everyone will be speaking about it. Perhaps even the Mad Baron saw you, and thinks that you are not the docile, chaste creature he envisioned."

"Thank you?" Olivia said, though it sounded to Prue rather like a question.

"Of course," Prue said, smiling. "What are friends for, if not helping to derail an unwanted marriage by causing numerous scandals in one night?"

But Prudence knew it was more than that. When her friend inevitably married, she would officially be the last graduate of Lady Penelope's School for Young Ladies who hadn't wed. The anniversary ball was just over a month away and she didn't have even *one* suitor. Not one. She'd need Olivia by her side for that event and ever after.

They could rent a cottage in Brighton and be spinsters by the sea . . .

If Olivia *loved* the Mad Baron, then she wouldn't interfere with a nudge or a push or a crazy scheme. But she knew Olivia didn't want to marry him, and unlike her, didn't possess a wicked mind, so it was her noble duty as a friend to help.

"Olivia, I have only your best interests at heart."

"I know. And I would do the same for you," Olivia said, smiling and affectionately squeezing her hand. Prue felt her breath catch. She had to remember this moment when everything was still amusing and lovely. Before Olivia inevitably wed someone and she herself was left on her own. It was a bittersweet moment, feeling this happiness but knowing it wouldn't last.

Forcing such maudlin sentiments aside, Prudence focused upon the quest of the evening. Cavorting with rogues. Plural.

"Remember that," she said, smiling mischievously.

"What? Why?" Olivia asked, now looking nervous.

"So you won't be angry when I do this," Prue said, giving a gentle—very well, firm—nudge to her friend, which sent her stumbling forward and into the arms of a rake.

OLIVIA SHRIEKED AS she pitched forward into the arms of . . . Whose arms were these? She looked up, into a wall of a man's chest clad in a cerulean blue silk waistcoat. Laughter reached her ears. She looked higher still, into the laughing brown eyes of a rather handsome dark-haired gentleman.

A man she didn't recognize provided some illumination on the matter: "What did you catch, there, Beaumont?"

Oh Lord Above, this was *Lord Beaumont*. She didn't think he even attended proper ton functions, preferring instead to frequent less formal events with much looser women. It was said—in hushed whispers—that he'd bedded a different woman every night since he'd turned fifteen. Prudence had once added it up, but Olivia couldn't remember the outrageously high number now. She couldn't remember anything. This was Beaumont and she was in his arms.

"I am terribly sorry," Olivia said, finding her feet and bearings to stand on her own.

"Are you all right?" he asked, still lightly gripping her arms as if she might topple over again. He peered closely at her with his dark eyes. What wickedness he must have seen! Her gaze dropped to his mouth—how many women had he kissed?

"Yes. Thank you. Terribly sorry," Olivia mumbled again. Lord, if her mother saw her talking to him, she would be locked away for weeks. In fact, if anyone saw this, it would certainly make the gossip columns.

When the Mad Baron learned of the reckless, dangerous company she kept, he'd never want to marry her.

It had to be noted that Lord Beaumont hadn't immediately turned his back to her.

"It's very crowded in here this evening," he said. "Lady Jenning certainly has outdone herself."

"Or overdone. It's dangerously crowded in here," Olivia remarked.

"Indeed, and perilous to young maidens throughout the ballroom," Beaumont murmured. Olivia eyed him warily: was he flirting or bamming her?

"The dangers have added a certain thrill to the evening," Olivia replied.

"Indeed." His gaze lowered to her breasts. She felt a blush creep across her cheeks. She'd always wanted a man to look at her lustily, had she not?

"Do you need a spot of air? Miss?"

Young ladies do not go onto the terrace unaccompanied by rakes.

Especially Beaumont!

Except that she was *trying* to break the rules. And lud, he was handsome. And if he had kissed so many woman, what was one more? Why not her?

Besides, Prudence would certainly follow at a discreet distance, wouldn't she? Never mind that Prue seemed to have vanished.

"That would be lovely, thank you," she replied.

And then, unbelievably, Lord Beaumont escorted her out to the terrace. Olivia felt her heart start to beat quickly, giddily. Was it always this easy to gain the attentions of a rake? If only

she'd known! If only Prudence had pushed her—
literally pushed her—into some man's arms years
ago. She could be celebrating her wedding anniversary, not her looming death on her wedding
night.

Perhaps this is when her romance would finally begin! Perhaps a footman might stroll past
with champagne and Beaumont would pluck two
glasses, handing one to her. They would talk of
the stars and the ball and whatever else one talked
about while falling in love. Surely, they would
discover that they liked all the same things and
were truly kindred spirits in spite of his black-
ened reputation. He'd whisper how beautiful she
was. Then, in the moonlight, he'd kiss her.

That was how it was supposed to go.

What actually happened: Lord Beaumont saw a
friend of his. His arm loosened as he drifted away
from Olivia and toward his old comrade. They
quite forgot she was there, as he disentangled
himself entirely and strolled away. Olivia looked
around for Prudence, who was still nowhere to be
seen. Olivia was left all alone on the terrace. And
that's when the Mad Baron found her.

THE RADCLIFFE TEMPER had been the bane of
generations of Radcliffe men. They were an easy-
going lot, able to allow almost any slight or frustration to roll like water off a duck's back. But
then—and one never knew when—something
was just too much and they'd erupt in a violent

explosion of fury. Phinn often attempted to calculate just how much pressure, how much force, how much frustration he could take before it was best for everyone that he make himself scarce. It was one formula he'd yet to perfect.

The constant setbacks of the evening—Olivia with that man, her mother, Rogan—were not enough to incite his temper on their own. But as the evening progressed, his resistance was fraying.

Then he saw her in the arms of yet another man.

Then he saw that man look lasciviously at Olivia's breasts.

She wasn't his, but he felt possessive of her—as if she were already his wife.

It was a good thing he'd seen Olivia's friend push her. While that did absolve Olivia, it begged the question of why her friend would do such a thing. Phinn didn't think he liked the obvious answer.

It didn't matter. None of it mattered when he finally found Olivia alone on the terrace. She looked beautiful. Her skin was luminous in the moonlight, and her eyes were wide and dark. She appeared a little lost. He wanted nothing more than to embrace her, hold her close, and whisper something devastatingly romantic.

But years of *not* wooing every female that crossed his path suddenly caught up with him.

Instead he said, "Lady Olivia. Good evening."

She turned slowly to face him. First she looked toward the right, then toward the left, and then behind her. After ascertaining that there was no one else with whom she might converse, she reluctantly focused on him.

"Good evening, Lord Radcliffe," she said indifferently. It ought to have been off-putting. Oddly, he felt more determined than ever to win her.

"Please, call me Phinn."

"Oh, I couldn't possibly—" she protested. He stepped closer to her, needing to be near, needing to bridge this distance between them.

"Phinneas is a ridiculous name," he said. Really, it was, and there was no pretending otherwise. "And Radcliffe is far too formal."

"Right," she said awkwardly.

She didn't want to speak with him, let alone marry him. That much was plain. But was it because of his reputation or because of himself? Phinn suspected it was because of his reputation— after all, before she knew who he was she had nearly kissed him. He wanted to go back to that night.

There was no turning back in this courtship— the rumors were already running wild, and it would reflect badly upon them both if things went awry. Phinn didn't give a damn for himself, but he did care for her sake.

That was the thing: he cared. All he had wanted was a nice, calm wife who would offer companionship and perhaps love.

He thought that woman had been Olivia.

What if she wasn't? The woman before him—

who'd been two steps ahead of him all night—
was not the docile, eager-to-please woman he'd
expected. Yet she still perplexed and intrigued
him. He couldn't say for certain that she wasn't
the one for him.

"I'd been hoping to find you alone this evening," he said quietly.

"Oh?" Her eyes widened.

"Of course. Why wouldn't I?" he asked, wondering why she'd seem surprised by this. She
didn't really think he'd do an injury to her on the
terrace at a ball with onlookers, did she?

"Well you haven't seemed very interested in me
thus far," she said, finding her voice.

"We only just met," he replied. Literally, they
had only just been introduced yesterday and their
initial encounter had been far too brief.

"Exactly," Olivia said flatly.

Phinn quirked his head, stared at her curiously and tried to make sense of what she'd just
said. Women. WOMEN. They defied all logic
and reason. He pushed his hands through his
hair and remembered why he'd waited so long to
marry again and why Lord Archer's suggestion
that they just marry and be done with it made so
much sense.

But then he remembered his first glimpse of
Olivia, standing on a balcony above the ballroom
looking so beautiful and so above the fray. He
hadn't forgotten how she felt in his arms either.

"Perhaps we can start anew. Getting to know

each other. We're alone and it's quiet enough out here for a conversation . . ." He said this because Rogan, who apparently understood women, suggested he do so.

Olivia just shuddered.

"But you must be cold," he said, even though it was a warm evening. "Would you care to take a turn around the ballroom with me?"

"I should find my friends," Olivia said.

Her friends, he thought, who had pushed her into the arms of unsuspecting gentlemen and who interrogated him about murder and dungeons in the midst of the ballroom. He would have to win over her friends if he wished to win Olivia's hand in marriage.

"Allow me to escort you," he said firmly.

She *thought* about refusing—he could see it in her eyes—but smiled slightly and murmured, "Of course."

OLIVIA RELUCTANTLY ACCEPTED the Mad Baron's offer for a turn about the ballroom, if only because it seemed preferable to the less sparsely populated terrace and practically desolate garden.

They linked arms, and she rested her fingertips lightly on his forearm. It was firm. Muscled. She could feel it through the gloves and his jacket. She thought he just mucked around with sciencey things. But now she found herself curious . . .

Also curious: everyone else in the ballroom.

They were staring again. Everyone. All the

lords and ladies invited to the ball were taking a long look at the shocking sight of London's Least Likely to Cause a Scandal arm in arm with a man so scandalous he hadn't been in town for the past six years.

She glanced up at him. *Phinn*. He didn't seem bothered in the slightest by all the stares. How could he *do* that? Was he so unfeeling that he cared not what the ton thought of him? Or like her, had he perfected the demeanor of one who wasn't bothered in the slightest? What if they were alike in some way?

He glanced down at her. Caught her eye. She looked away with an embarrassed blush.

"I've heard you have many hobbies," he said. "Tell me about them?"

Olivia felt a flush of anger. *I've heard about your hobbies.* Did they tell him of her reputation for speaking endlessly about the dullest subjects imaginable? Was he bamming her? But another sidelong glance at the Mad Baron told her he was completely earnest.

She spied an opportunity to utilize a tried and true method for repelling men.

"Oh, I enjoy the usual activities for ladies," Olivia said. In other words, he could find another woman with the same hobbies. "I embroider, play the pianoforte, and paint watercolors."

She peered up at him, expecting to see his eyes glaze over and the vague expression of polite disinterest. But no.

"What do you paint?" he asked.

"Still lifes, mainly. An endless combination of flowers, fruits, and decorative home items," she said, sounding bored. Indeed, she had long ago tired of her inanimate watercolor subjects. "However, I would like to paint portraits of the male nude."

Beside her, the Mad Baron started coughing, and Olivia didn't even try to restrain her smile. Lud, it felt good to finally say that aloud!

"I'm sorry, my lord. Have I shocked you?" she asked ever-so-sweetly.

"I thought you would say landscapes," he said in a strained voice.

"I suppose you're going to tell me the landscapes in Yorkshire are beautiful and perfect for painting."

"Yes," he said simply. "I have no skill at painting, but I appreciate the talent in others."

"Well, I'm sure if you practiced every Monday and Thursday for two hours since the age of six, you'd excel at it as well," Olivia replied dryly.

"Perhaps that's why I'm good at mechanical drawings," Phinn said, not bothered by her dry retort. "I've been working on them since I was young and it still occupies much of my time."

Olivia was reminded of a line from the broadside. The Mad Baron would, apparently, spend days and weeks in a barn on his property, constructing strange machines and instruments of torture.

"What things do you build?" she ventured, curious as to how he would explain building dangerous and deviant machines.

"Currently, I'm assisting the Duke of Ashbrooke in constructing the Difference Engine he designed. Should we be successful, this machine will be revolutionary."

"That must keep you very busy." Honestly, she couldn't believe that Emma and her husband had a hand in bringing this dangerous man to town. Perhaps he would be too busy to court her and she might somehow find another man to elope with.

"Yes. But you have your own interests to keep you occupied," he said, and Olivia smiled faintly as hopes for companionship and company from a man she loved drifted further and further away. Everything about this possible looming marriage was the opposite of everything she'd ever dreamt of.

Phinn came to a stop before a slight alcove made from two pillars, a settee in its dim recesses. It was the sort of dark, secluded, intimate and romantic spot that would be ideal for a lovers' interlude. Or something more nefarious.

Her heartbeat quickened.

Olivia couldn't help it: she gazed up into his green eyes even though she knew the intensity of his gaze made her *feel* things that were very inconvenient. It was just that for so long, no one ever looked at her anymore. And then, out of nowhere, he'd appeared, apparently captivated by her from across the ballroom. *Why* did the one handsome stranger to notice her have to be none other than the Mad Baron?

Her gaze inevitably drifted to that menacing scar. What happened? She wanted to ask, but she didn't really want to know. It was too bad he was so dangerous. He wouldn't murder her in the ballroom, would he? No, there were too many witnesses.

"Lady Olivia, I don't mean to frighten you. I just want to know you. When we first met, I felt myself drawn to you," he said in a low voice that sent shivers up and down her spine.

"I as well," she confessed. "Yet . . ."

He took a step closer and she was all too aware of how large he was. She blushed, remembering the firmness of his chest when she'd fallen into him and his kiss upon her hand. What if tonight he dared more? Her heart pounded at the prospect—but was that desire or fear?

If it weren't for his dangerous past . . .

"I really should get back to my friends," Olivia said a touch breathlessly. Besides, the less the ton talked about her and the Mad Baron, the better her chances of escaping this courtship before it was too late.

"Of course," Phinn said obligingly. Ever the gentleman. Wasn't that at odds with his murdering past? She became aware that he was aware of her efforts to lose him. And yet, would he still endeavor to court her or would he step aside?

They had taken but a few steps when another gentleman stepped into their path. He was almost as tall as Phinn, but not as fit. He had unruly blond hair and a grin upon seeing them.

"If it isn't the happy couple," he said with a laugh.

"Go away, Rogan," Phinn said, sounding exasperated. Olivia found herself intrigued. This jovial wastrel didn't seem like the company a brooding, murderous recluse would keep.

"You're not going to introduce me to your lady?" Rogan asked, nudging Phinn in the ribs.

"Lady Olivia, may I present my friend, Lord Rogan. Ignore everything he says."

Lord Rogan just grinned wickedly and said, "Phinn has been speaking highly of you."

"Except that. Don't ignore that," Phinn countered.

"It's nice to meet you," Olivia said as this Lord Rogan bowed and kissed her hand and then winked at her. Finally, gentlemen were starting to notice her! Unfortunately, it was the friend of the man courting her.

"We were just returning Lady Olivia to her friends," Phinn said, starting to walk away and leading Olivia with him. "She is eager to find them."

"I'll join you. I'd love to make their acquaintance," Rogan said, falling into step beside them. "Especially before the wedding breakfast."

They strolled through the ballroom, weaving

through the crowd, on their way to where Olivia
had spotted Prudence and Emma in their usual
spot. Just a few more steps to safety and freedom
when—

She slipped on something. Her daintily slip-
pered feet flew from underneath her. Olivia's
arms flailed wildly in a desperate attempt to
right herself. She was aware of looking foolish
and she was aware of falling backward . . . falling . . . falling . . .

And then she was caught. Strong arms closed
around her, hands splaying across her belly where
no man had ever touched her. She'd fallen against
a strong, firm chest behind her. This chest and
these arms were more muscled and more assured
in their hold than Beaumont's. A giggle escaped
Olivia's lips as she realized how marvelously odd
it was that she, Prissy Missy, should know the embrace of two different men in one night.

When she'd embarked upon her quest to cavort
with men of dubious reputation, she had no intention of winding up here, swept off her feet
and into the arms of the Mad Baron. Strangely, it
wasn't horrible. Not horrible at all.

"Feats of strength, man, what did I tell you!"
Rogan said gleefully as onlookers peered curiously at them.

"Feats of strength?" Olivia echoed. Then she
put the pieces together. "Are you saying that I am
extraordinarily heavy?" she asked. She struggled
awkwardly to untangle herself and stand on her

own two feet. If they had shared a moment, it was certainly over. "I am not a feat of strength!" she protested.

"No! I told you to ignore everything Rogan said." Phinn punctuated this with a hard glare at his friend, who attempted to appear chagrined.

"Phinn tells me you're beautiful," Rogan said. For a fleeting second she softened. *He thought her beautiful!* But why couldn't anyone else have noticed that, ever?

"Except for that," Phinn grumbled. "Don't ignore that."

Olivia looked from one to gentleman to the other. They were mad, both of them.

Then Phinn bent over to pick up the sheet of paper she had slipped on. Waxed parquet, satin slippers, and sheets of paper were a dangerous combination. Why was there a piece of paper on the ballroom floor? Had someone been exchanging love notes, planning a secret assignation? Then she remembered Dudley and his smirk as he handed her—

"The Mad Baron: The Gruesome Story of an Innocent Maiden's Tragic Love and Untimely Death. A True Story," Rogan read aloud, peering over Phinn's shoulder.

Phinn straightened to his full height. Shoulders broad. Jaw clenched. Olivia's heart started to pound. The fury in his gaze made her want to flee in the opposite direction. And yet, oddly, she also wanted to tear the sheet of paper from his hands and rip it to pieces. As if that might console him.

He took a deep breath. She could hear it because a hush had fallen over the ballroom. Very well, she *definitely* wanted to flee. Somehow he seemed taller and harder and meaner. There was a distance in his eyes that terrified her more than anything—as if, in this strange, bewitched state, he would be deaf to voices or pleas.

Abruptly Phinn turned on his heel and stalked out of the ballroom. No one stopped him.

Chapter 6

"You know, Rogan, I think she actually believes this rubbish," Phinn said, holding aloft the copy of *The Mad Baron*. It was the worst sort of penny dreadful gothic horror mongering rubbish. Given that the whole sordid mess occurred six years ago, Phinn assumed that by now the broadside would be used for wrapping fish and lining trunks. Who the devil had seen fit to keep such drivel?

"Everybody does, my friend," Rogan said, happily settled into a chair with a full glass of brandy in one hand and a lit cigar in the other.

"Well that explains why Olivia is in a constant state of anxiety around me," Phinn said dryly.

"Either that, or such an innocent maiden cannot help but tremble before such an example of masculinity as yourself," Rogan scoffed.

"Much as I'd like to believe that, this damned broadside and those stupid rumors are a more likely explanation," Phinn replied. He pressed his whiskey glass against the scar.

"Well, a name like the Mad Baron is hard to live down."

Phinn glanced warily at his friend. "When were you going to tell me all of this?"

"I thought you knew," Rogan said, drawing on the cigar. "You know, since everybody does."

Phinn elected to ignore that questionable logic. "This broadside explains a lot. Like why she tried to avoid me all evening, especially when I sought a moment alone with her. As *someone* had advised."

"I suppose women wouldn't want to be alone with a known murder," Rogan mused. Phinn bit back a growl of frustration. But had Rogan ever been known for his rational faculties? No. "Not even at a ball when hundreds of people are close enough to hear her scream."

"'Alleged' murderer," Phinn corrected. They'd never charged or tried him. The magistrate had ruled it wasn't his fault, though Phinn knew he was guilty and that there was a black mark on his soul that nothing would ever erase. "And for God's sake, you're not helping."

"All right, all right," Rogan said, waving his cigar dismissively and scattering ash everywhere. "What you need now is to reassure her that you're not inclined to violence against women, despite numerous publications to the contrary."

"Numerous? Are there more?"

"You're legendary, Phinn," Rogan said, raising a glass in toast. Phinn just downed his drink and focused on the burn of the whiskey and not the numerous publications detailing his alleged murderous exploits circulating the country.

"Should I just tell her that I didn't do it? 'Olivia it has come to my attention that you think I'm a murderer. I'd like to assure you that is not the case. Marry me.'"

"You may want to soften her up a bit first," Rogan said. "She'll probably be too terrified to listen. Pay her some pretty compliments."

"You make it sound so simple. Compliment the lady, assure her of my innocence, live happily ever after." Yet everything thus far with Olivia had been anything but easy.

"Fortunately for you," Rogan began, "it's even easier than that, for I have compiled a collection of tried and true compliments. Ladies fall for them all the time. Lady Olivia will be throwing herself at you."

He glanced dubiously at Rogan. Only hours ago he had idiotically referred to Olivia as a feat of strength. But while Phinn had been unlocking the mysteries of various scientific phenomena and using the knowledge to build new machines, Rogan had been chasing after women. Granted, given the type of women he chased, his success was questionable. But Phinn had no plans of his own to woo this intriguing if maddening beauty.

How bad could a few compliments be?

The following day
Drawing room, Archer House

Even though the construction of the Difference Engine was behind schedule, Phinn returned to the Archer household, armed with compliments and determined to woo and wed Lady Olivia.

This would be his last effort, and if she adamantly refused him—well, then he would have to find a woman who would make a sweet and kind wife.

Of course, every time he considered abandoning his courtship, he couldn't quite shake the image of Olivia as he'd first seen her: so lovely, beautiful, and above the fray. There was also the matter of how she felt in his arms. He'd been up a while considering the sensation of her against his chest and under his palms and just how much more pleasurable it would be to touch her bare skin.

If she truly didn't want him—fine. But a woman had never intrigued him the way Olivia did, so he wasn't about to slink off to Yorkshire just yet.

That she didn't appear with her face caked under layers of paint, he considered a successful start to tea. That they were stuck in her drawing room with her parents serving as chaperones, he considered a detriment to his efforts.

For a quarter of an hour they discussed the weather (warm and sunny, except for when it was cold and rainy), and Lady Archer apprised all of them on her plans for the wedding, completely disregarding the fact that Phinn had neither proposed to Olivia nor had she shown even an inkling of accepting.

He and Olivia exchanged alarmed glances, which led to shy smiles. She was so pretty when she smiled. *Make smile + Add compliments = Win girl.*

Lord Archer drank his tea, stole frequent glances at the clock, and otherwise appeared uninterested.

When he could stand it no more, Phinn interrupted Lady Archer by turning his attentions solely to Olivia. He smiled. She eyed him curiously.

"Lady Olivia, is your father a thief, perchance?" Phinn inquired. Immediately, his misstep was clear. Lord Archer coughed and sputtered, spewing his sip of tea.

"I beg your pardon!" Lady Archer gasped, clutching a handkerchief to her chest as if she'd been wounded.

"I ought to call you out for that!" Lord Archer bellowed. His face had become an alarming shade of red, not unlike wine.

Inwardly cursing Rogan, Phinn hastily carried on with the rest of the, er, compliment. Looking at Olivia, he added, "Because he must have taken the sparkle from the stars in the sky and put them in your eyes."

Then he vowed to make Rogan pay for failing him with these stupid compliments.

"What?" Olivia was confused. But then he saw the moment it made sense to her. She gasped, "Oh!" and smiled faintly. And then she unfurrowed her brow and grinned when she glanced at her parents, who were quite possibly on the verge of apoplexy. It seemed that upsetting Lord and Lady Archer was a faster way to her heart than flattery.

"Yes, that was a compliment," Phinn said. "You have very pretty eyes, Lady Olivia."

"She gets that from me," Lady Archer said, now sufficiently recovered from the shock to flutter her lashes. Phinn grinned when he caught Olivia rolling her eyes.

Lord Archer seemed to notice, too. After a disgruntled look at him, then his daughter, he said, "Lady Archer, let's you and I step out for a moment."

"Isn't it improper for me to be unchaperoned?" Olivia asked. Her eyes widened when she saw his annoyed frown. He was definitely going to put this matter of his alleged murderous past to rest. Today.

"I don't think we should leave them alone," Lady Archer murmured.

One had to wonder why she feared leaving them alone together now when she was so eager for them to be wed. One also had to be thankful to Lord Archer for impressing that upon his wife.

"If this bloody wedding ever happens, they'll be alone together for the rest of their lives," he said gruffly. "Might as well get started now."

"Well, leave the drawing room door open," Lady Archer said. Olivia didn't reply, for she had bitten into a pastry, which her mother then admonished her about, telling her that ladies restrained their appetites. Olivia contrarily took another large bite.

Given that Rogan's compliment wasn't a complete failure after all, Phinn thought he'd try another. Were they ridiculous lines that he felt foolish uttering? Absolutely. But was it worth it when Olivia smiled? Yes. A thousand times yes.

"Could I implore upon you for some directions?" he asked Olivia after her parents had left the room.

"Whatever do you mean?" she said, tilting her head as if confused.

"To your heart. Directions to your heart," he said.

And then she laughed. He wasn't sure if she was laughing at the joke or at him, but he didn't care. He had made her happy if only for a second. In that second, when all seemed right in the world, he knew he couldn't let her go. Not yet. Not without a fight.

With some reluctance, but knowing it was the right thing, Phinn brought up the inevitable subject.

"Lady Olivia, it has come to my attention that some still persist in calling me the Mad Baron."

"Everyone," she said, taking another bite of pastry.

"I'm sorry?"

"You said some people, but everyone does," she replied, confirming what Rogan had said. Apparently, he ought to pay more attention to London gossip columns instead of reading scientific journals.

"I'd hoped that enough time had passed for the moniker to be forgotten," he said. "It's been six years."

Olivia just shrugged. "I have been called Prissy Missy for four seasons now and London's Least Likely to Cause a Scandal for three," she replied. "I have no hope that these things ever fade."

"I know. I like what those names say about you," Phinn said.

But that seemed the wrong thing to say, for she smiled faintly. And sighed. And availed herself of another pastry.

"Given that is likely the case with my unfortunate name," he began, "I want you to know that you need not be afraid of me. I would never harm you."

"Is this the part where you tell me that you did not, in fact, murder your wife?" Olivia inquired.

That was the thing. He couldn't just *say* that and not feel like a liar.

"Something to that effect," he answered. Olivia's eyes widened considerably. *Wrong* thing to say.

"A resounding denial might be more effective in alleviating my distress and, frankly, utter terror at being courted by an alleged murderer," she said frankly.

"I can't give you that," Phinn said softly, with some anguish. "I wish I could but I cannot in good conscience."

Olivia's only reply was to select another pastry and take a bite. She peered at him expectantly. Ah, this was the part where he was to tell her the entire sordid story. But where to begin with the dramatic and disastrous Nadia? It wasn't the sort of story one told over tea in the drawing room.

"I did not kill her, but her death was my fault." The whole mess with Nadia was a knot so tangled he still couldn't unravel it. All of the what ifs he asked never led him to an answer. The damned broadside was littered with lies and exaggerations and gross inaccuracies, but enough of the truth remained. His wife. His temper. His machines.

"Was it an accident?" she asked.

He hesitated. Neither he nor Nadia had *planned* her death. By all accounts it was an accident—one he held himself responsible for. But then again, Nadia had been a smart, devious woman. She didn't do anything by accident.

Olivia finished that pastry and helped herself to still another. She stared at him, waiting for more of the story.

"It was not exactly an accident," he admitted.

"What, pray tell, does that mean?"

"This is a difficult subject for me. I generally try to avoid it. I had hoped that it wasn't necessary to mention it, but Lady Olivia, I would like to assuage your doubts about our upcoming match. Given your temperament, I'm sure we shall get along peacefully."

"My temperament?" Olivia seemed alarmed, perhaps even angry, even though he'd only meant it as another compliment. But she didn't know Nadia's temper. Or his. "Are you saying that if I behave myself and avoid *bothering* you, then I needn't fear for my life?"

He could see how she would interpret it that way, but—

"I can explain, Lady Olivia. You're so different than my first wife. You're London's Least Likely to Cause a Scandal, and she was—" No words he could use to describe Nadia were polite enough to mention. Not that Olivia even gave him a chance to answer.

"And if I'm not the obliging, docile, deferential wife you're looking for, then what?" she asked, crossing her arms over her chest, doing marvelous things to her breasts. It took no small effort to wrench his gaze and imagination away and focus on the angry woman before him.

"Olivia, I just thought we might suit," Phinn said, exasperated by the unfathomable reasoning she presented.

"Based upon my reputation, and upon gossip," she said angrily. "You don't know me."

"Just like how you think we won't suit based on my reputation and gossip," he challenged, with a lift of his brow. It brought a scowl to her face, probably because he was undeniably right. "You don't know me either."

"What do we do?" Olivia asked.

"We get to know each other," Phinn said.

"And if we do not suit then?" She arched one brow in challenge. His heart started thudding hard. This was the moment he lost her. Or perhaps the moment he secured the chance to win her.

"It'd be a terrible fate for us to marry if we didn't suit," he answered cautiously. It was a fate he'd already suffered.

"I'm pleasantly surprised that you agree," Olivia replied. "I cannot think of anything worse."

"But an even worse fate would be to miss our opportunity . . ." he went on. And then, lowering his voice because he was the sort of man who didn't just *say* such things, he added, " . . . for love."

"Love?" Her eyes flashed, surprised to hear him say that.

"Would you rather I mentioned my ten thousand a year and your dowry?" Phinn asked dryly. He didn't do much wooing of women, but he knew to err on the side of romance and less on the side of economic and practical considerations. "Would that persuade you?"

"It would persuade my father," she remarked tartly.

To which he replied, "I wouldn't be married to your father, now would I?"

"You'd be married to me," she declared. "Prissy Missy. London's Least Likely to Cause a Scandal."

"You say that as if those things are deterrents. But I like those things about you."

"And if I caused a scandal?"

She lifted her brow. This was a challenge. Phinn held her gaze.

"I think you underestimate my talents for dealing with wild and unruly women," he said, essentially daring her to acts of outrageous behavior. He had survived Nadia. Never in a million years would Olivia be able to upstage her. But she didn't know that. What was the worst she would do, anyway?

Opposite him, Olivia sat in a perfectly pressed and modest day dress. Her back was ramrod straight, her posture perfect. She daintily sipped her tea. He couldn't imagine her causing trouble.

"I think I might surprise you," she said. "Perhaps even scare you off."

The words were out of his mouth before he could consider the pros and cons and consequences: "Would you care to wager about that?"

Chapter 7

A young beauty, were she as fair as Hebe, and elegant as the Goddess of Love herself, would soon lose these charms by a course of inordinate eating, drinking, and late hours.

—THE MIRROR OF GRACES

British Museum

THREE PARTICULAR YOUNG ladies sought a diversion in the antiquities room of the British Museum. They lingered before the pottery, particularly the ones painted with the most intriguing scenes of naked men and women dashing about. They chatted in hush whispers, as befit both the setting and the topic of conversation.

"I am more convinced than ever that the Mad Baron did indeed murder his wife," Olivia confided in Prudence and Emma. She'd gone over their conversation in her mind repeatedly. He did not declare his innocence—not in any way that made her feel safe enough to close her eyes in his presence, let alone marry the man.

"He was awfully determined to whisk you off alone to a secluded place at the ball the other night," Prudence said. "Presumably for nefarious purposes."

"That isn't even the half of it," Olivia added dramatically. "We had a conversation about the murder allegations."

"You did not," Prudence said, eyes wide.

"Honesty. Always the best course of action," Emma replied.

"Says the woman who faked her betrothal," Prudence remarked.

"I married him, so it doesn't signify anyway," Emma said with a shrug. "And anyway, it was *your* idea to fake the betrothal."

"Olivia was the one who wrote the letter," Prudence replied.

"Hello!" Olivia said, waving her hands in front of her bickering friends. "*He said the death was his fault,*" she whispered frantically. Both Prudence and Emma obliged her with appalled gasps and exclamations, which attracted more than a few curious stares from other museumgoers. "And he said that because of my docile and obliging temperament, he was sure we would suit because, presumably, I wouldn't drive him into a murderous rage."

"He has no idea what you have in store for him, does he?" Emma asked, shaking her head in pity for the poor Mad Baron.

"He might expect some trouble," Olivia confided with a smile on her lips. She had all but promised him that she wasn't going to behave as London's Least Likely to Cause a Scandal. "And he all but dared me to."

"You and the Mad Baron locked in a battle of

epic proportions with your life on the line," Prudence said. "Be still my beating heart."

"My heart does race whenever he's around," Olivia confided. She felt a heightened awareness of his green eyes upon her when he was near, like a prey animal being stalked. It was torture. Just waiting. For something to happen. Something bad. Presumably.

"Are you certain you do not find him attractive?" Emma asked, tilting her head curiously. "He *is* handsome, Olivia. I quite like his eyes and his tussled hair. It gives him quite a rakish air."

Olivia knew she might have, too, if everything were different. Like, say, if he hadn't essentially confessed to murder in her drawing room over tea.

"I also have trouble breathing," she said. Really, in the past few days, morning, noon, and night, she couldn't quite catch her breath.

"So you're saying he leaves you breathless?" Emma asked. "Really, Olivia—"

"Your corset could be laced to tightly. Or you could . . ." Prudence let her voice trail off and she awkwardly looked away. She and Emma exchanged a nervous glance.

"Or I could be what, Prudence?"

"You might be filling out your dresses more," she said, wincing.

Olivia opened her mouth to protest. Then she thought better of it. She glanced down at her figure. Was it fuller? All those pastries she no longer refrained from eating, and all those extra helpings at meals—despite the disapproving comments from her mother—had to go somewhere. It seemed they went toward her breasts and generally giving her a rounder figure.

"It's possible, given that I abandoned all efforts to restrain myself to ladylike portions. Extra cake and biscuits at tea has been one of the better parts of breaking the rules," she agreed, smoothing out her skirts. "However, I truly believe my symptoms are because I am constantly left alone with a notoriously violent man. He's likely to strangle me and leave me for dead in some dark corner of the ballroom. Or perhaps in my very own drawing room! I fear for my life. My heart is racing just thinking about it."

"But why would he do that *before* the wedding?" Prudence asked thoughtfully as they strolled through the gallery housing the pottery and into a large, airy room lined with ancient marble statues.

"Prudence!" Emma exclaimed. "That is not helpful."

"But it's logical. You're definitely safe with him at least until the vows are said," Prudence said. "If he wanted to simply go around murdering young ladies, why go through all the bother of courtship first?"

"He just doesn't seem that terrible," Emma said. "I had a nice conversation with him at the ball. He answered my questions about the murder. He confirmed that he doesn't have a dungeon. I can't imagine that Blake would work with him if he were guilty of such a crime."

"He is handsome," Prudence admitted. "For a murderer."

"He does seem a bit shy," Emma said. "Probably because he hasn't spent much time in the throes of the social whirl."

"You know what they say. It's always the quiet ones," Olivia said gravely.

"I have heard that," Prudence agreed solemnly.

"Oh, for Lord's sake, Prudence! You're distressing Olivia." Emma's vexed cries echoed around the room. A few other museum patrons turned to peer at them.

"Prue isn't making me any more distressed than I already am. He basically confessed to the crime. And he wants me only because I am the perfect lady who won't bother him. The kind of woman who won't put up a fight," Olivia said with a sigh. Then, brow furrowing, she added, "And he and his friends made such a joke about his show of strength."

"All the better to carry you off, ravish you, and then . . ." Prudence said, letting her voice trail off. She mimed strangling herself. It was not pretty, and Olivia shuddered. Nearby, a mother urged her child to turn away.

"If he's very strong, he must be very muscled. Like these," Emma said, gesturing toward the array of statues before them.

Naked. Male. Statues.

Young ladies do not gaze upon naked men.

Olivia felt her cheeks redden and she fought the urge to avert her gaze. Most men she was acquainted with didn't seem like they were hiding physiques like these under their jackets, waistcoats, shirts, and cravats. Even the men whose arms she stumbled into the other night didn't seem to hint quite at *this.* The Mad Baron, on the other hand . . . from what she had felt, she thought that he might be harboring such a chiseled chest and abdomen under this clothes. Not that she would ever know.

"Do you think he is like this?" Prudence asked in a hushed whisper.

"I haven't even considered it," Olivia said, cheeks reddening. *Young ladies do not lie. But young ladies do not possess such wanton thoughts.*

"Oh, I think you must have," Emma said, grinning at Olivia's blushing cheeks.

"Perhaps you noticed when you fell into his arms at the ball," Prudence said pointedly. "And now you are wondering . . ."

"You'll know on your wedding night," Emma said. Still with that naughty grin.

"My wedding night. I thought I'd always look forward to it," Olivia said glumly. She might end up married to the Mad Baron and he might have muscles like this. She'd be left alone, at his mercy, and in no way a match for this sort of strength. She took a calming deep breath.

"You needn't wait for the wedding night itself,"

Emma pointed out. Prudence looked mildly appalled. "You could always . . ."

"Highly unlikely, given that I am determined not to encourage him," Olivia said. "In fact, he practically dared me to prove that we will not suit. More to the point, we have wagered about it."

He'd surprised her with that dare. And that grin of his, which didn't make him seem like a murderer *at all*. She couldn't help but wonder: what if he had adamantly defended himself from her charges? What if he had explained everything? What if he were innocent? But if he was, he would have said so, and he did not.

"Is that so?" Prudence asked.

"Quite an interesting plot twist," Emma remarked.

"So you see, I must do something desperate, and time is running out," Olivia said. "My mother hopes for the banns to be read this Sunday. So what shall I do to prove that I am London's Latest Scandal?"

"You know what you have to do," Emma said. "Act scandalously. Improperly."

"Nudity," Prudence stated. "And I'm not merely speaking of leaving your gloves at home or giving a gent a glimpse of your stocking-clad ankle, either."

"I beg your pardon?" Both Emma and Olivia peered curiously at their friend after her mad suggestion.

"Lady Clarke once wore a gown that revealed

more of her bosoms and back than it covered. The ton talked for weeks. Lady Thurston is said to dampen her gowns—and all the gents throw themselves at her while respectable women never invite her to tea."

"Nudity, Prudence?" Olivia winced, imagining herself streaking through a ballroom with *nothing* on.

"We could take a cue from these statues," Prudence said, waving toward them.

"I am not strolling naked through a ballroom with naught but a sheet wrapped around me."

"But you could be a bit more revealing," Prudence said with a pointed look at Olivia's exceedingly proper and modest day gown. "Show your ankles. Lower your bodice. Somehow procure a diaphanous gown and dampen the skirts."

"You might just cause a sensation," Emma remarked thoughtfully. "And perhaps attract a new beau."

"One who will whisk you away to Gretna or procure a special license," Prudence pointed out.

Olivia's immediate, unbidden thought to that plan was to picture Phinn looking forlorn. *Disappointed* in her, even. He'd probably push his fingers through his hair, mussing it up, and look at her with those eyes and ask her, pained, *why* she would do such a thing. He would rue the day he wagered with her.

What did she care what he felt?

If she was going to fall in love and live happily ever after, she'd have to stop waiting for it to happen to her. She'd have to start making her own opportunities. If she didn't want to be London's Least Likely to Cause a Scandal—and keep the groom that came with it—then she'd have to show a little skin.

"I like this plan," she said resolutely. "I can scare off Phinn and attract a new suitor. But how do I get out of the house dressed immodestly without my mother having a hysterical fit?"

The three women fell into a long silence. Their thoughts may have been distracted by the proximity of all the tall, impeccably muscled statues looming over them. What was under that fig leaf, anyway?

Finally, Prudence spoke. "This is where your skill with a needle and thread will finally be put to good use."

Later that evening

Rogan succeeded in dragging Phinn to Brook's, where there were all sorts of entertainments for gentlemen. Rogan seemed at ease in the club and familiar with more than a few patrons, making Phinn fear for the man's inheritance.

"You wagered with your betrothed that you would suit?" Rogan lamented as they strolled through the club.

"It seemed like a good idea at the moment,"

Phinn admitted. It had been positively electric. Not for the first time did he feel a connection to her, as if drawn by an unseen force, like gravity.

He knew all about gravity: it was futile to resist.

"You have basically given her every incentive to try to break with you," Rogan said. "I think I need a drink."

"I might have also told her Nadia's death was my fault," Phinn added, turning to watch Rogan's exceedingly appalled expression. He couldn't help but grin.

"There's nothing funny about telling a woman you'd like to woo that you're a murderer," Rogan said. No. There wasn't.

"It seemed logical at the time. I tried to explain that Nadia's death was an accident and that because Olivia has such a different temperament she needn't be afraid. However, I think I succeeded only in offending her and convincing her that I am a cold-blooded killer."

"I definitely need a drink," Rogan said, glancing about for a footman with a bottle of brandy. "Are you trying to make this impossible for yourself? Do you not want to marry her?"

"I do want to marry her. Perhaps even more than when I first set eyes on her."

At first he'd simply thought her beautiful. There was such an innocence about her, and in her white dresses, she just radiated sweetness and purity. She was everything Nadia hadn't been. Olivia was poised, refined, and exceedingly well-mannered. Nadia had been a dark-haired vixen, never speaking when she could weep, shout, plead, or demand. Instinctively, he craved Olivia.

Or, rather, the Olivia he first set eyes upon, and the Olivia he had been told about.

"Well seems like you are trying to give her every excuse to flee," Rogan said. "You practically dared her to act scandalously. Fortunately, I don't think Prissy Missy is capable of it."

Phinn wasn't sure about that. He saw the sparkling intensity in her gaze. The excited upturn of her lips. She might not succeed, but Lord help them all, she was going to try.

"Is it wrong that I'm curious to see what she will do?" he mused.

"No. I confess I'm intrigued as well. It ought to liven up an otherwise dull season," Rogan replied. "But you have other problems, my friend."

"What was I to do about that drama with Nadia? Lie?"

"Yes!" Rogan said. Phinn scowled.

"I don't want to start my marriage on false premises," he said. "It'll be doomed to fail. Like constructing upon a weak foundation, or a simple mathematical error that throws off all subsequent calculations."

"At this point you'll be lucky to start your marriage at all," Rogan muttered. "If you keep talking about mathematics and whatnot."

"You needn't be so dark about it. I'll just . . . keep wooing her."

How, he was not quite sure. He could probably build a machine to do the job before he could figure out just what Lady Olivia Archer wanted.

"I'll continue to help you," Rogan said with a sigh. "Seeing as you desperately need my assistance."

"Thank you."

"That's what friends are for," Rogan said. Then after appearing to give the matter some thought, he grinned and said, "I'll probably spike the lemonade at Almack's. After a few drinks her defenses will be down and—"

"Do *not* finish that sentence. Do not speak it. By God do not ever do what you were about to suggest I do."

"All right. So you want to win a woman without being the slightest bit roguish?"

"What would that entail?" Phinn asked.

All his life he'd endeavored to be calm, steady, and reliable. Like a machine. Like a gentleman. More to the point: utterly unlike his father, mother, and brother, all of whom had been inclined to hysterical, highly dramatic and irrational behavior.

"You'd have to flirt with everyone. Right in front of Olivia," Rogan said, grinning, presumably, at the genius he perceived in himself. Not that Phinn had a better suggestion.

"Lady Olivia to you," Phinn said, and his friend ignored him and continued on with his plan.

"Women love it when men play hard to get," Rogan said. "And nothing gets their attention like competition with other birds."

"Won't other women be put off by my reputation, the way Olivia is?"

"Not the ones I have in mind. As long as you're all right looking and can keep up a conversation while hinting at *more*, they'll give you *all* the attentions you want."

Chapter 8

*On no account must they be too short; for when any
design is betrayed of showing the foot or ankle, the idea of
beauty is lost in that of the wearer's odious indelicacy.*
—The Mirror of Graces

Almack's assembly rooms

It was not difficult for Prudence to spike the
lemonade at Almack's. After all, whoever paid
attention to Prude Prudence? No one, that's who.
Most young ladies would have had a terrible time
coming across a bottle of gin, if they even managed it. But not her. Given that the household cook
was given to drink, Prue easily nipped a bit of it.
She discovered that flasks easily fit in one's reticule. Convenient, that.

Thus Prudence waltzed into Almack's . . .

No, she never waltzed. No one ever asked
Prude Prudence if she would like to dance, and
she was fine with that.

She walked in, hoping, as usual, that no one
would notice her.

At the first possible moment, still quite early in
the evening, Prudence spiked the lemonade.

Why, why, *why* would she do such a thing?

To help her dearest friend, of course. Olivia was so distraught about this business with the Mad Baron. While Prudence applauded her efforts to act unladylike, she also knew a hopeless case when it hit her in the face and then apologized profusely afterward. Olivia was too good. Deep down, bottom of her heart, good. Her instincts were to be polite, gracious, and kind. For years she'd watched Olivia never act abominably toward Lady Katherine, even though she'd had every justifiable reason to. Nor did Olivia ever speak ill of her mother, whose overbearing manner was the reason she couldn't catch a gent's eye.

In the very best way, Prudence lacked faith in her friend.

While waiting for said friend to arrive, Prue graced the wallflower patch with her presence. Emma had arrived at the ball already, but she was off dancing with her duke. Soon she would engage in her frustrating new habit of trying to force introductions between her friends and eligible gentlemen. It was awkward for everyone.

When Olivia finally arrived, Prue took one look at her and was glad she'd spiked the lemonade. She was going to need it.

Olivia wore the most modest, most demure, most unprovocative dress she had ever worn, which was really saying something. It was white muslin and silk. There was a large lace ruffle along the hem. Instead of a fashionably—and seductively—low bodice, she wore a white lace fichu that covered her up to the neck.

"You look nice," Prudence said, her voice hollow. "You are the picture of a young, virginal, modest woman. What of our plans?"

But then she caught the wicked gleam in her friend's eyes. Her confidence was restored. Marginally.

"For now," Olivia drawled. "By the end of this evening, if I haven't given my mother a fit of the vapors, I shall consider myself a failure."

"Your mother won't be hard to shock. I do hope that is not your only measure of success."

"True. Then I hope to read how I have thoroughly tarnished my reputation in the next issue of *The London Weekly*."

"Whatever have you planned?" Prue asked, excited.

"Let's just say the stitches holding this fichu and this flounce are not the strongest ones I've ever sewn. I might have shortened the hem and lowered the bodice, too. They have lasted long enough to get me out of the house and past my mother's approval. At any moment now, I hope the stitches fall out and I lose all this ghastly lace. I should also add that my coiffure won't last long either. I have removed half the hairpins my maid used. I'll look a tawdry wreck before the night is through."

"One hopes. One dearly hopes," Prudence murmured. "I feel parched. Shall we fetch some lemonade?"

"Wait!" Olivia suddenly stopped short and grabbed Prue's arm to hold her back. They had been weaving their way through the guests, onward to the lemonade table.

Following her gaze, Prue said, "Ah. I see."

The Mad Baron was there. *Phinn.* Olivia didn't want him to see her like this: the demure, proper, and biddable girl he sought as his demure, proper, biddable wife. Not when she vowed to prove otherwise.

She had imagined how tonight was supposed to go: later in the evening, after she'd lost the stupid fichu and the hideous flounce at her hem, he'd spy her across the ballroom, surrounded by a mass of suitors. As she laughed while men vied to kiss her hand, he'd realize that she was not the woman he sought and thus not worth the bother of courting her.

"That is quite a gown, Lady Olivia." It was Lady Katherine, flanked by her pack of friends, giving her a disparaging stare. In her slinky blue silk gown decked with glass beads, she made Olivia feel frightfully unfashionable in addition to the way she usually made her feel: unfortunate, simple, and slightly ridiculous. Katherine smiled cruelly. "Already dressing for your spinsterhood, I see. Won't even the Mad Baron have you?"

It hurt, that. Especially given that it might be

true. But rather than wallow, Olivia tipped her chin up and finally came up with a retort to Lady Katherine.

"Oh look!" she exclaimed, pointing toward the far side of the ballroom. "I think I see someone who cares."

Behind her, Prudence burst out laughing. Lady Katherine's friends could be seen biting back laughter.

Lady Katherine just stared at her. Olivia stared right back. It was not clear who was more shocked by Olivia's outburst. But when Katherine scoffed and slinked off, Olivia felt triumphant.

"You bested Lady Katherine!" Prudence exclaimed. "After all these years of her cutting remarks, someone has finally stood up to her. I am so proud."

"Funny what comes out of my mouth when I stop being polite," Olivia replied, somewhat awed by herself. Honestly, what if she had acted thusly sooner?

"And to think, the night is still young," Prudence said. "Now, onward to the lemonade?"

Olivia glanced that way and stopped in her tracks. "No, he's still there."

"Is he giving a lemonade to Lady Ross?" Prudence asked, tilting her head curiously to one side.

"By all accounts it would appear to be so," Olivia replied, as if she didn't quite believe her eyes. He was supposed to be the most feared and loathed man in the ton.

Yet there was no denying that Phinn and his friend Rogan were engaged in an apparently charming conversation with Lady Ross, a handsome widow who got along famously with all the gentlemen. She loved to wager, be it on cards or horses, and she reputably possessed a bawdy sense of humor that appealed to men.

Whatever were they discussing so animatedly? Olivia couldn't imagine it, thanks to her dreadfully limited knowledge. Not for the first time did she curse her Perfect Lady's education.

"Who is his friend?" Prudence asked.

"Lord Rogan," she answered. "I think he's a bit of an ass."

"Olivia!"

"I know," Olivia replied, smiling. "Young ladies do not use such language."

"My heart is nearly bursting with pride," Prudence said, ginning. Olivia's smile faltered when she saw an unconceivable sight.

"Is she *laughing*? Why is he smiling?" she asked, aghast. "Is he *flirting* with her?"

The question she didn't dare give voice to was: *Why did she seem to care?* She had to admit that she did. She couldn't wrench her gaze away from the unfathomable sight of the Mad Baron having a perfectly lovely conversation with another woman. She'd just never expected it. She thought he was a brooding recluse from whom all women ran screaming in terror, and yet . . .

Phinn caught her staring. It was just a glance at

first, but she saw the double take. Then his gaze settled on hers and he looked her up and down in a bold, almost possessive manner. It went without saying that no man had ever looked at her that way. What surprised her was how much she liked it. She felt him take stock of her gown, more modest than the ones she usually wore. Then he lifted one brow questioningly, as if to ask, *That's the best you can do?*

Olivia gave what she hoped was a wicked smile that promised he hadn't seen anything yet.

"He couldn't possibly be flirting with her," Prudence said. "It must not be what we think it is. Let's get closer and see if we can eavesdrop."

As they pushed through the crowd, Olivia was shocked to see what happened next. The Mad Baron and Lady Ross linked arms and strolled off —but not before he caught her eye again. *And winked at her!*

Olivia gasped. What did this mean? What was happening? The lace across her bodice started to itch, and she wanted to rip it off right then and there. But Prudence was nearly dragging her over to the drinks table now that Phinn and Lady Ross had gone.

ROGAN DIDN'T MAKE an effort to follow the lively conversation between Phinn and Lady Ross. Then again, he didn't make an effort to follow most conversations. While they were deep in conversation on mathematical something or other, he took ad-

vantage of their distraction. There were some pre-
cautionary matters he had to attend to.

His friend Phinn was a capital fellow, especially when he didn't go on about his scientific
whatnot, which was known to happen until
someone shoved his head in a privy. Well, that
hadn't happened since their first year at Eton, but
every once in a while Rogan had half a mind to do
it. He just didn't have much attention or appetite
for serious conversation, especially when out at a
ball. He reckoned the ladies didn't either. Given
that tonight was all about chatting up The Ladies,
he thought a little extra something would assure
success.

So in the best interests of everyone at Almack's
that evening, particularly Phinn and Olivia,
Rogan poured the contents of his flask into the
tureen of lemonade.

Honestly, someone ought to have done this
sooner. Rogan grinned, imagining all the stuffed-
up marriage-minded mamas a bit tipsy.

He glanced around to make sure no one saw
him. Phinn, however, chose that moment to
look over at him still lingering by the lemonade,
furrowing his brow. Rogan gave him his best
nothing-to-see-here smile. And then he availed
himself to the lemonade before sauntering off to
the card room.

"LEMONADE?" PRUDENCE SAID, offering a glass
once they finally reached the table.

"I beg your pardon?" Olivia asked, still trying

to seek out Phinn in the crowd. He'd surprised her, that was all. She thought he would have immediately sought her favor and she'd spend the entire ball avoiding him. Perhaps, once she made the alterations to her gown, she would almost certainly spend the rest of the evening dancing with other gentlemen. Why, she could have a new beau by the end of the evening and be married to someone else by the end of the week.

As Prudence said, the night was still young.

Prudence interrupted her thoughts by handing her a glass of lemonade, full to the brim.

"Oh, right. Thank you," Olivia said. She drank the lot of it one swallow, noting that it tasted a bit sharper than usual this evening. Perhaps someone didn't measure the sugar correctly.

Prudence smiled. "More?"

Olivia held out her glass for Prudence to refill it. It was gone in one long, unladylike sip. It was time for her to show the ton the new, scandalous, Lady Olivia Archer.

A short while later

Olivia's blood hummed in her veins as she and Prudence strolled through the ballroom, on the prowl for scandal. She sought out the Mad Baron—it wouldn't do to act indecently if he wasn't watching. She saw him standing near a pillar, now speaking to Lady Hatfield and, if she wasn't mistaken, his gaze was not on her face but just a bit lower. Olivia's eyes narrowed. He was supposed to be courting *her*.

Well, he had dared her to act outrageously. And she did want to be rid of him. It logically followed that she wouldn't be jealous that he was lavishing his attentions on other women. And yet . . .

But she did want to be married before Lady Penelope's Ball. Obviously, she would need to attract the attentions of another gentleman—two could play at Phinn's game—but none were giving her a second glance. The exceedingly modest fichu wasn't doing her any favors. It had to go.

She ought to take a trip to the ladies' retiring room where she might carefully remove it in privacy. But tonight was about breaking the rules. Besides, she felt bolder than usual this evening.

"Why are you stopping?" Prudence asked. "And you look like you're considering something wicked."

"Because I'm about to do something wicked," Olivia said. She grabbed a fistful of lace and gave it a good tug. The whole thing came right off, leaving a large portion of her back and bosom exposed. Olivia breathed deeply—freedom!—or as deeply as she could mange, given how tightly her corset was laced tonight.

Then she tossed the lace up into the air.

A hush fell over the people nearby as they saw the scrap of white fabric rise high above their heads. The whispers and murmurs and second glances began immediately.

"Did she . . . ?"

"Prissy Missy did what?"

It was happening. London's Least Likely to Cause a Scandal was officially causing a scene. Young ladies did not forcefully remove offending parts of their garments in public. If anyone knew better than to divest herself of her garments in a ballroom, it was she.

"Your eyes do not deceive you," Olivia declared "Prissy Missy just ripped off part of her dress. It was altogether too confining."

The matrons clucked their disapproval. The younger ladies wore expressions of obvious shock. Were they jealous? Olivia wondered. And the men—they stared. And not in a horrified way. Olivia felt her heartbeat quickening and her temperature rising as the men's gazes raked over her, *considering* her.

She'd never been considered before, and it was oddly disconcerting.

"Do you feel liberated now, Lady Olivia?" Prudence asked.

"I do, Miss Payton," Olivia replied. "Shall we be off? Who knows what trouble I might find myself in before the evening is over."

Prudence and Olivia linked arms and strolled away. Gossip traveled faster. People turned to look and stare and whisper to their companions. Even Mr. Middleton took a leisurely second look as she strolled by.

"I feel quite strange, Prudence."

"That might be because of the gin I poured into the lemonade," Prudence replied.

"That would explain it," Olivia said, feeling the effects of the wicked lemonade even more now.

"I am quite sure they are questioning my sanity," Olivia remarked in a low voice.

"The important thing is that the Mad Baron does," Prudence replied.

Olivia glanced up, looking around for him. Had he witnessed her strange display?

Their gazes met. Smoldered. He had.

There was no denying it, especially when his gaze dropped to her breasts, now swelling slightly above the low bodice of her gown. There was a storm of emotion in his expression—she could see that. But was he angry? Legend had it he had one hell of a temper. Or was that desire?

Her heart, oddly, began to race at the prospect of being desired.

Even though she was supposed to be scandalizing him.

"Are you all right, Olivia?"

"Yes, fine."

Olivia breathed deeply. She was *fine*. She'd just caused a slight scene, which perhaps would lay to rest her awful moniker of Prissy Missy. But she feared they'd replace it with Crazy Lady. Meanwhile, she had possibly, inadvertently, made herself desirable to the man she was trying to repel.

She glanced at the clock. It wouldn't be long now before her mother got wind of this, had a fit, swooned, was brought to, and hustled her home. Then she glanced around the ballroom until her eyes rested on Phinn. He was still with Lord Rogan, only now he was speaking with yet another woman—Lady Elliot, an older widow who broke no rules of ladylike behavior, other than having acquired a reputation as a bluestocking with a particular interest in the sciences, which meant she and Phinn would have loads to talk about.

Good. But she might have been scowling. Even though ladies did not scowl.

"Olivia?" Prudence interrupted her thoughts.

"What is it?" she murmured. Really, Lady Elliot? Why wasn't he looking her way anymore?

"You're staring," Prudence said flatly.

No, what she was doing was waiting for him to look up and notice that she was acting scandalously. Thus making Lady Elliot seem an even more perfect match for him than she. But he wasn't looking. Not at her. Not anymore.

Olivia was under the throes of a very dangerous mixture: gin and jealousy. Had anyone tried to explain this, she would have laughed. How could she possibly be jealous of Lady Elliot over the attentions of the Mad Baron?

Already she wasn't enough for him. Wasn't right for him. If he didn't come to his senses and realize that, she didn't know what she'd do when he absconded with her to his remote and desolate country estate. Her determination thus renewed, Olivia glanced around, looking for mischief.

Not accustomed to the effects of spiked lemonade, Olivia found the ballroom and everyone in it a bit blurry. And it seemed the floor had become uneven, which was quite strange.

She happened to catch the eye of Lord Harvey, a young buck who had probably been forced to attend by his marriage-minded mother, and who'd presumably prefer to spend the evening tangled up with opera singers and playing high-stakes games of cards. He was precisely the sort of man her parents disdained.

A wicked idea occurred to her.

Bowing before Lord Harvey and only stumbling slightly on her feet, she asked, "My lord, would you care to have this dance with me?"

Ladies *never* spoke to gentlemen with whom they were not acquainted, and they *never* asked strangers to dance. But tonight Olivia thought it a fine idea and she felt more bold, daring, and fearless.

Beside her, Prudence groaned and muttered, "Oh dear Lord."

Olivia extended her hand. Really, Lord Harvey had no option but to smile politely and escort her to the floor—throwing a confused glance back at his laughing companions.

A waltz was conveniently beginning.

Olivia's lips curved into a smile. This was her chance to show the haute ton that she was a gifted and graceful dancer. After all, she'd had private dancing lessons thrice a week since she had turned twelve. *And no one ever asked her to dance.*

Why, she could probably dance every step with perfect poise and precision whilst on a ship. At sea. During a squalling storm with hundred foot waves. What she could not quite manage was dancing whilst under the effect of very spiked lemonade. The floor had strangely become uneven.

His grasp on her hand was light, as was the pressure of his palm on the middle of her back. There was a vast height difference between them, which made it all the more possible for them to do the steps of the waltz in slightly different time.

Given the awkward circumstances of the initiation of this dance—and the, oh, significant fact that they had not been introduced, ever—Olivia did not quite know where to look. Directly into his cravat? No, that was dull. She glanced up at his face and saw his jaw firmly set. He also seemed to be glancing here and there, but not at her.

She felt her cheeks starting to flush with mortification.

The blush deepened when she managed to glance around the ballroom. She saw faces staring at her. She saw men murmuring discreet and obviously inappropriate comments, judging by the smirks on their faces. Olivia became all too aware of the vast amounts of skin she had exposed.

The collective attentions of the ton were fixed upon the spectacle that was Olivia, quite underdressed, waltzing disastrously. She lifted her head high and carried herself as proudly as she could manage. Ladies snapped open their fans, covering their mouths whilst whispering what Olivia presumed to be the most cruel remarks. She started to burn with a horrid combination of embarrassment and remorse, then she caught herself. The ton had always made snide comments about her, if they bothered to spare a thought for her at all.

Because she and Lord Harvey were waltzing while trying not to acknowledge each other as they missed every cue to turn here or spin there. More than once did they collide with another couple—Lord and Lady Farnsworth seemed particularly put out. Both versions of them.

Olivia was now, strangely, seeing everything double. All the whirling and spinning was making her very dizzy and, truth be told, rather nauseous.

Young ladies do not cast up their accounts during a waltz, in the ballroom.

She caught a glance of Phinn, with Rogan and yet another woman by his side. Olivia recognized her as Lady Bellande, a notoriously merry widow. She preyed ruthlessly on every available—and even unavailable—men. And now she was after Phinn!

His expression was inscrutable. Round and around Lord Harvey whirled them both. Was Phinn angry? Jealous? Embarrassed? Round and round and round they went. Or did he feel nothing because he was a monster and would murder her on their wedding night or soon after?

With that, she stumbled, falling face first into Lord Harvey's cravat. It smelled like fresh linen and bergamot. Why did she know that? She really did not wish to know that.

"Excuse me," a male voice cut in. Olivia peered up at the one and only Duke of Ashbrooke, Emma's husband. Well, two of them. She was having such trouble seeing clearly. And someone ought to do something about the uneven floor at Almack's.

Ashbrooke was tall, devastatingly handsome, and incredibly imposing. The sun rose and set at his command. Lord Harvey fled.

Ashbrooke swept Olivia into his arms.

"If you're trying to cause a scandal, you're doing a bang up job of it," he remarked. But he grinned as he said it.

"Huzzah," Olivia said flatly, which only made his grin broaden.

Unlike Lord Harvey, Ashbrooke was a master of waltzing. His grasp was just firm and possessive enough. With the duke as her partner, Olivia could have had three more of those wicked lemonades and waltzed on a ship, at sea, during a squalling storm with hundred foot waves without missing a step.

They moved in perfect time to the music.

Olivia's heart sort of broke with happiness for Emma that she should have the steadfast and eternal love of this man. And she was so glad that he was so good as to extend his kindness to her friends. And to her dismay, she was jealous. Oh, she didn't covet Ashbrooke, but she coveted the sort of love they possessed.

That was what she wanted. That was what she'd never have with the Mad Baron. Not when he'd spend all his time at work on his bizarre machines, leaving her to manage the servants and embroider. That is, before her murdered her.

She spotted the Mad Baron in the crowd. There was no woman with him now. He stood alone, brooding. Watching her. With that dark scowl and the scar, he seemed far too dangerous.

As they waltzed around—without too many spins, because he was Ashbrooke and was probably an expert at dancing with slightly intoxicated women—Olivia alternated between staring at his cravat and everyone in the ballroom.

Most people had gone back to minding their own business. The Mad Baron still brooded, even though Olivia was no longer making a spectacle of herself. Everyone knew Ashbrooke had married her best friend, and thus there was nothing untoward to be made of the association. It was completely and utterly unremarkable.

The orchestra closed the song with a flourish.

"Thank you," Olivia said, not too intoxicated to recognize a real gentleman.

"My pleasure." And then, leaning in close, Blake murmured, "He's not so bad, you know."

THE MAD BARON was waiting for her on the terrace, cutting a devastatingly handsome figure as he leaned against the balustrade. Broad shoulders. Long limbs. Strong features. Eyes that saw her when no one else did. And a scar that could never let her forget what he'd been accused of, and what he had not denied.

Ashbrooke delivered her to him and then went off in search of his wife, leaving Olivia alone with the man she'd been trying to avoid . . .

. . . and the man she couldn't stop fixating on.

Once again she felt that connection between them, like that first night. She felt his gaze upon her, *all* of her. Soft strands of her hair had tumbled down and brushed against her shoulders. She must look ridiculous. Looking into his darkened eyes, she felt terrified.

Nervously, she waited for him to speak. Causing trouble, and the subsequent ache in her stomach, was an unfamiliar feeling. She'd never really gotten in trouble before, or forgot to prepare for lessons, or really done anything *wrong*.

All she wanted was to be different; she hadn't stopped to consider the consequences.

"You didn't need to do all that, you know," he said softly, surprising her. She expected him to be enraged. A small part of her feared he might hurt her in front of everyone.

"But I did," she said softly. "For me."

Then she wavered on her feet. It seemed the paving stones on the terrace were as uneven as the ballroom floor.

"Olivia, are you alright?" Phinn asked. He

peered down at her with concern. Or was the spiked lemonade still affecting her vision? He was a bit blurry.

"I'm fine," she replied. Because ladies were always *fine*.

But she wasn't. He wasn't angry with her at all, even though she behaved abominably. She'd made quite a spectacle of herself, what with ripping off bits of her dress and asking a complete stranger to waltz, both of which were things were just Not Done.

He was supposed to be furious because she wasn't what he wanted and she had embarrassed him by embarrassing herself. He was supposed to pull her away and rage at her or worse because he was the Mad Baron and that's what he did, according the broadsides and the gossip.

Phinn then did the most surprising thing: he reached to push a wayward strand of hair away from her face. It ought to have been a tender, romantic gesture.

If only she hadn't flinched.

"Oh, Olivia," he murmured. "I'm so sorry."

She didn't know quite what he was apologizing for.

"I didn't think Rogan would actually spike the lemonade," Phinn said grimly. "I told him not to in no uncertain terms. And because of that, you have gotten everyone talking."

Again she swayed on her feet. Prudence and Rogan spiked the lemonade? That would explain why the world was terribly out of sorts. She might have felt emboldened before but she felt faint now. Just as she lurched toward the balustrade for support, Phinn shouted her name and lunged forward to catch her.

As she tumbled into his arms, he happened to step on her loosely sewn flounce. The swath of lace hardly attached to such delicate fabrics as silk and muslin were no match for the force of a man's step. The entire thing ripped off, stuck under Phinn's boot, leaving Olivia's ankles and bare legs quite exposed.

Horrors. Truly, horrors.

Phinn apologized profusely and dropped to his knees, apparently with some vague notion of reattaching the flounce to the dress, seamstress though he was not. And then something happened.

Olivia glanced down and caught the way he stared at her ankles. Then, slowly, he lifted his gaze to hers. His eyes had darkened considerably. And lud, the way he looked at her . . . she *felt* it. The warmth of his gaze, like a caress. The heat smoldered in her belly and radiated through her limbs, going straight to her head. She became aware of how tight her dress was—she wanted to tug the rest of it off. She also became aware of how light-headed she felt, and thought about fainting. In his arms.

In this moment, her fear was no match for a feeling quite like desire.

This is why young ladies ought not drink to excess.

In the moment—the most inconvenient, inappropriate, and deuced uncomfortable moment—Phinn could only think about how badly he wanted to touch Olivia. He wanted to reach out, clasp his hands around her ankles and skim higher and higher until he was able to show her true pleasure. But if she was too afraid to be alone with him, and flinched when he only meant to caress her, she wouldn't trust him enough to surrender to the pleasure of his touch.

But really. Now was *not* the moment to have such thoughts.

He wasn't sure who had caused a bigger scene tonight. Olivia, propelled by Rogan's idiotic notion to spike the lemonade, or him, on his knees before a woman in a torn dress.

And then their gazes had locked. Her eyes on his proved a powerful aphrodisiac. He hated that she feared him. He hated that their courtship had been one disaster after another. But he didn't feel any of that hate as strongly as he felt a raw desire to touch her and possess and love her.

For the moment—in this absurd, oddly wonderful moment—he thought she might have felt the same way.

But then a woman's distressed cries pierced through. "Olivia! Dear Lord above, Olivia what has happened to you?"

It was Lady Archer, in all her bustling, fussing glory.

For a perfect, fleeting second Phinn swore he

and Olivia shared the same thought: *Run!* It was there, in her eyes. But then whatever it was that Rogan snuck into the lemonade stole over her and she wobbled again.

"Oh my lord," Lady Archer gasped.

"Lady Archer, good evening," Phinn said.

"Good evening. Olivia, we must get you home immediately before anyone sees."

Phinn exchanged an uneasy glance with Olivia. The truth was that everyone was already witness to London's Least Likely to Cause a Scandal doing precisely that, from tearing off bits of her dress to asking a gentleman to dance.

"I'll help you," he offered. Because, while he was not deeply acquainted with drunk women, he suspected that one might require assistance making it from the terrace to the carriage to her house. If nothing else, he wanted everyone to see that the Mad Baron was standing by his future bride, her scandalous actions that evening notwithstanding. It was the least he could do, given that he'd driven her to such outrageous behavior.

She might not give a damn about her reputation tonight. But she probably would in the morning.

Chapter 9

PHINN FELT A pang of sympathy for the lecture Olivia must have endured the following morning—and the pounding headache she must have suffered, too. He remembered the time when he and his brother George had gotten revolting drunk on their father's stash of French brandy. There was the lecture—and then the belt. But they had endured it together, as brothers.

That was long ago. Before Nadia ripped them apart.

He had come to the workshop on Devonshire Street where everything was governed by logic, where he knew and understood everything and he wasn't the Mad Baron but the expert machinist. But he had trouble focusing on his plans for the Difference Engine; his thoughts kept straying to Olivia. Perhaps he should let her go. While he knew her behavior last night had been worsened by the punch and prompted by his stupid wager, he also knew that she wanted *out*.

Like Nadia.

But such thoughts were banished once Ashbrooke tossed the mornings' papers on his desk. Cringing, Phinn read one of the gossip columns.

For the first time in the history of London, Almack's was the place to be. Some rogue spiked the lemonade, resulting in all sorts of amusing and shocking behavior—none more so than that of Lady Olivia Archer. Prissy Missy took the ton by surprise when she shredded her gown, leaving many to question her wits. But none were more surprised than Lord Harvey, who accepted the young lady's invitation to waltz.

The gentlemen of White's are considering a revision to their famed betting book. Will Lady Olivia retain her title of London's Least Likely to Cause a Scandal or will she be renamed London's Lowest Tolerance for Spiked Lemonade or London's Most Entertaining when Under the Effects of Spirits?

The patronesses of Almack's have announced that all beverages will be served by footmen to prevent a reoccurrence of "the deplorable activities of the previous evening." We the editors beg them to reconsider, especially if they want to draw a crowd of young eligible men who would consider attending of their own volition . . .

Phinn might not have been as finely versed in the laws of society as in the laws of physics, but even he knew it did not bode well for one's marital prospects to have their wits questioned in a gossip column. It was his fault. He ought to apologize.

As with Nadia, he had the power to avert greater scandal. He could make everything right with a proposal of marriage.

There was just one problem: Olivia was certain to refuse his offer, especially if it were motivated by his intentions to save her from herself. Until he figured out how to apologize and propose in a remotely romantic way, he dared not risk her wrath.

He tried to focus on his work and finally lost himself in drafting a design for a crucial piece of the engine when the duke approached.

"How are things coming along?"

"Excellent. I am working on a way to ensure that all the screws are cut identically," he answered. It was the little things like a lack of standard screws that slowed down construction.

"Better and better. Now we have just a few thousand more pieces to design and construct."

That was the problem with building an intricate machine that would stand eight feet high, seven feet long, and three feet deep. It would require as many as twenty-five thousand separate parts, many of them identical. The engine would be larger and more intricate than any machine that had been made previously.

"Good thing you secured as much funding as you did," Phinn quipped.

"You wouldn't believe what I had to do to get it," Ashbrooke said, sighing dramatically. Phinn had heard the story and found it quite remarkable. Worthy of a book.*

"All for a good cause, though," Phinn replied.

"Profoundly changing everything from accounting to navigation," Ashbrooke went on. "Just by being accurate. It's so tragic how many lives have been lost because of miscalculations and errors in the ready reckoners."

Phinn looked away from the duke, not wanting him to see how the words affected him. He could feel his jaw clenching and the familiar tightening in his chest when he thought of Nadia and how she'd died. His machines, his mistakes, had killed her. He was guilty, because he was cold and calculating like a machine—until his temper got the better of him.

He and Nadia were doomed from the beginning. From the minute he slipped the ring on her finger he'd known as much, with the same deep certainty that he knew how to calculate the force of gravity. He just hadn't foreseen how tragically it would end.

I'm sorry, Nadia. He thought the words often.

"The Difference Engine is just the beginning," Ashbrooke went on. "By eliminating the risk of human error, we can always be sure that

---

*The Wicked Wallflower

our calculations are correct. And once we finish this, and the debut at the Great Exhibition is a smashing success, I have an idea for an analytical engine that will perform ever more complex calculations."

"One thing at a time, Duke," Phinn said with a smile before picking up his pencil and turning back to work. He'd drawn just one carefully executed line when Ashbrooke interrupted again.

"So how do things fare with your courtship of Lady Olivia?"

"Horribly," Phinn answered grimly. There had been moments here and there—but at this rate it'd take seven years before they could spend one civil day with each other. And yes, he might have performed those calculations. "I must thank you for waltzing with her and saving her from even more trouble."

Phinn didn't waltz because he spent too many hours working on his scientific endeavors, instead of learning the steps to various dances. His brother George had been the one who knew all the steps and all the ways to charm a woman.

Besides, there was nothing like a public display of approval from the Duke of Ashbrooke, the ton's darling, to ameliorate any damage done by Olivia's drunken antics.

"It was my pleasure," the duke replied. "Besides, Emma would have my head if I didn't. At any rate, Lady Olivia is a lovely girl."

"Is she?" Phinn had to ask. "When I first saw

her I thought her lovely, pretty, kind, restrained, and sweet. And now . . ."

The duke grinned and said, "When she's not deliberately trying to cause a scandal to scare you off, yes, she is all of those things."

"I might have encouraged her to do that," Phinn muttered.

"Why would you do such a thing that would deliberately thwart your own aims?"

"She's determined to prove we won't suit. I'm determined to prove that we will."

"That's absurd. Of course you'll make a splendid match. She'll give you an excellent reason not to work so much, and you'll treat her to all the romantic moments women love. At any rate, you'll have to suit. Given what the gossips are saying in the papers."

"I know," Phinn said, deeply regretting how he'd challenged her. Never once did he think it would have the opposite effect: that they'd be duty bound to wed.

"And yet, you are here. Drafting designs for the perfect screw," Ashbrooke remarked.

"I'm not yet certain how to proceed with Lady Olivia," Phinn said.

"There's more to those wallflowers than meets the eye," Ashbrooke remarked. "One minute you think that because they're London's Least Likely they'll be so glad for the attentions. And the next you've gone mad with love and trying to win them."

"I'll say," Phinn murmured. The aloof beauty he'd first set eyes on was turning out to be a wickedly enchanting, maddening creature. She was exactly what he didn't want in a wife, and yet he still wanted *her.*

Which was a damn good thing, since it looked more and more like they needed each other.

"So what are you going to do?" Ashbrooke asked, ambling over to a sideboard where he kept a store of brandy and glasses for precisely those conversations that made a man crave a drink.

"Marry her. Somehow, someway. She'll see it's the right thing for us to do now. And then we'll make the best of it."

"Yes, but how are you going to woo her so that she'll say yes?"

Phinn shrugged. "Rogan's been giving me advice. Pay her compliments, make her jealous, that sort of thing."

"And is it working?" Ashbrooke asked, handing Phinn a glass of brandy.

Phinn took a sip and thought back to the ball. He'd actually enjoyed speaking to Lady Ross, Lady Elliot, and others. He just hadn't felt the same pull—like gravity—that he felt with Olivia.

Even more, he'd enjoyed the feeling of Olivia's eyes on him. Every time he glanced around seeking her out, she was watching him, which was a marked contrast from their first ball, when she went to great lengths to avoid him. She was still making a spectacle of herself trying to repel him, but it was progress.

But the rest of Rogan's advice had not worked. In fact, it was a failure.

"Let's just say that I'm open to other suggestions." Phinn shrugged and sipped his drink.

"You've come to the right place, Radcliffe," the duke said, smiling broadly. "In addition to being a gifted mathematician and inventor, I'm also a renowned rake. At least I was before I married."

"What do you suggest?"

"The thing with women is they like to be swept off their feet," Ashbrooke said matter-of-factly.

"Feats of strength," Phinn said, nodding. "That's what Rogan advised."

The duke looked appalled. "*Never* refer to lifting a woman as a feat of strength."

"Right," Phinn said. He took a long swallow of his brandy. What other stupid advice had Rogan given him that he had unwittingly followed? Not for the first time did he regret all the hours he'd devoted to science. He ought to have been devoting himself to studying the seduction of women.

"Never. Ever," the duke added.

"Never," Phinn repeated.

"They like a man who is confident, self-assured," Ashbrooke declared. "Dominant, if you will. A man who decisively determines a course of action and always ensures a woman is cared for so that she has nothing to do but fall in love with you."

"Is this what you did?"

Judging by his expression, Ashbrooke seemed to be thinking back fondly over his courtship with his wallflower. Phinn sipped his drink and didn't dare consider he might one day do the same.

"Emma was determined to resist my charming efforts to seduce her. But I knew she was the one, and eventually she realized that I was the one for her."

"That's all well and good, Ashbrooke, but I'm looking for specifics."

"First of all, you have to get her away from the prying eyes of society and her overbearing mother. These wallflowers are painfully aware of what the ton thinks of them. It makes them far too self-conscious, which will never do when you're trying to be romantic."

"London's Least Likely," Phinn remarked. So they internalized that. Had he thought of himself as the Mad Baron and acted accordingly? Was it self-fulfilling prophecy? What if Olivia was railing against everyone's perceptions of her, and not against him?

"Exactly," Ashbrooke agreed. He took a sip of his drink and then said, "Here is what you should do: plan a romantic outing. And plan every last detail—the luncheon, wine, etcetera—so that she doesn't have to think about anything other than falling in love with you. You do not want her thinking about how you forgot wineglasses or napkins."

"I see," Phinn murmured. If he could sweep

her off her feet with romance, she might forget her fear, and not be so determined to prove she wasn't Prissy Missy.

"When they start thinking, they employ a logic that is so complex and convoluted that no man will ever be able to follow each twist and turn to the surprising conclusion. Trying to sort it out is like getting trapped in quicksand."

The duke finished his speech by draining his brandy and setting the glass down on the table. Phinn pushed the drawings to the side.

"Perhaps I could take Olivia on a picnic," he suggested.

"An excellent idea," Ashbrooke agreed enthusiastically. "I know the perfect spot. In the far corner of Hyde Park there are the ruins of an ancient gazebo. Take her there."

"This could work," Phinn said. "We've had some moments that lead me to believe there is hope yet. Perhaps if we just have one nice afternoon we'll have a chance at happiness."

Given his reputation, and hers, they might be each other's only shot at happiness.

"One more tip," Ashbrooke said, lowering his voice. "If you must have a chaperone, insist upon a maid and bribe her to look the other way. You must ensure that Lady Archer does not accompany you. For reasons I trust I need not speak aloud."

Chapter 10

To wear or not to wear the bonnet. That is the question.
        —THE DELIBERATIONS OF LADY OLIVIA

IN ANTICIPATION OF an outing with Phinn, Olivia had spent the better part of an hour fussing over her bonnet. According to her well-worn (but not beloved) volume of *The Mirror of Graces*:

> *No lady should make one in any riding, airing, or walking party, without putting on her head something capable of affording both shelter and warmth.*

The bonnet in question was indeed capable of affording both shelter and warmth. It was decked in a bright canary-colored ribbon and festooned with an assortment of yellow and white silk flowers. For an added bit of flair there were large white feathers jutting out along with bits of lace. The thing was monstrous.

Usually she avoided wearing it because of said monstrous decorations. Today she reconsidered because of the exceptionally large brim that would prevent any attempts at kissing, should the Mad Baron be so inclined.

She did not want to kiss him.

Olivia touched her fingertips to her lips, which had, tragically, never been kissed.

Or did she want to kiss him? If she just weren't so scared, perhaps.

Involuntarily, she considered his firm, sensual mouth. And the way he'd gaze at her so intently and how his gaze had a way of making her feel things. Warmth. Wanting . . . or was it terror?

The bonnet. She must focus on the bonnet. Perhaps she wouldn't wear it at all, which would be scandalous, as would the ensuing freckles and sunburn. It might be nice, for once, to venture out of doors without an object capable of providing shelter and warmth upon her head.

There was also the matter of the satin ribbons—they trailed right now to her waist, they were so long and wide. Why, if he were so inclined, the Mad Baron could certainly strangle her with these ribbons. Why, he could even hang her from a tree!

Olivia gasped and paled at the gruesome thoughts. Her heart started to pound and her palms became damp. Would he ravish her first and then murder her? Or would he fly into a fit of rage, insensible to decency and reason, and pull the ribbons so tight she couldn't breathe? She'd forevermore be known as the girl who met her untimely demise by bonnet ribbon.

Then again, should she have to flee on foot through the treacherous wilderness of Hyde Park on a summer's day, she'd be able to wave the bright yellow ribbons to attract attention as she shouted for help. In fact, now that she considered it, this headpiece could quite possibly double as a weapon.

A servant discreetly entered the room, and Olivia nearly gave a shout, having been caught off guard while thinking terrifying thoughts.

"Lady Olivia, Lord Radcliffe insists you come down now."

"Thank you, Nancy."

He *insists*, does he? Olivia scowled. She was supposed to do his bidding, was she? Hadn't she shown him that she wasn't the docile creature everyone believed her to be?

Speaking of weaponry, should she fill her reticule with rocks? But there was no time for her to venture out into the garden. All she had were embroidery scissors. Olivia stuffed those into her reticule. At the last moment she applied a bit of lip paint.

And then she donned the bonnet and ventured forth to meet her fate.

As PER THE suggestion of the Duke of Ashbrooke, Phinn planned every last detail of a romantic picnic. In the park, he scouted the location of the ancient gazebo. It was indeed in a far corner, and he had the devil of a time finding it. But it was private, beautiful and perfect.

He consulted with Rogan's chef on the menu and personally determined which footman would accompany them. He wore one of his new jackets, which the tailor had only just finished. He procured a carriage with matching horses.

Now all he needed was his betrothed.

"I'm sure Olivia will just be a moment, Lord Radcliffe," the terrifying Lady Archer said, again. They were sitting in the drawing room, discussing the weather, and had been doing so for the past quarter of an hour.

He was not sure of it. In fact, he was sure that Olivia would take every excuse to delay. If she were suddenly stricken with a serious, rare, and highly contagious illness, he would not be in the least surprised.

Phinn leaned back against the settee, allowing himself to comfortably settle in. Oddly, her every challenge only made him more intrigued and more determined to win her. In other circumstances—namely, without Lady Archer present—he might have indulged in fantasizing about when she finally surrendered and the pleasure they'd find together.

But first this damned picnic. Fortunately, he had Ashbrooke's advice to follow. The man was a legend. How could he go wrong?

He would just be decisive and certain. He'd be commanding. Lord of the Castle. He'd make sure everything was perfect. Olivia wouldn't have to do to anything but be wooed.

If the stubborn chit ever deigned to make an appearance.

Phinn addressed one of the servants, "Tell Lady Olivia it is time to depart. Please."

"Yes, of course," the maid said meekly before vanishing.

A moment later Olivia appeared, dressed in a perfectly respectable day dress of blue and white stripes. He thought fondly of the wildly inappropriate dress she'd worn at the ball the other night. She also wore a massive bonnet that dispelled all thoughts of kissing her, as did the lip paint that made an unfortunate reappearance. Good God, were they back to that again?

But still . . . he did want to kiss her. Rub that stuff right off her lips with the pad of his thumb and then claim her mouth for the kind of kiss that left one completely senseless.

Lady Archer bustled about, fussing with the enormous bonnet strings as if Olivia were still just a girl, managing to annoy both her daughter and himself. Did she not know that Olivia was very much a woman?

"Make sure you have your gloves, Olivia. And perhaps a parasol, you do not want to freckle for the wedding."

Olivia pulled a face revealing how she felt about that, but still accepted the parasol her mother handed her and clutched it to her chest.

"Let's be off," he said.

"I'll get my bonnet," Lady Archer said brightly. His heart sank. Lady Olivia looked at him with a tortured expression.

Be decisive and commanding.
Do not involve Lady Archer.

"Actually, Lady Archer, Lady Olivia and I would like some time alone to get to know each other. Perhaps we could all picnic another time, but today it will be just Lady Olivia and myself."

"But it's improper, " Lady Archer said. "The gossips are already saying the worst things." Phinn was quite certain he might have hurt her feelings. But really. A man couldn't woo a girl with parents hovering about. And they'd already meddled enough as it was.

"Perhaps a maid might accompany us. But I would like to get to know Lady Olivia. Alone."

He heard a gasp from under the bonnet. He was aware that she turned to glance up at him. Was she still afraid of him murdering her? Or was she shocked to hear him stand his ground with her mother?

"Good day, Lady Archer," Phinn said, nodding to her. "We shall return later this afternoon."

PHINN EXTENDED HIS hand to help Olivia climb into the high perch phaeton. There was no way that she would ever manage to board on her own. For a second she thought of running. Not that there was anywhere she could go, and not that she'd get very far with skirts tangling around her ankles and this behemoth of a bonnet obscuring her vision.

Reluctantly, she reached out and placed her

gloved hand in his. His grasp was firm—but not the viselike death grip she had feared. For a moment he was just a handsome gentleman helping a lady into his carriage. It should have been a lovely moment.

Why could it not just be a lovely moment?

Then she remembered that she'd worn her most atrocious bonnet and applied lip paint again. Funny, that all she did was plot ways to repel him so completely that he'd break the marriage contract, and yet she only felt foolish doing it. What if being wicked didn't suit her? What if she was Prissy Missy and she was rebelling against an inevitable fate?

She sighed, her dreams of a lovely courtship and whirlwind romance drifting away . . .

Phinn drove the carriage, and it wasn't long before they reached the perimeter of the park. Her heart began to pound. He guided the equipage along Rotten Row and Olivia shrank down in her seat, mortified that the ton should see her in this ridiculous bonnet and with lip paint very liberally applied.

Just when she thought there couldn't be anything worse than being seen in such a ridiculous state with the Mad Baron for company, the carriage took a turn down a remote road she didn't recognize.

"Where are we going?" Her voice wavered as she inquired.

"I have planned a picnic for us in the park,"

Phinn answered, keeping his eyes focused on the road.

"It's a good thing I have brought the parasol," Olivia replied. "I redden terribly in the sun."

It could also double as a weapon just in case . . .

If only she'd had a parasol with a secret knife blade that emerged with a click of a discreet button, instead of this one that was so refined, delicate, and purely ornamental. It wouldn't protect against the rain, let alone the violent advances of a murderous madman.

"You needn't worry. I have determined a shady, secluded spot for us," Phinn said, giving her a glance and smile. Was that a cryptic smile? A kind one, or a malicious one?

"I would feel more comfortable if we were in a more popular location," she said. He wouldn't dare harm her in public.

Perhaps he wouldn't at all, her conscience argued. At the ball the other night, she had made a complete spectacle of them both. He had every reason to be furious with her, for she'd embarrassed them with her inappropriate attire, drunken antics, and practically throwing herself at Lord Harvey (the memory of which still made her wince). When Phinn had reached out to touch a strand of her hair, she'd flinched, expecting to be hit.

But it'd only been a tender touch, in which he brushed aside a wayward strand. It was the intimate gesture of lovers. Olivia glanced at him and dared to imagine, for the very first time, if Phinn and she made love. Sitting beside him in the close quarters of the phaeton, his muscled thigh was pressed against hers and she could feel his strong arm. Arms that might hold her—or harm her? She glanced up to his mouth—a full, sensuous mouth—and closed her eyes, imagining his lips pressing against hers.

The carriage hit a rut in the road and she was jolted from her thoughts. Her appalling, wanton, *unladylike* thoughts, which left her feeling quite the same as she'd felt when her dress was torn and Phinn, on his knees before her, had given her That Look. Which is to say, a strange heat now stole through her limbs. She caught herself inhaling sharply, once again aware that her dress was far too tight. She wished she could remove it, along with the bonnet, for the ribbons were chafing around her throat. If they married her dress would come off. Along with that jacket of his and everything else. She'd be alone, defenseless, and completely at his mercy.

"You will like it, I am sure of it," Phinn said.

"I beg your pardon?" Olivia asked, alarmed that he had somehow read her mind.

"The picnic. I'm sure you will like it," Phinn said. Then, turning to peer curiously at her, he asked, "Why, what else were you thinking of?"

"It doesn't signify," Olivia said, shrinking back against the seat. She wondered if he noticed that she was blushing, and if so, could she pass it off as too much sun? Not with this horrid bonnet and the stupid lip paint. She sighed. Just sighed.

"You needn't worry about whatever is troubling you," Phinn said. "I have taken care of everything. You needn't concern yourself with thinking at all."

She supposed that was meant to be reassuring. It was accompanied by a kind smile. But it only just reminded her that he wanted a biddable wife. A boring, docile creature who wouldn't need to use her brain for anything other than to follow his commands. It went without saying that while she didn't quite know what she wanted, she knew she didn't want that. She wasn't a child, or a little soldier or a servant. She was a woman who wanted love.

Then the carriage went off the road entirely. She didn't want this either, she thought, gripping the rail tightly in one hand and desperately clutching the parasol in the other. The horses trotted along, pulling the phaeton over the grass, then back onto another utterly desolate path.

"Where are we going?" she asked.

"Ashbrooke told me of the ruins of an ancient gazebo," Phinn said. "I thought we might go there."

Olivia knew of it. The duke had built it—illegally and at great expense—as a testament to his love for Emma. Olivia was happy for her friend. Truly. If anyone deserved such love and happiness, it was Emma.

But what about her? Didn't she deserve true love, too?

Phinn swore under his breath.

"Are you sure you know the way?" Olivia inquired, even though young ladies never second-guessed a gentlemen. "Because you seem lost."

Phinn turned to face her. He fixed those green eyes of his on her face. Lifted one brow. Issued his challenge. "Do *you* know the way?"

She felt quite taken aback.

"No," she admitted in a whisper. At this point she didn't even know the way back to Rotten Row.

"Ah, there it is," Phinn said with a sigh of relief.

There it was indeed. The strange edifice was constructed of stone, which had been made to look old. Thick branches of wisteria wound around the pillars. A dome roof provided shelter from the sun. She would need neither parasol nor bonnet.

A footman had come in advance to set up a table and chairs. After helping her alight from the carriage, Phinn carried the picnic basket that had been secured to the back of the carriage.

"Is that heavy? It seems heavy," Olivia said. The hamper was enormous. He must have packed a feast, which was just as well since she was a bit hungry. And as part of her quest to break all the rules of ladylike behavior, she had quite enjoyed indulging at mealtimes. Especially when it was likely her last supper.

"Yes. It's very heavy," Phinn said. But he carried the thing effortlessly. Olivia tried, in a moment of charity, to be impressed with his strength and not, say, consider how he might easily hoist her away and have his way with her.

That thought made her blush. She wasn't thinking about murder. For once.

The table had been set with plates, cutlery, and wineglasses. There wasn't much room for the veritable feast that Phinn unpacked from the hamper. In addition to an enormous amount of food, there were bottles of chilled white wine and jugs of cool water.

"That is quite a feast," she said, surveying all the food before her.

"I wasn't sure what you liked," Phinn said. Her heart reluctantly softened at his consideration. "Or what you were in the mood for."

"That is very considerate of you. Thank you," she said, providing him a glimpse of the ladylike manners she was famous for. Or had been. She'd caught a glimpse of the gossip columns saying: *At Almack's, Lady Olivia Archer failed to display any of the grace, refinement, and manners we had come to expect from Prissy Missy.* Afterward, her mother had taken to bed with a vial of smelling salts for an afternoon. Olivia read all the gossip rags she could get her hands on and then considered taking to her bed as well.

"I also noticed that you have quite an appetite," he said.

She was suddenly beset by a fit of coughing. To be fair, she had endeavored to eat an ungodly amount of food in his presence, all the better to scare him off. But still, that was really something a man should never comment on.

"Terribly sorry," he said, looking earnestly pained by what he'd said. "That was the wrong thing to say."

"Yes."

"I just meant that—"

"It's all right, Lord Radcliffe." Olivia sighed. She had expected the picnic would be a disaster. At the very least it was only her pride that was wounded and not her person.

"Phinn. Please, call me Phinn." He smiled. And her heart fluttered. He was handsome when he smiled . . . if only that scar of his didn't remind her of his dangerous past.

Seated at the table, Olivia eyed the spread before them. A gentle breeze rustled through the trees. Other than the slight birdsong, there was no other sound. She was keenly aware that they were very much alone in a very remote location.

In anticipation of the meal, she removed her gloves. So did the Mad Baron. She saw that his hands were riddled with scars, as if warning her of his violent activities.

"What happened to your hands?" she asked.

"Oh, little accidents when working. Some are burns from dealing with hot metals as I forge tools, others are due to cuts from sharp machinery."

"That is not as nefarious as I had imagined," she replied.

"Terribly sorry to disappoint you," he murmured. "Would you like some wine?"

"Please," she said. Perhaps just one glass would soothe her nerves. She must take care not to have more than that.

Phinn poured a liberal amount of chilled white wine into both their glasses.

"Cheers," he said, raising his glass to hers. They shared a smile—his hesitant, hers slightly petrified. Their gazes locked.

His eyes were really something. They were green and shadowed by dark lashes. And they knew things, those eyes. They were at once intriguing and terrifying.

She took a sip of wine. And he was handsome—Emma was right about that. He was *trying* to win her. She could see that, too. Men didn't plan elaborate picnics in romantic locations if they weren't intent on marriage to the lady in question.

And yet, he had basically confessed to murdering his previous wife. And now she was alone with him. In this secluded place. No one would hear her scream.

Phinn proposed a toast: "To seeing if we will suit."

Ladies take small, dainty sips. She took a long swallow of wine. Then another, until her glass was nearly empty.

Phinn peered at her curiously.

"Would you like some more?" he asked, offering the bottle.

"My mother discourages me from drinking wine," Olivia said, taking another sip. "She says it makes a woman forget herself."

"Drink enough of it and you'll forget everything," he quipped, which made Olivia smile nervously.

What did he want her to forget? Her heart started drumming in her chest.

"Here, if you are going to drink thusly, you ought to eat," Phinn said.

"Of course," she murmured, availing herself of the meal before her—and the fork and knife in her hands, which could double as weaponry just in case. Between the cutlery, the embroidery scissors in her reticule, the parasol, and the bonnet with its ribbons, she was a veritable artillery of lady weapons.

Thus, she felt able to experience a measure of relaxation. The wine soothed her. The food was delicious. The scenery was lovely.

"Olivia, I owe you an apology," Phinn said, surprising her.

"Whatever for?"

"I never should have suggested our wager," he said. "It seems to have had some unintended consequences that I did not foresee."

"Whatever do you mean?" She sipped her wine, wondering about these unintended consequences.

"You've read the gossip columns, I assume."

"Of course," she replied. She breathed as well.

"Your reputation has suffered because of the antics I provoked in you at Almack's. Also, the lemonade was spiked, thanks to Rogan."

Wait—hadn't Prudence added gin as well? No wonder she'd felt so unconstrained.

"I have erred in judgment," Phinn went on. "For that, I apologize."

Olivia bit back a smile. This was the moment! He erred in believing her a biddable girl; she had proven otherwise. Now he no longer wished to marry her because of the reports in the gossip columns. Her brilliant plan was a success.

Taking care not to appear too happy, she replied in a carefully modulated tone: "I understand if you no longer wish to court me or marry me because of my tarnished reputation."

"To the contrary, Lady Olivia," Phinn said, his gaze settling on her. "My honor impels me to stand by you."

"But . . . but . . . but . . ." Olivia stammered. This was not how it was supposed to work! "But we do not suit!"

Phinn sipped his wine. He looked at her with those eyes. Aye, he was no fool.

"Tell me, Olivia, how we do not suit."

Was he serious? Olivia leveled a stare at him. Was that the slightest hint of amusement in the upturned corners of his mouth, or was she imagining things? She rather suspected he was bamming her, but if he wasn't, then she could not pass up this opportunity to point out how she'd be the worst wife for him. Especially since he had declared his attentions to stand by her—presumably at the altar.

"Well, I am rather forward with gentlemen," she said, thinking of all the rogues she had cavorted with: Lord Gerard, Beaumont, Harvey. "Surely you wish for a wife who is more devoted to you. And you alone."

"That would be preferable," Phinn agreed. "I wouldn't care to share my wife's company with other men."

"I also drink to excess," Olivia said. To punctuate this she took another sip of a very unladylike size. When she set the glass down she felt marvelously warm and quite dizzy. She wished to lie down, in fact. But she had to point out all the ways they were wrong for each other. "If you wish for a respectable wife, you mustn't shackle yourself to a drunk who cavorts with rogues."

She had never imagined saying such things about herself. She also had never imagined that she'd be so desperate to prove to a man that she was unsuitable and he definitely should not marry her.

It didn't escape her notice, however, that there was a grain of truth in what he said—the papers had been cruel and would quite possibly ward off all other suitors. If Phinn didn't marry her, she'd be a spinster. She would be the one failure in the history of Lady Penelope's School for Young Ladies. But a true love match seemed more important than that.

"I cause scenes, as you know," she carried on. "I'd probably drive you mad with all the scenes I would cause. I suppose your previous wife drove you mad."

"Sometimes," Phinn admitted. "But I had taken a vow. Till death do we part. I took that very seriously. So I did my best to honor that vow."

Olivia paled. And reached to her reticule to ensure that the embroidery scissors were still there just in case she needed them. Assured, she took another sip of wine. It wasn't quite making her forget herself, but it was loosening her tongue tremendously.

"Did you murder her because she drove you mad?" she asked in a whisper.

Phinn sighed. He sighed! What did *that* mean?

"Are you *still* hung up on the whole 'mad baron murdered his wife' gossip?"

"Yes! Yes I am. Any woman would be. Is that why you spoke to my parents about courtship before even meeting me? Because you knew I would refuse?"

"What the devil are you talking about?" Phinn asked, pushing his fingers through his hair. "Ashbrooke warned me—"

"You were talking to Ashbrooke about me?"

"Obviously. How else would I have known about this place?"

"While exploring for secluded places where you might ravish and dispose of a young woman. Obviously."

Phinn scoffed. "Fond of gothic novels, are you?

If you want to know, the duke offered a bit of advice about wooing reluctant women. He said that Emma said—"

"Emma said!" Olivia exclaimed incredulously. "I cannot believe her!" she muttered.

She took another sip from her wineglass. Found it empty. She reached for the bottle, but Phinn stopped her.

"I think you should have some water," he said.

"No thank you," she replied. "I am a wanton lady who drinks to excess, remember?"

He cracked a smile. Completely disregarding her wishes, he filled her wineglass to the brim with water.

"I find it interesting, Lady Olivia, that all your reasons we might suit focus on you. I can't help but notice you haven't mentioned anything in my character."

"Well . . ."

"Do you find my appearance objectionable? I know the scar is a bit frightening. It was just the result of an unfortunate collision with a broken dish."

Olivia looked at him, really looked at him. The scar wasn't that frightening at all—just a white line slashing from his temple to his eye. Otherwise, his skin was flawless. His hair was dark and tussled. He pushed his fingers through it when he was frustrated, she had noticed. Given the state of his hair now, she had been bothering him quite a bit today.

"No," she said softly. She did not find his appearance objectionable.

"Do you find me dull?"

She considered their interactions. He'd terrified her. Made her laugh. Vexed her. But he didn't bore her.

"No," she admitted.

"Is your heart set on another?"

"No."

Phinn pushed his fingers through his hair. Gave a short exhale. He was growing impatient with her. She could see that, even with the ridiculous bonnet that obscured her vision.

"Do you truly fear that I will hurt you?" he asked. Since he *asked*, she thought she might as well give him an honest answer.

"I have brought my embroidery scissors in my reticule. Just in case."

Phinn stared at her. Then he burst out laughing.

"Do you really find it amusing?" Olivia demanded.

Once he stopped laughing, he answered. "It's not funny at all. But the alternative to laughter . . ."

Phinn leaned forward. "I am drawn to you, Olivia. You must marry someone. I would like to marry, and I'd like a different marriage from my first. In spite of all the ways you claim we will not suit, I think we will. For example, I was so glad to hear from you, your parents, and everyone, really, that you had so many hobbies you enjoyed. Pianoforte, painting, floral arrangements. You won't need me to keep you amused all day, so I'll be able to focus on my work."

"And at night?" She realized she must be drunk to actually voice such a question.

"I want a wife at night, too," Phinn said in a low voice. It sent a shiver up and down her spine. A sudden warmth inside. A curious longing. And fear. She couldn't be that for him. She was too scared to be at his mercy like that. Naked, under him . . .

She turned a furious shade of red, then took another sip of her drink. Then she desperately wished to be elsewhere.

It wasn't fair that she'd gone to great lengths to tarnish her reputation—and it hadn't mattered. And he was the *one* man who wasn't bored to tears by her ladylike pastimes. The unfairness of it all was suddenly just too much.

"I hate embroidery," she burst out. "If I never sewed another sampler in my life, I'd die happy. I find the pianoforte dull. I've spent hours practicing the same scales over and over and I only play the same songs that my mother thinks are suitable for young ladies. Sometimes I think about playing bawdy songs in a proper musicale, but I am never asked to play because I am not as popular as the other girls. If I have to paint another assortment of fruit, flowers, and precious keepsakes I will go mad."

"What do you like?" he asked, as if it were as easy as that. As if he wasn't at all ruffled by her outburst.

"I don't know. I never had a chance to know. And I never will know if I am shut up in the attics of your remote Yorkshire estate while you build all your dangerous contraptions! All the while, I shall be cowering in fear of the day that I meet the same violent fate as your first wife!"

Olivia clamped a hand over her mouth.

Young ladies do not have emotional outbursts.

PHINN HAD ONCE performed an experiment that did not yield the intended outcome. He thought it a failure until a year later, the knowledge he'd gained proving to be essential in solving a far greater problem. This picnic was similar. He'd hoped to know her better. It seemed he did now, though not how he had expected.

She was afraid of him, still. Fear drove people to do things they'd never imagine themselves capable of just to avoid it. Perhaps she wasn't Prissy Missy. Perhaps she wasn't, deep down, a painted, wanton woman prone to drink, in spite of the persona she'd endeavored to project. Somewhere in between those two extremes was the real Olivia, the one he was drawn to. She was scared.

He could, perhaps, assuage her worries by telling her the truth about Nadia, the accident, the end. He was about to do just that.

And then everything went to hell.

Phinn's attentions were wrenched away from Olivia only by the sound of intruders. He saw Rogan driving an open carriage, full of lords and ladies engaged in tests to see how far they could lean out of the vehicle without toppling to the ground. He suspected they were not factoring calculations of weight, gravity, and other such physical matters, as he would have, but leaving everything to chance.

"Hello there, young lovers!" Rogan called out, interrupting everything. Just this once, Phinn did consider murder.

Rogan tossed the reins to his companion, jumped down from the carriage and strolled up the steps of the gazebo. As if he had been invited. Which he most definitely had not been.

"Olivia, you remember, Lord Rogan, a man I used to call a friend," Phinn said sharply.

"Partner in crime is a more apt description for the likes of a rogue like me," Rogan said, which was exactly the wrong thing to say. Olivia's eyes widened as she looked from one man to another. Then she took the bottle of wine to her lips and took a long sip. Rogan eyed her curiously, and when he spoke next his tone was more subdued. "Just thought I'd see how your romantic picnic was faring."

"We're fine. Be gone with you."

Olivia set down the empty bottle of wine on the table with a thud that rattled the cutlery and china. Phinn glanced warily at the carriage of people avidly watching Prissy Missy drinking wine straight from the bottle.

"Does anyone need any more wine? I can fetch more from the carriage," Rogan answered. Phinn did not want to know why he was driving around at midday with bottles of wine tucked away.

"Actually, I should like to go back to the carriage," Olivia said, standing and holding onto her chair. "I'm feeling a bit out of sorts. My eyelids feel heavy. And my brain feels . . . fuzzy."

"Drinking wine on a sunny afternoon would make anyone feel drowsy and unwell," Phinn said as she wavered on her feet. He jumped up and linked their arms together, intent on escorting her back to the carriage or perhaps on a short stroll away from these intruders.

She gazed up at him, her blue eyes full of questions. Once he got rid of Rogan, he would provide the answers she sought.

Olivia found herself leaning against Phinn. She was oh-so-drowsy and a bit unsteady on her feet, and he was a strong, solid, towering wall of support that she could lean on. Drinking the last of that wine had been a terrible idea; she hadn't wanted more but felt it was necessary to prove her point.

What was her point? All she knew was that it was happening again: desire warring with fear. His gaze was so warm and affectionate now, but she'd seen the cold distance in his eyes when he'd become angry.

For a moment it was easy to forget about the picnic crashers and just focus on Phinn's lips. He dipped his head. Would he kiss her? Olivia's heart started to pound. People were watching! And if they weren't?

"Put something in her drink, did you?" Rogan asked with a grin. "Clever."

Olivia looked from one man to the other.

"Did you poison me?" Olivia gasped. She did feel awfully drowsy and weak. "Oh goodness, I'm dying," she muttered.

"Olivia, you're fine. I would never do something like that," Phinn said insistently. "I would never hurt you. Rogan doesn't know what he's talking about."

"But I feel so ill," she mumbled. She yawned and rested her head on his shoulder, inadvertently swatting him in the face with her atrocious bonnet. She was too tired to care.

"It's just the effects of the wine," Phinn explained.

"How much did you give her?" Rogan asked. He shifted his concerned gaze from Olivia to one much more critical at Phinn. "She looks like she must be suffering from alcohol poisoning."

"Wrong choice of words, Rogan," Phinn said sharply.

Olivia felt him tense. His grasp on her arm tightened. Peering up at him, she saw his jaw clenched shut. His breaths were short and shallow. Rogan was making him angry. If Rogan had any sense, he would stop. But she was too tired to say that. Besides, what if Rogan was right?

Rogan peered curiously at her. She looked blankly at him.

"And what are you still doing here?" Phinn

managed to ground out the question through a fiercely clenched jaw.

"She does look ill, Phinn. Definitely alcohol poisoning."

"Poisoned? Have I been poisoned?" Olivia gasped. She struggled to keep her eyes open. What was she to do? Rogan wasn't any help; she'd have to save herself. She tried to disentangle herself from Phinn so she might fetch her embroidery scissors.

Phinn held her steady.

"You have not been poisoned," he said firmly. And then he turned on Rogan.

"And you—what the hell do you think you're doing here?"

"Only trying to help," Rogan said, carefully stepping backward. Phinn's grasp on her tightened. This is what she was afraid of.

"You know my temper Rogan. You have precisely ten seconds to make yourself—and your friends—scarce. Otherwise . . ."

"I'll just be off, then," Rogan said, attempting to sound jovial. Then he scrambled off to his carriage as Olivia felt faint.

Between her tightly laced corset, confining gown, wine, and the afternoon sun, she was simply overcome. Vaguely, she was aware of her knees giving way.

Phinn caught her.

She was aware of him lifting her up, holding her like a precious damsel in distress as he carried her to his carriage. Her head rested against his chest. The steady beat of his heart lulled her. She stirred a bit when she realized he was carrying her off and everyone was watching . . .

"Feats of strength!" Rogan called out after him. Had she more strength, she would have bashed Rogan with her parasol. And then she fell asleep.

"Never refer to a woman as a feat of strength, you fool," Phinn said through gritted teeth.

He glanced down at Olivia's peacefully slumbering face. The tightness in his chest eased. He drew a deep breath. His pulse started to subside. She soothed him. And thus, slightly soothed, Phinn could see that Rogan meant to help but only had a knack for making things worse.

For example: the carriage load of loud, gossipy companions now bore witness to the sight of the Mad Baron carrying an unconscious woman from a secluded location to his awaiting carriage.

He expected rumors of her death at his hand within the hour, which would inevitably be confirmed by everyone who saw him attempt to drive the carriage back to the Archers' house with one hand, whilst using the other to keep Olivia upright. Her body was limp. Her eyes were closed. He knew how this looked. And he cursed his luck—or did he?

Chapter 11

*Lord Radcliffe, better known amongst the ton as the Mad
Baron, did nothing to dispel rumors that he murdered
his late wife when he was seen carrying the unconscious
form of Lady Olivia Archer from a secluded gazebo in
Hyde Park, where they had been enjoying a picnic. The
word poison was overheard. It is now impossible that
Lady Archer not marry him, given that she has been
so thoroughly compromised. Whoever thought she'd be
London's Least Likely to survive the wedding night?*

—"FASHIONABLE INTELLIGENCE"
BY A LADY OF DISTINCTION,
THE LONDON WEEKLY

"THIS IS NOT good," Prudence said, setting down
the newspaper after reading the latest installment
of "Fashionable Intelligence" that had the ton
talking of nothing else. Prudence and Olivia had
rendezvoused at Emma's as soon as they'd read
the papers.

Olivia groaned and buried her face in her hands.
No one had to tell her how "not good" it was.

"In fact, I would even go so far as to say this is
bad," Emma said grimly. Olivia flung herself back
on the settee.

"Also not good," she said, "my mother fainted when Phinn brought me home, limp and nearly lifeless in his arms after our disastrous picnic. Even worse: my father has had a word with him. Given that I doubt they fought a duel, I am sure the archbishop has been called upon."

Not good. Bad. Terrible.

"Olivia, what exactly happened?" Emma asked.

"Besides the part where I was poisoned?" Olivia replied.

"With what?" Prudence asked, greatly intrigued.

"Wine," Olivia said. "Perhaps something else."

"You were just drunk," Prudence scoffed. "Why were you drunk at a picnic? It's one thing to be intoxicated at Almack's when one has spiked the lemonade. But in the afternoon?"

"I was a nervous wreck, fearing that he was going to ravish and murder me in the woods," Olivia confessed. "The wine seemed to soothe me."

"You'd think you'd want to keep your wits about you in that instance," Prudence remarked.

"Thank you, Prudence, for telling me that *now*."

"Obviously he did no such thing," Emma pointed out. "Neither poisoning, ravishment, nor murder."

"No. We merely conversed," Olivia replied. "At his request, I listed all the ways in which we would not suit."

"And did he agree with your assessment and offer to break the match?" Emma asked.

"No," Olivia said glumly. "He pointed out that because of our little wager, it was *his* fault I had been provoked into tarnishing my reputation, thus, he was honor bound to stand by me."

"Very noble of him," Emma said. "If dreadfully inconvenient for you."

"I didn't see that coming," Prudence said softly. "Who knew the Mad Baron was a man of honor? Makes one wonder what else we might have underestimated about him."

"It's worse," Olivia muttered. She told them everything—from her agonies over whether to wear the bonnet, to the minute Lord Rogan showed up to spoil everything. If it weren't for him, and his gossiping friends, she and Phinn might have had a chance of returning to her home undetected. Everyone saw. Everyone talked.

No one would have her now. Perhaps some tradesman's son or solicitor would, but then she'd be cut off from society just as much as if she'd been whisked away to a dungeon in Yorkshire.

"I'm afraid I'll have to marry him," she said with such a forlorn sigh she made herself even sadder. "In spite of all our efforts."

She'd never know the first blush of true love, the delicious anticipation of waiting for a suitor to call, or the sweet pleasure of waltzing with an adoring beau who didn't terrify her. It was too late for her to know herself now—she'd wasted so much time being the perfect lady when she could have been the perfectly lovely Olivia. As the Mad Baroness, alone in Yorkshire with her household to manage and while doing embroidery, she'd never know, never share a meeting of hearts and minds with a man who made her heart beat faster with love, not fear.

"You really do not wish to marry him, do you?" Emma asked softly, her expression full of concern.

Olivia shook her head no. The vision of her life as his bride saddened her. The man himself scared her. Why, everything seemed to go horribly wrong when they were together. Oh, there were moments when she was intrigued about his work or his past, even tempted by a kiss or his touch. But were mere moments enough to base a lifetime on?

"Even if it means you would be unwed for Lady Penelope's Ball?" Prudence asked.

"I'd rather attend Lady Penelope's Ball as a ruined spinster," Olivia declared, sounding more convinced than she felt.

Her future happiness was at stake, and she couldn't see a way for her and Phinn to be happy together. They'd make each other miserable and what happened with his first wife would happen to her. The madness. The desperation. The end.

"Then you have very little time to cause a scandal so great that you never recover from it," Prudence said.

"And one night to meet another man, fall in love, and elope to Gretna Green," Emma added.

"Given that I haven't managed to do that in four seasons, for it to happen in one night would be a miracle," Olivia pointed out. "Much as I want the plan to work."

"You'll have to take a risk, won't you?" Emma asked, tilting her head with the slight dare. "Especially if he's so horrid."

"I thought you and Blake liked him," Olivia replied.

"I do like him," Emma said. "But I love you and I would hate to see you miserable."

"Also, we don't fancy having to go all the way out to Yorkshire to visit you," Prudence added. "We'd much prefer you here in London."

Olivia also preferred herself in London.

"Even if I don't meet a man to run off with, I want just one night where I can be free," Olivia said. "I don't want to be Prissy Missy, London's Least Likely, or the future Mad Baroness. For one night, I just want to be *me*."

The tightness in her chest eased at the prospect of doing something drastic and daring just for herself.

"So we have one night in which to thoroughly and completely ruin Prissy Missy," Emma said. "There is only one problem with that plan. Possibly several."

"Will I never find happiness?" Olivia lamented. "What are the problems? Can I not just wear a scandalous gown and contrive to find myself in a compromising position with a known rogue?"

"Of course. But what happens next? You'll be ruined. You basically are ruined after that incident in the park. Marrying anyone else will be . . . unlikely."

For a moment Olivia wavered. *Should she just marry him and hope for the best?* He couldn't possibly murder two wives. What were the odds?

"You'll live with me," Prudence said, squeezing Olivia's hand. "We can live our spinsterhood in a nice cottage by the sea."

"And your aunt?" Emma asked skeptically. Prudence's aunt was Something Else.

"It's either my crazy aunt or the Mad Baron," Prudence said. "Take your pick."

"My father has probably procured a special license already," Olivia said flatly, as the truth was harder and harder to avoid. There'd never been a chance at something else, from the moment Phinn sought permission from her father to court her. Now that she'd been seen unconscious and possibly dead in Phinn's arms, there really was no hope for any alternative.

Lovely as living by the sea in a neat little cottage with Prudence would be, Olivia couldn't hinder her friend's chances at true love. Prue deserved more than being saddled with her downfallen friend who, as a ruined spinster, wouldn't be received by anyone.

The Mad Baron was her most likely and possibly only option for matrimony. Unless by some magical twist of fate she met someone else, fell in love, and ran off with him in one night. The odds of that happening were very low indeed.

She felt a sob stick in her throat. Which meant . . .

"I have only one more night of freedom," she said. "One night to dare to try to be anyone else. One night where I might waltz with rogues or steal kisses or flirt outrageously."

"I have an idea," Emma said, grinning. "It's either perfect or disastrous."

"Or perfectly disastrous," Prudence mused.

"There is a masquerade ball tomorrow night," Emma said, which was news to the others.

"I did not receive an invitation to that," Olivia said, dejected. "I am already being cut for my association with the Mad Baron."

"Neither did I," Prudence muttered. "And I have no such excuse."

"That's because it's being held by the demi-monde," Emma explained with a mischievous smile. "Blake was invited through his scientific friends. I have heard that such soirees are always much more *lively* than ton events."

"Do you think the Mad Baron will be there?" Olivia worried. "It wouldn't do if he were there on my night of freedom, and possible elopement."

"It's possible, I suppose," Emma replied. "But being so dark and brooding, he doesn't seem like the sort to attend such raucous parties. At least, I am led to believe they are raucous."

"Just to be safe," Prudence said, "we can ensure you are unrecognizable in your dress and mask. That way you will be free to dally with all sorts of disreputable gentlemen. No one will ever know you were there until you return from Gretna with a ring on your finger and a man on your arm."

"What will I tell my mother?" Olivia asked. For a second she imagined informing her that she would be attending a demimonde ball without a chaperone. Her mother would shriek, swoon, and take to her bedchamber with a stockpile of smelling salts—leaving her free to go.

"Tell your mother you are coming to stay with me," Emma said. "And then we shall dress in costume and attend the masquerade. You will have one night in which you can be anyone you want, Olivia."

"One night of freedom," Olivia said with a sigh. "My first and last night of freedom."

Lord Rogan's Residence

"I'm sorry," Rogan said, possibly for the thousandth time.

Phinn ignored him. If the Difference Engine hadn't fallen so far behind schedule because of the distractions and delays of his courtship, it would be finished by now. Then he could use it to add up Rogan's every apology. The decent thing to do would be accept at least one of them.

But the Difference Engine hadn't yet been built. It seemed he would be marrying Olivia under the worst circumstances. He'd had a word with her father about that. They had no choice in the matter now, after her shocking behavior at the ball, their disastrous picnic, and the subsequent scandal.

He'd come to London with two intentions: take a wife, build the engine. He hadn't quite failed, but he also couldn't shake the feeling that he should have stayed in Yorkshire.

"I am deeply, deeply sorry," Rogan carried on.

Phinn glanced at him out of the corner of his eye. The man did seem to genuinely regret the damage he'd done by inviting a dozen gossips to witness yet another romantic failure. Then he had to go and mention *poisoning*. Rogan not only terrified Olivia after he had managed to assuage her fears, but he got tongues wagging. *The Mad Baron offs another bride.*

Poisoning was such a miss-ish way to kill people, too, Phinn thought meanly. Insult to injury. Not that he injured anyone, ever. That was the most ridiculous thing of all—he had a temper, but he'd never raised a hand to anyone.

"I had only the best intentions."

Rogan was, inexplicably, still talking. Phinn was just trying to cool his boiling blood and calm his pounding heart. He'd lost his temper earlier and hadn't quite gotten it back.

Miss-ish or not, if he had some poison right now . . .

Instead he focused on breathing in and out. And staying seated in this chair. He glanced down at his hands—the knuckles had gone white, he was gripping the arms so tightly. It was either that or pummel his friend within an inch of his life.

Not exactly what his reputation needed right now.

Not for the first time did Phinn curse the Radcliffe temper.

"It was Ralph's idea to pop 'round and see how you two were doing," Rogan explained. Phinn had no idea who Ralph was, and thought it was probably for the best that he never knew. Because of his temper.

He had lost it the night Nadia died. She had been harping on him, nagging incessantly. He'd been distracted, for his work wasn't going well. Making matters worse, he'd been slightly drunk and in need of a good meal. And she kept on and on at him about leaving her alone at supper, embarrassing her in front of the servants, boring her . . .

He'd just snapped. It was the Radcliffe temper. He hadn't laid a finger on her. But he had roared. Sent her running.

The thing was, Nadia had a temper, too. And she went running to his workshop, intent on revenge. Or attention. He wasn't sure.

He hadn't mentioned any of this to Olivia. He might have if Some People hadn't interrupted him. He might have shown her his past and shown her his remorse. Instead, he revealed how quickly he could turn from gentleman to beast.

"I didn't think Ralph would want to crash your picnic," Rogan added.

Phinn finally fixed a steely gaze upon his friend, who shrank back.

"And how did he know that I was taking Olivia on a picnic?"

"I might have let it slip," Rogan said, shifting uncomfortably in his chair. "But you didn't say it was a secret."

"I like to keep my personal affairs private," Phinn said. "Always. As a rule."

A rule that no one followed. Witness: *The Mad Baron: The Gruesome Story of an Innocent Maiden's Tragic Love and Untimely Death. A True Story.* Witness: the gossip columns since he'd arrived in town.

"Look, I'm sure it's not as bad as you think it is," Rogan said in a conciliatory tone.

"Really? Are you certain of that?" Phinn challenged. He picked up on the newspapers that lay strewn about his feet. "The 'Man About Town' writes, 'The Mad Baron couldn't wait for the wedding night. His new bride has suffered the same fate as his first—without even a trip down the aisle first.' "

"Dreadful stuff," Rogan confirmed, mopping his brow with a handkerchief.

"It's libel and slander and I should call them out for it," Phinn said in a steely voice.

"I'll be your second," Rogan offered eagerly, as if presented with an opportunity to earn Phinn's forgiveness.

Dueling wouldn't help anyone. Phinn ignored him and picked up another paper out of the dozens that lay crumpled beneath his boots. One paper was one thing. But just to confirm, he had purchased a selection. They all related variations on the same horrid theme.

"And this one says Olivia is now known as London's Least Likely to Survive the Wedding Night," Phinn said dryly.

"You'll have to issue a challenge to that author as well," Rogan said. "Impugning on Lady Olivia's honor like that."

"That author is a woman," Phinn said flatly. "I don't think it would improve my reputation to challenge a woman to a duel."

"No, best not," Rogan agreed.

Silence befell them.

"Brandy?" Rogan offered.

"No," Phinn said. "The last thing I need is the wicked, noxious effects of alcohol on my already fiery temper."

"I could use a drink," Rogan muttered. He ambled over to the sideboard and poured a glass for himself. "I have an idea," he ventured.

"I don't want to hear your ideas," Phinn said. "In fact, I'm beginning to think that all of your ideas are utterly devoid of merit."

When Rogan didn't reply, Phinn glanced over at him. He looked genuinely hurt as he nursed a glass of brandy.

"I was only trying to help," Rogan said quietly. "I only want the best for you. Don't forget that I knew Nadia, too."

This was true. Rogan had come to visit a time

or two. They'd all been down to London—he, Rogan, his brother, and Nadia—and they'd marveled at her petulant, demanding behavior. His brother lived to serve her. Phinn had seen right through her. Rogan had, too. Only George had been blinded by her charms; he couldn't see her flaws.

Rogan had even tried to talk Phinn out of marrying her. More than once Phinn wished he had listened.

"She wasn't easy, Phinn. You did the best you could. And Olivia hasn't made things easy for you either. How was anyone to know a wallflower would get such a bee in her bonnet about getting married?"

Phinn's rage started to recede, leaving guilt behind. He'd spoken cruelly in anger, and he shouldn't have, even if Rogan did deserve it.

"There's a ball tonight," Rogan said.

Phinn groaned. He'd had enough of balls and soirees full of vapid guests with their accusatory stares and gossipy whispers.

"Not a tedious ton affair," Rogan corrected. Then, with a smile, he added, "A Cyprian's ball. A masquerade. Do you know what that means?"

"Everyone stumbles around, overintoxicated, and with limited vision because of the masks?"

"Besides that. It means that you can go out in disguise. One night when no one is whispering about you being the Mad Baron." It'd been years since he'd been out without being known thusly. As if sensing that Phinn was tempted, Rogan pressed his advantage. "Olivia's mother definitely won't be there, introducing you to her boring friends. Hell, there's no way Olivia would be there. You'll have the rest of your life to woo her. This is your last night of freedom! After this, you will be a staid, respectable married man."

"But I *want* that," Phinn protested.

"But don't you want a spot of fun first? Perhaps let off some steam?"

Phinn knew what happened when pressure continued to build without any release. Explosion. Thus, he decided to go to the party.

Chapter 12

These good natured kisses often have very bad effects, and can never be permitted without injuring the fine gloss of that exquisite modesty which is the fairest garb of virgin beauty.

—THE MIRROR OF GRACES

Young ladies did not sneak out to attend demi-monde balls.

By some magical alignment of the stars, Olivia managed to convince her parents to allow her to spend the night with Emma, who had miraculously convinced Blake to escort the wallflowers to a Cyprian's ball.

"If word gets out about this, I'll be ruined," Blake grumbled as they all climbed into his fine carriage emblazoned with the ducal crest.

"We'll all be ruined," Emma said brightly. "But we'll have the best time until then."

"Just please stay out of trouble. I beg of you," Blake said, addressing the three young women across from him in the carriage.

Young ladies kept their word.

They murmured vague promises and exchanged glances full of mischief. But Olivia felt a tightening in her chest. All at once she felt truly happy because she loved her friends. *This* is where she belonged—not in some secluded estate in Yorkshire. And yet the happiness was bittersweet, for who knew if they would ever share moments like this again? Packed into a carriage, dressed in their finest, on their way to a scandalous ball . . . surely, she wouldn't have moments like this as Mrs. Mad Baron in Yorkshire.

Yet it was settled. A license had been procured. Unless . . .

That was why it was so important that she live every moment to the fullest tonight, and why she could not truly promise that she'd be on her best behavior. After all, she'd been on her best behavior her whole life and where had it gotten her? Tonight she was determined to be her true self.

Away from the overbearing gaze of her mother, she already looked different.

She wore her hair only partially swept up, leaving long tendrils of soft blond curls trailing down her back. The dress she had managed to procure at the last minute was unlike anything she'd ever worn. It was a cerulean blue silk edged in black tulle. The bodice was scandalously low, revealing the swells of her breasts. Unlike her old dresses, this gown clung perfectly to her curves. For the first time, she felt sensual. Seductive. Womanly. Not like some doll that had been dressed in white lace and curled and starched within an inch of her life.

With the dark blue satin mask she wore, she also felt like a woman of mystery.

The air in the carriage was positively sizzling with excitement.

"I mean it, ladies," Blake said. "Please do not give me cause to regret this."

"Or get you in trouble," Emma said, chiding her husband. "As if you've never had the irate parents of proper young ladies calling for your head."

"That's all in the past, and I prefer to keep it that way," he replied.

Emma and her duke only had eyes for each other. The way he looked at Emma made Olivia's breath catch in her throat every time she saw it. His eyes positively sparkled with love for her. Prudence said they smoldered. Sparkle or smolder, the duke loved her and he couldn't hide it. Didn't even try. That was why she was here tonight—to find a man who looked at her like that.

"Perhaps they should get another carriage," Prudence murmured.

"Or a room," Olivia added softly.

The two laughed softly. Blake and Emma demanded to know what was so funny.

Then, finally, they arrived.

Olivia hadn't been clear on who was hosting this party, perhaps Lord Richmond, newly returned from India with his scandalous Indian mistress, Shilpa. Whoever it might be, it was clear to her from the moment she alighted the carriage that she was not in Mayfair anymore.

Young ladies do not gawk. But it was impossible not to.

A thick throng of carriages and horses blocked the courtyard. Footmen and drivers lounged about, smoking, drinking, waiting, and basking in the orchestral music wafting from the house. The stone mansion rose above them, four stories tall. Every window was lit up. The sound of men and women carousing and laughing rained down from all the open windows. Men smoked on the balconies and women in barely there gowns leaned seductively against the balustrade.

"We're not in Mayfair anymore," Prudence murmured.

"Let's go," Olivia said with a surge of uncontainable excitement. She grasped Prue's hand and led the way through the carriages and up to the main entrance of the house.

Inside, the scene that greeted them was breathtaking.

The foyer was a vast, decadent scene. Open to all four stories, the large space was dominated by a massive marble staircase spiraling higher and higher. There were open balconies where men shouted down or across to each other and women blew kisses. Olivia even spied a couple kissing openly.

Hand in hand, she and Prudence tailed behind Blake and Emma through the foyer and into the ballroom. The orchestra loudly played lively songs. Was it her nerves, or did they play every song faster? She'd have sworn she could feel the deep, low bass and cello playing in time with her heartbeat.

And then the gowns! And jewels! Everywhere she looked another woman sashayed past, decked in richly hued silks and satins draped to make all manner of indecent suggestions. Under the candlelight, jewels glittered, beckoning.

Olivia accepted a glass of champagne from a passing footman.

"Sip that slowly," Ashbrooke warned. "And don't have another."

"Of course," she murmured. In her head, she heard her mother lecture. *Young ladies do not drink. It makes them forget themselves.*

She took a small sip, savoring the explosion of tiny bubbles on her tongue. Like stars. Like magic. She took another small sip and let her gaze roam the ballroom, noting the men. They were young and brawny, dressed in officers' uniforms or less formal evening clothes. No one was very old, or very respectable, or even on their very best manners. All the rakes and rogues who would never show their faces at ton events were here, gallivanting with the kind of women who would never gain a voucher for Almack's.

There was a certain frisson in the air. An undercurrent of danger and wicked pleasure. Men draped over women, women draped over men. Gowns were lower. Cravats quickly lost their starch and men's shirts opened at the neck. All of them dancing wildly, too close together. *Oh . . .* If only she had attended a party like this earlier.

But then, she knew she wouldn't have been able to enjoy it. She'd have tapped her foot under her skirts. Or watched longingly, thinking she could *never* dance with such abandon, or so closely to a man with whom she wasn't acquainted, or display such intimacy in public. After all, what would people think? And if people didn't think well of her . . .

She'd had a good reputation. She'd endeavored successfully to tarnish that reputation. Both would result in marriage to the Mad Baron. Thus, tonight she'd act as she wished and wouldn't give a care for what anyone thought. Tonight was just about her.

The French doors were thrown open to a terrace where guests mingled and the men smoked. Beyond that she could make out a garden with torches lighting the paths. Danger. Trouble. Pleasure. Adventure.

"If your mother finds out I participated in this," Ashbrooke grumbled, "I will fear for my life."

"I am already forever in your debt, Duke," Olivia said, utterly awed by the scene before her. "And I can assure you, if she learns of your involvement it will not be from me."

"Stay out of trouble," he admonished with a pointed look at her and Prudence. Then he whisked Emma off to dance.

"We'll see about that," Olivia replied, perhaps smiling wickedly.

For the first time in her life, men noticed her and didn't look away. She felt her temperature rise from their dark, curious gazes. More than one rakish smile was directed at her. By the third or fourth time she stopped peering over her shoulder to see which gorgeous lady behind her had been the object of their affection. While all of the glances pleased her, none affected her as deeply as that first connection with Phinn. But tonight wasn't about him.

"Let's take a turn about the ballroom, shall we, Prudence?" she said.

Prue smiled as they linked arms and strolled through the melee.

"This is madness," Prue said, awed.

"I think it's wonderful," Olivia exclaimed. "This is the best party we shall likely ever attend. Do you feel something positively electric in the air, Prue? I think I'll fall in love tonight. In fact, I am quite sure of it."

"The champagne must be going to your head," Prue remarked, laughing.

"So what if it has?" Olivia mused. "Tonight I shall enjoy myself. Thoroughly."

"Just be careful, Olivia," her friend cautioned. "These are not gentlemen."

One of the not-gentlemen, a handsome young man with dark tussled hair, caught her eye. He smiled when he saw her. There was a gleam in his eye, especially after his gaze dropped to her bodice and then slowly raked back up to her

face. She felt hot and shocked, as if he'd actually
touched her.

"No, they certainly are not," she murmured.
She sipped her champagne and glanced at him
again. He wore a red jacket. A soldier.

Her heart started thudding as the man snaked
his way toward her through the crowd, his gaze
ever fixed upon hers.

*Young ladies do not associate with men to whom
they have not been introduced.*

When he was a few feet away he bowed, then
took her hand, gave her a wicked grin, and asked,
"May I have this dance, Angel?"

Olivia simply handed her half-empty champagne glass to Prue and followed her soldier into
the swirl of dancing couples.

She threw herself into it with a vengeance,
dancing with her soldier, then another and another—a whole regiment, mayhaps. She danced
with younger sons of peers, men who earned
their living, or all sorts of not-gentlemen whose
attention made her feel beautiful and enchanting.

Her cheeks were pink and hurt from smiling so
much. This never happened at all those ton parties, where she was hardly ever asked to dance.
Such a pity for hours and hours of dance practice
to go to waste. She put it to good use now.

This was what she wanted. Every joyous,
wicked, wonderful moment was underscored
with an awareness that this was the last. She'd
only just begun and it was already the end.

THERE WAS CERTAINLY nothing like this in York-shire, Phinn thought as pushed his way through the crowds. Women he didn't know beckoned at him with bedroom eyes and blew kisses with painted lips. If that weren't forward enough, more than one woman allowed her hands to stray across the expanse of his chest or caress the length of his arm.

Within minutes of arriving, he'd lost Rogan to one of these lovely, vivacious sirens. As for him-self—he honestly couldn't say he didn't enjoy the attention. If any of these women recognized him as the Mad Baron, they didn't seem bothered. Here, he was just another rake, just another rogue. He was a possible tumble, a quick diversion.

Truth be told, he couldn't say he wasn't tempted. "A machine," Nadia had called him. But he was a man, red-blooded and wanting as any other. But the woman he wanted was Olivia. So while a lithe little blonde might have caught his eye, or a buxom brunette purred "Hello," he didn't stop. He didn't stray.

Phinn accepted a drink from a passing foot-man. He did enjoy the orchestra, playing with much more vigor than at any of the ton parties he'd attended. Finally, he found a spot by a pillar where he could just watch the kind of revelry he'd never even imagined. Men whirled women around, much to their delight, only to pull them in close. This was dancing that would give the patronesses at Almack's the vapors. And in the middle of it all a woman in blue gown and a mask caught his eye.

Phinn sipped his drink and watched her dance. She moved with an uncommon grace and a liveliness that was unmatched. She smiled, her cheeks pink. Her hair tumbled down her back in pale gold curls. She *looked* like an angel but . . .

His gaze slid down to her breasts, swelling above the bodice of her gown. She breathed heavily from all her dancing. He wasn't the only one to notice the rise and fall of her breasts. Phinn didn't like all these men staring at her.

Forcing his attentions back to her face, he found his gaze drawn to her mouth. She smiled—a wide, rosy-cheeked smile—and he couldn't look away. No, he was involuntarily drawn to the smile of a beautiful, happy woman. He was suddenly insanely jealous of the solider she danced with. He wanted Olivia to smile at him like that—like she was having the time of her life with him.

Like an angel.

The lucky bastard she danced with slid his hand around her waist. Something knotted in Phinn's gut.

He had imagined those blond curls that Olivia kept so tightly restrained. He had imagined her breasts, which were always covered up in respectable white frocks. And he had imagined her stumbling adorably into his arms . . .

Even though it was outrageous to suppose Olivia was here, at a raucous party like this, he suddenly knew it was her.

The Radcliffe temper flared, as if all the champagne at this party had been tossed onto a fire.

He forced himself to turn away.

Nearby, he noticed another women who looked familiar and also certainly did not belong here. She bore a striking resembles to Olivia's friend, Miss Payton. Like him, she was watching the raucous debauchery from the sidelines. He caught her eye, but she looked away, intent upon watching the couples—or one in particular—dancing. The girl in blue and the soldier in red.

YOUNG LADIES DO not drink to excess.

As Olivia sipped her second glass of champagne, she wondered how many it would take to drown out her mother's voice in her head, reciting all the rules of what a lady did or did not do. With every sip, with every whirl around the dance floor, with every tempting smile from this soldier, the voice became a little more faint. And she had much more fun. It was quite possible that she'd never been as happy as she was in this moment, with Brendon (or was it Brandon?) holding her in his arms and gazing at her as if he were thinking all sorts of sinful thoughts.

"I don't know about you, darling, but I could use some air," Brendon (Brandon?) said.

"Yes, please," she said, breathing heavily. She'd been dancing for the past hour—or two? Her soldier linked their arms and led her to the terrace.

Young ladies do not stroll on the terrace with gentlemen.

The terrace was crowded with people. Gentlemen stood in groups, puffing away on cigars and cheroots. Women lingered, drawing men away for private tête-à-têtes. There were so many people out for a spot of air that they spilled down the stairs, into the gardens.

Brendon (Brandon?) smiled at her in the seductive way she had always wanted a man to smile at her. There was a sparkle in his eyes. She smiled back, utterly happy, but all too aware of not knowing quite what to *say* to him. Already they were more physically intimate than she'd been with any other man—his hands may have strayed during their dance, *not* that she minded. But they hadn't really talked. Perhaps she'd break the ice with a jest.

"Was your father a thief?" she inquired, tilting her head inquisitively as she'd seen other flirtatious women do.

"What?" He seemed perplexed. A bit of her died inside when he didn't immediately seem to understand. Then she felt an intense pang of empathy for Phinn, who'd encountered much the same reaction. Had he also feared dying from embarrassment?

"The sparkle from the stars," she said, stumbling over the words. "In your eyes."

The rogue grinned, then burst out laughing. Was he mocking her or laughing at her cleverness? Well, Phinn's cleverness. Would these floorboards kindly open up and swallow her whole? Now? Please?

"I'll show you stars, darling," he said, holding out his hand.

"Very well." She put her hand in his.

Olivia wasn't quite sure how he managed it, but one thing led to another—crowds, light in his eyes, avoiding one person and trying to say hello to another, finding a place to rest their feet, seeking a better view of the stars—and she found herself alone with him.

What was his name? Good Lord, she did not know his name. But did she need to? For that matter, did he even know hers? It was best if he did not.

Young ladies do not wander into the gardens at night. Especially without a chaperone. One mustn't do anything, ever, without a chaperone.

She was alone with Brendon (Brandon?). The stars sparkled. The bubbles of the champagne had gone straight to her head. She ought to be inside. She ought to be home, tucked into her bed. But she was tired of what she ought to be: an obliging and demure paragon of virtue.

Tonight she wanted passion. Wild, wanton, leave her breathless, make her dizzy, heart-pounding passion.

And stars. Sparkling, twinkly, make-a-wish, remember this moment stars.

And a kiss—the kind that she'd always been warned about. The kind that made her weak in the knees, forget her own name, and with enough pleasure and passion to last her a lifetime.

"Darling," he murmured, pulling her into his

arms. He definitely did not know her name. Nevertheless, Olivia's heart started thudding in a pleasant way because her first kiss was so close she could almost taste it.

"Darling," she repeated, because she wasn't quite sure of his name. This was horribly wanton of her. But she didn't care. She was done being a good girl, a perfect lady. So very done.

And then he pressed his lips against hers.

Finally, finally, finally, oh God, finally, one of London's Least Likely had her first kiss. His lips were firm and insistent against hers. Olivia yielded, eager to follow his lead, for what did she know of kisses?

And then she had more than she bargained for.

Young ladies do not find themselves at the mercy of a rogue.

He tugged her into his arms. She stumbled forward, giggling. His chest was firm and his hands were warm and determined as they explored her in places no one ever dared to touch her before. It was exciting and thrilling and wonderful.

Until it wasn't.

His touch became insistent. Bodice, *down*. Skirts, *up*. He thought her a light-skirt, and obviously had no idea that she was one of the more innocent girls ever to make her debut. They didn't call her Prissy Missy for nothing. She could not disrobe for a stranger, in a garden, no matter how many glasses of champagne she had drunk. She just could not.

She didn't *want* to. She wanted to dance and kiss and flirt and only now did she realize that was all she wanted. The rest scared her. *This* scared her. If she was going to do such an intimate, scary thing it ought to be with a man whose name she knew.

"No," she said, pushing him away. Because tonight was about her pleasure, and this wasn't it.

"No?" The rogue laughed. And then pulled her closer, held her tighter, kissed her harder.

"Stop That Right Now," Olivia said, summoning the voice her mother used when dealing with wayward servants and troublesome children.

Brendon (Brandon?) laughed softly in her ear. She felt the rush of his hot breath on her skin. Warm. Dangerous.

"No," she insisted, now struggling in his arms. Her heart was pounding, and not in a good way. "No." This was fear. "Stop." This was everything she'd been warned against. This is why girls didn't drink to excess or wander into the gardens with strange gentlemen. This is why they wore demure gowns and did not speak with men to whom they had not been introduced. This is why they had chaperones. This was why they followed the rules.

"Stop. *Please.*"

But he didn't. Tears pricked Olivia's eyes. *Where* was a pair of embroidery scissors when she needed them?

"The lady said no."

A man's gruff voice cut through the night air.

It was stronger than her stupidly girlish protests, and the scoundrel gripping her tightly stopped only for a moment to say, "Get your own, mate."

Olivia winced as the crack of the stranger's fist connected firmly with the jaw of Brendon (Brandon?). She winced again when the soldier stumbled back uttering swear words she'd never imagined. And she gasped when, after rubbing his jaw for a moment, Brendon (Brandon?) lunged, hurling himself at her savior.

It was dark but she could hear the grunts and smacks and the crack of fists meeting flesh and bone. A nest of ducklings seemed to have been disturbed in the fight; the mother and chicks came running in search of a safer nesting spot, giving her a terrible fright until she realized what they were. But first she shrieked.

Eventually the fight sounds ceased and there was silence, save for the faint, faraway party sounds from the house. A cool breeze rustled the leaves on the trees. A cloud passed away from the moon, revealing a man who was tall—but not too tall. Muscled, but not overly so. He wore evening clothes, and a black domino obscured his face. But she could see he was handsome. A firm sensual mouth, a clenched jaw. Was he angry with her? He didn't even know her.

"Are you all right?" he asked.

"I think so," she said softly. She was such a fool, courting danger like that. She *knew* better. She was so very lucky this man had turned up when he did. Although she was now at *his* mercy, and she sensed that while his anger was receding, he wasn't entirely a virtuous angel of goodness and light. "Thank you."

He didn't say "You're welcome" or make a quip about saving a damsel in distress, or lecture her on her exceedingly foolish decisions that evening. She deserved every possible lecture or to be dragged unceremoniously back to the ballroom *or worse.*

He exhaled slowly, as if frustrated and trying to control his temper. When he spoke, the words were clipped, gritted out.

"You just wanted to have fun," he said.

Yes. Yes that was it exactly. This man understood that she only wanted to have a spot of amusement before she'd never enjoy herself again. Who was he?

She gazed at him.

He gazed at her.

Young ladies do not fall in love with mysterious heroic strangers the night before their wedding . . .

Chapter 13

It is the height of folly for a young woman to find herself
alone in a darkened garden with a gentleman.

—COMMON KNOWLEDGE
AMONGST YOUNG LADIES

HERE, IN THE depths of the garden, there was
only silence and the sound of a man breathing
deeply and exhaling slowly.

Her eyes, adjusting to the light, saw this mystery savior toe the unconscious form of Brendon
(Brandon?). He might be dead. At the moment she
only cared that she had survived. She'd kept her
innocence and her virtue and her *self.* Thanks to
this man.

He cut a dashing figure, broad-shouldered, tall,
and mysterious. The domino obscured most of his
face, but she saw his firm jaw, his mouth.

Olivia gazed at him.

He gazed at her.

"Would you like me to escort you back to the
ballroom?" he asked. He certainly wasn't leaving
her to fend for herself out here.

This man intrigued her. Strangely, she felt safe
with him, perhaps because he'd just come to her

defense even though they were perfect strangers. Not that she trusted her judgment at the moment. Which is why she said, "Yes. But I think I just need a moment to collect myself."

Then she took a few steps and sat on a nearby stone bench. Weak knees. Like him, she took deep breaths. What would she have done if he hadn't come? She didn't want to think about it.

He, whoever he was, took the liberty of sitting beside her. Out of the corner of her eye she watched as he gingerly flexed his fingers. There was a sharp hiss and intake of breath. He had hurt himself. For her.

Whoever it was had suffered because of her wanton disregard for ladylike rules, common sense, and decency. Because of her selfish and stupid behavior, people had been hurt. The first sob came, unbidden. And then another and another as it dawned on her what a truly horrible fate she had barely escaped. She was a fool. But she was lucky. A lucky fool. She'd gone courting magic, adventure, and romance. Instead she'd nearly been broken.

And still, she didn't know *this* man! He could be even worse. Nevertheless, she turned and clasped his coat and buried her face in his wool jacket. Vaguely, she noted that it smelled of clean wool and something she couldn't quite identify, but that she liked.

Then he wrapped his arm around her shoulders and pulled her closer into his embrace. She nestled against his chest. She'd never been so intimate with a man before. Not even with Brendon (Brandon?). She'd never been held before. Not like this. This just felt so right.

And she was betrothed to another.

She sobbed even harder.

"It'll be all right," he said.

"It won't," she replied. Not that he even heard her, given that her face was buried in his cravat as she wept.

"Are you lost?"

"I am," she said, lifting her head to peer up at him. "I am lost. And confused and wretched."

He frowned.

"Because it's so strange to see an angel so far from heaven," he said.

Then it was her turn to frown.

"Oh, I'm no angel," she told him. "I have behaved wretchedly. Everything is ruined. I am ruined. My whole life is ruined."

"Tell me about it." Olivia felt her heart sigh—and realized she definitely had overimbibed champagne, because hearts did not sigh. But she *felt* as if hers had done so because this man wanted to know about her, her life, and her feelings. No one—not her mother, father, or the Mad Baron—had ever really asked her about those things.

"Oh, where do I begin?" she sighed.

"The beginning?" he ventured. She smiled slightly.

"My parents are forcing me to marry a man I

don't love," she said sadly. It was a terrible fate. Almost as bad as the one she'd just averted. But when the Mad Baron started doing those things to her, she wouldn't be allowed to say no.

"Could you love him?" the man asked.

"Never," she said vehemently. She felt his grip tighten around her shoulders. Was he heartbroken by this tragic, star-crossed turn of events, too?

"Never?"

"Never," she said firmly.

"Perhaps—"

"No, I despise him. We do not suit," she said. He was terrifying and she was terrified, for one thing. And he never asked what she felt or thought, like this man did.

"What is so dreadful about him?"

"He is overbearing. Why, he just decides we're going on a picnic. He doesn't even ask if I wish it. He just decides and I'm supposed to be told what to do, like a child. And he says the worst lines."

"That bastard," the man said. She wouldn't have used quite such strong language. But then again, deep down in her bones she was A Lady, despite all behavior to the contrary.

"And he plans to take me away to his desolate estate in rural Yorkshire where we will live in utter solitude. I'm sure I'll go mad, especially for want of company while he is consumed with his work and I am left to embroider and manage the servants."

"I'm sure you won't go mad," he said consolingly. Then, to her surprise, he asked, "Would you prefer to remain in London?"

She leaned her head against his shoulder and smiled, in spite of the tragic situation she'd related. This man asked her about her preferences. Unlike her parents or the Mad Baron, who just decided for her. Why couldn't she have met him sooner?

"Yes. At least I shall have my friends for company," Olivia answered. Marriage was a huge change; she wished to smooth the transition. Lowering her voice, she added, "And there will be people around, just in case . . ."

"In case what?"

"I think he might be dangerous and violent," she said in a grave whisper. "In fact, I am sure of it."

"That's terrible," he said. And then, protectively, he asked, " Has he ever hurt you?"

"No," she admitted. "But the gossip—"

"Has he lost his temper at you?" the man asked softly.

"No," she said. "But the broadside—"

"Has he threatened you?"

"No, what is your point?"

"Perhaps you needn't be afraid of him," her mysterious midnight rescuer said. She had decided to call him Mysterious Midnight Rescuer in her head until she learned his real name. This man she could love. She knew it, deep down in her soul.

"But everyone says—" she protested.

"Everyone has said that the world is flat, when it is round."

"What does that have to do with anything?" Olivia asked.

"They have said the sun revolves around the earth, when the opposite is true," he explained.

"Very well, I take your point," she said. "I oughtn't listen to gossip. I should only trust what truths I discover myself."

"Yes," he said gruffly. "Trust yourself and your own experiences."

"My mother says ladies do not gossip."

"I'm afraid your mother is wrong," he replied, which no one ever said. Questioning her parents was Not Allowed.

"You're right," Olivia said, surprising herself by agreeing. "She said if I was well-behaved and a proper lady a nice man would want to marry me. And now I am betrothed to the Mad Baron. See, she is wrong."

"I suppose you've tested this theory of yours," he said, which confused her. It wasn't a theory. It was just life as she had lived it.

"Whatever do you mean?"

"Have you tried to act very unladylike? Have you set about breaking all the rules?" She had to laugh at that. If only he knew!

"Yes," she admitted, a little smile playing on her lips. "I have tried to break as many as possible. I have cavorted with rogues, drunk to excess, and worn absurd amounts of face paint."

"And what are the results?"

"Besides this unusually frank and intimate conversation with a stranger in a garden?" It was quite possibly the longest conversation she'd had with a man. It was certainly the most honest. Olivia sighed. "I have been drunk, made a fool of myself, and was nearly ravished by a scoundrel whose name I am not quite certain of."

"Following all the rules of being a proper lady hasn't made you happy. Breaking the rules, I'm assuming, hasn't made you happy. Perhaps you ought to make your own rules, Angel."

Olivia leaned her head against his shoulder. *Make my own rules.* Rules were always the creation of someone else: her mother, high society, the conduct books she was given each year for her birthday.

"Make my own rules," she mused, the thought occurring to her for the very first time. What would her own rules be?

"Do only what pleases you, Angel."

"And if I don't know? I've never had a chance to know. Now I fear I never will. The Mad Baron will make me follow his rules. He wants a biddable wife."

"Men say they want a biddable wife," he said, "but then they realize they want a woman who fascinates them, who cares for them. They want a woman to love. So I promise, you'll be able to make your own rules and your husband won't try to stop you."

"How do you know?"

"I just know," he said, giving her shoulders another squeeze. "On behalf of decent gentlemen, give your betrothed a chance. Perhaps he isn't awful. Then if he is very awful, run away."

"You are rather kind," she said, turning to face him. They both wore their masks, still. As if neither wanted to be themselves in this moment.

"We're not all rogues," he replied.

"If only I'd met you sooner," Olivia said with a soft sigh.

He turned. She turned. His gaze dropped to her lips.

She thought about kissing. Despite all logic and reason, she wished to kiss this man. Even though she had just discovered how dangerous kissing gentlemen could be. But she felt drawn to this man in a way she'd never felt before, and in a way the poets spoke of. Wanting to kiss him simply felt right. And besides, she still wanted to know what the poets (and other girls) had been talking about when they were in rapture over a kiss.

It was an awkward moment—she didn't think he meant to kiss her. But their lips collided and then there was no way she could stop.

This kiss was gentle. The pressure of his mouth against hers was so light, she found herself leaning closer to him in want of more. This kiss was slow. His lips lightly brushed against hers, so lightly she shouldn't have felt it but she did, all over, as if her every nerve was attuned to the slightest touch.

And then the kiss deepened. He teased the seam of her lips. She opened for him, ready to follow his lead. Ready to experience the pleasure of this kiss. Already she knew this one would be different. *This* was the first kiss she'd dreamt of and was meant to have. And she trusted him, whoever he was.

Because she was now making her own rules, she did what she wanted to do, which was to thread her fingers through his hair. It was soft, like silk, through her fingers. As if it were the permission he needed, her Mysterious Midnight Rescuer deepened the kiss. Their tongues touched and teased as they tasted each other. She was starting to know this man in a way she didn't know any other.

Gently, he clasped her face with his hands. Had it been Brendon (Brandon?), she might have felt trapped. With this man she felt cherished and wanted. Most men hadn't even wanted to talk to her, but this one—he didn't want to let go. *This* is what she wanted. *This* was why she risked reputation and virtue. And now that she found it, how could she ever let go?

Olivia broke away from the kiss to ask this perfect stranger—this perfect match—an utterly mad question. Caressing his cheek with her palm, her gaze dropped to his mouth, then lifted to his eyes.

Her heart was pounding. But she had to ask: "Will you marry me?"

In the darkness, she saw his darkened eyes and the slight, wistful smile as he said, "Not tonight."

Chapter 14

The only thing one can politely say about the wedding of Lady Olivia Archer and Lord Radcliffe is that it happened. It was quite uncertain for a moment.

—"MISS HARLOW'S MARRIAGE IN HIGH LIFE,"
THE LONDON WEEKLY

AT ELEVEN O'CLOCK that morning it was official. She was now Lady Radcliffe. Mrs. Mad Baron. The fate she had feared and protested so vehemently was now hers.

During the small, intimate ceremony in the drawing room, she had stumbled over the words "submit" and "obey." The vicar didn't seem to mind. Neither did her parents. And Phinn? His expression was inscrutable. There was just that scar, which was so menacing. And the firm line of his mouth. And those green eyes of his she couldn't bear to gaze into.

Make your own rules, her midnight rescuer had said. Perhaps she'd try that tomorrow. Today, she felt too much all at once—sadness that *this* was her wedding day instead of the joyful occasion she had long dreamt of; regret that she hadn't met that man from the garden sooner, for he seemed to understand her; and fear for the future.

For what would tonight would bring? And every night ever after? Every time she considered it, her corset felt far too confining. She couldn't breathe. Would the kissing be rough and unyielding, as with Brendon (Brandon?). Or would it be the perfect slow dance, as with her Mysterious Midnight Rescuer? Would the Mad Baron even kiss her at all?

She fully expected to be whisked away to Yorkshire immediately after the wedding breakfast. Thus, she was confused when the carriage rolled to a stop but a few moments later in front of Mivart's Hotel on Brook Street in Mayfair.

"We're here," Phinn said.

"A hotel?" she inquired, lifting her gaze to his, surprised. "I thought we would travel to your estate and live there."

"We might do that one day," he said. "But I have business in London and I thought you might prefer to be near your friends while we are still getting to know each other. I did not wish to rent a house without consulting you first."

At this unexpected reprieve, Olivia felt the tightness in her chest ease. Her mad wandering of his remote estate would wait. She would have the comfort of her friends in these early days of her marriage.

Perhaps . . .

Phinn had more to say, "That is, if you are amenable. If there is something you would prefer, please tell me."

Perhaps he wasn't as horrid and unfeeling as she had feared.

For the first time all day, she managed a full breath. Perhaps she would not be so lonely after all. Perhaps he was not overbearing and commanding all the time. Perhaps he would consider her wishes. In this instance, he had somehow managed to just *know* what she wanted.

Like the man in the garden. He had understood her, even when she was least deserving of it. If only she'd found him sooner. If only she hadn't lost him.

She hadn't had a clue how to find him, though Lord knew she'd wracked her brain over the matter ever since. Her mother hadn't given her a moment to herself in which she might find him— had she even known where to look.

Thus, she was here now—the grandly decorated lobby of Mivart's Hotel—on the arm of her husband. Well-dressed men and women lounged in settees, many holding conversations in foreign languages.

They were shown to a beautiful suite of rooms, with two bedchambers adjoining a large drawing room that was decorated in soothing shades of pale blue and green. Large windows overlooked Brooke Street.

Olivia strolled around the room taking in all the fine furnishings and paintings. Phinn was either beggaring them with every night spent in this suite—or he was rich indeed. She had never paused to consider it. She discreetly cast glances his way, noting the calm and efficient manner with which he dealt with the servants. What else did she not know about him?

"Will this do?" Phinn asked, coming to stand beside her, referring go the suite. He clasped his hands behind his back. She was suddenly aware of how tall he stood. How broad his chest. How strong he was. For once, she thought not of how he might overpower her, but how she might curl up in his arms seeking comfort.

"It's lovely," she said, offering him a shy smile. "Did you see your friend Lord Rogan has left us a bottle of champagne?" She had noticed it during her perusal of the room. "That's kind of him."

Not that she was quite in the mood for champagne after the Cyprian ball. Or that night at Almack's. Now that she was making her own rules, she rather thought she wouldn't drink to excess.

"Meddlesome, more like it," Phinn replied dryly. He glanced about the room with narrowed eyes, as if searching for more "gifts" or "meddling."

"I'm not quite sure I can make sense of the note he left, though," Olivia said, plucking the small vellum card.

"What does it say?" Phinn asked, standing close behind her and reading over her shoulder. With him so near, she could not concentrate on deciphering Rogan's handwriting. Instead, she puzzled over the urge to lean back against his chest and into his embrace. It had been so lovely and comforting when the good man from the garden had held her. Would it be the same with Phinn?

"Oh, that bastard," Phinn swore.

"What is it?" Olivia asked, turning to face him, and now even more intrigued.

"Nothing," he said, shoving the card in his pocket. "Let me show you to your rooms." He clasped her hand and led her through a set of double doors.

Her bedchamber was beautiful. The spacious room also had large windows, pale butter yellow walls, a small furniture set before the fireplace, and a fine four-poster bed. Upon which were strewn an assortment of books and periodicals. While Phinn gave directions to the maid about her luggage, Olivia curiously picked up one of the periodicals.

The first thing she noticed were the pictures. Were these fashion periodicals? If so, they were a lovely gift. She'd happily spend her first day of married life in this bed, perusing the latest fashions, deciding which to buy now that she didn't need her mother's approval.

But upon closer look, Olivia noticed that the women in the pictures were not wearing clothes. In fact, neither were the gentlemen. What on earth was *this*? She peered even closer. What *strange* activities were they engaged in?

The men and women were stretched out on the bed with their limbs tangled together . . . and bent over writing desks . . . and bent over settees. It started to dawn on Olivia that these were depictions of The Act.

She tilted her head and turned the page. So that's what was under the fig leaf on the statues at the British Museum.

She glanced over at Phinn. Did he mean for them to do all these things? Her mind immediately conjured up an image of them in such positions. A man kneeling before a woman who sat on a chair with her legs spread to an unladylike degree. A woman straddling a naked man lying on a mattress. A woman's mouth on a man's— She quickly shut the publication, cheeks burning.

She felt an unsettling feeling in her belly and a flush of heat spreading throughout her limbs. It wasn't unlike the sensation she'd experienced when she'd kissed her Mysterious Midnight Rescuer. Was it the pictures themselves or her imagination picturing she and Phinn in such states? Did he mean for them to do all these things?

"What are these?" she asked, gesturing at the array of publications. Her voice sounded odd to her ears. Goodness, would he notice?

"Let me see," he said, sounding as curious as she. Olivia handed him the one she'd been looking at and picked up another, a book, entitled *50 Ways to Sin*.

She gasped when Phinn immediately snatched it out of her hands.

Instead she picked up another.

"Are these things you wish us to do? Are these

instructional?" she inquired. Was he concerned that she wouldn't know anything? She was supposed to be innocent, wasn't she? Was this a new ladylike art that she was now to perfect, after careful research and daily practice? Her mother had just said, *Ladies lie still and oblige their husbands.*

Olivia had questions. Phinn did not have answers.

"No. Just never mind," he said in a rush, turning very red. "You shouldn't see these."

"Because if this is depicting what I think it is . . ." Olivia said, frowning, unsure how to finish the thought. "My mother said I had to lie very still. But she didn't mention lying still over a desk while . . ."

She wasn't quite sure what to make of the strange sensations the pictures afforded or how to interpret Phinn's clenched jaw and darkened eyes.

"Say no more, I beg of you," he said. He sounded, oddly, as if he were being strangled. Then he rushed to gather up all the publications by the armful, but some kept slipping out and falling. As he tried to catch them, more fell to the floor. Olivia bent to help retrieve them. Their heads collided in the process.

"Oh!" she gasped, rubbing her cheek just below her eye, where it had connected solidly with his forehead.

"Are you all right?" Phinn asked, dropping them all to the ground to reach out to her, concerned. He tenderly touched the spot where they'd hit. She winced—but not from his touch.

"I'm fine. Are you?"

"Yes," he said, rubbing his own forehead. That's when she noticed the bruises on his swollen knuckles. "What happened to your hands?"

"Nothing," he said, even though something had obviously happened. He rushed on, collecting all the scandalous materials. She noticed *50 Ways to Sin,* again, and the title *Wicked Wanton Women.* One book fell open to a page of illustrations. Upon closer inspection, her mouth dropped open in shock as she took in prints of women with their skirts pulled up, exposing everything. Gentlemen, also in a state of undress, clasped and fondled the women.

"Are these yours?" she ventured.

"These are definitely not mine," he said vehemently. "They belong to a friend."

"A friend?" she asked, alarmed. "What kind of friend?"

Did he have a mistress already? What did she care, anyway? He could at least be discreet about it on their wedding night.

"Rogan. This is all Rogan's doing," Phinn said tightly. "And it'll be the last time he meddles . . ." His voice was tight. His jaw was clenched. There was a faraway look in his eyes that frightened her.

"Phinn," she said softly.

"I apologize," he said stiffly. Then he fixed his gaze upon her face and took controlled and measured breaths, as if trying to restrain his temper.

"Perhaps you'd like to lie down." When she must have widened her eyes in alarm, he hastily added, "To rest! Just to rest. I have to go out for a moment."

"Where? And when will you be back?"

"Just stay here," he said sharply. So sharply that she was taken aback. In that moment she realized that until this moment Phinn had never spoken harshly to her.

Stay here, wife. Wait.

She'd been married for less than a day and it was already everything she'd been afraid of.

PHINN DIDN'T GO very far because apparently Lord Rogan couldn't leave well enough alone. She was alerted to his arrival by Phinn's enraged bellowing.

"What the hell are you doing here?"

Olivia looked up from studying the one book that had slipped under the bed and that Phinn had failed to collect. She stuffed it under the pillow, opened the door just a crack and peered out.

"Just on my way to my club," Rogan said jovially, as if oblivious to Phinn's rage. "Thought I'd see how things were faring."

"Has it never occurred to you to leave a man and his bride alone on their wedding night?"

"Found the champagne, did you?" Rogan asked. Then, dropping his voice, "And the other things . . ."

Phinn paused in his furious pacing to yell, "What the hell were you thinking, Rogan?"

"I thought I'd be helpful," Rogan said, sounding remarkably impervious to Phinn's temper. She wasn't the object of it, yet still her heart raced as she stood hidden behind a lockable a door. How the man could stand there immune to Phinn's rage was mystifying. He was either incredibly brave or very daft. Or he knew that Phinn was all bark and no bite, though the bruises on his fist suggested otherwise.

"You thought you'd help by terrifying her?"

"It's supposed to be inspiring. Stimulating, if you will," Rogan said, rocking back on his heels.

"Not to virgins." Phinn bit out the words.

"And their prude husbands." Rogan's jest fell flat.

"Oh, that is *not* true," Phinn raged, which Olivia found immensely intriguing. Of course he'd been with other women. He'd been married. Had they done the things in the pictures? She wasn't quite sure how she felt about that. "What is true is that you have overstepped. You've gone too far this time, Rogan. I don't know what's worse—that you left such offensive materials in my wife's chamber or that you've returned to see how we've fared."

"Is that the thanks I get for all the advice I've given you?" Rogan replied, wounded. "The advice, which I might point out, has helped you land the girl."

"There are so many things wrong with that statement I don't even know where to begin." Olivia watched through a crack in the door as

Phinn pushed his fingers through his hair, frustrated. "Your advice was terrible."

"What, showing her how strong you are?" Rogan asked.

"Not exactly the most brilliant idea when she thinks I'm a murderer," Phinn said. And Olivia remembered that strange comment about "feats of strength." And her fear of being carried off by him. "I'm not sure what's worse: that or your suggestion that I impress upon her how large and remote my estate is."

"How was I to know all the young chits were still gossiping about that?" Rogan challenged.

"And all those stupid lines!" Phinn went on. "Is your father a thief? Stars in your eyes? My God, what an ass I've made of myself at your direction!"

Olivia's lips parted as the pieces started to come together. He'd been taking Rogan's advice all along. Rogan's terrible, horrible advice. But *why*?

"They've worked for me," Rogan challenged, which only seemed to enrage Phinn more. In a more conciliatory tone, he added, "And anyway, I was only trying to help you out."

"I don't want any more of your help. I can't believe what you have done," Phinn said. And then, growling, "And that you are *here*."

"Look, I just thought that if things didn't go well—" Rogan said, suddenly sound uneasy.

"What?" Phinn spat the word. "What did you think?"

"That you'd want some company," Rogan said softly. Olivia ached for them both. He'd only been trying to help. But why did he think Phinn needed it so badly? Probably because she had reacted so horribly to all his previous efforts to gain her affections. She touched her lips. He'd only been trying to woo her with advice from his well-meaning but daft friend, and she'd made it impossible.

"Some confidence you have in your friend," Phinn muttered grimly. Her heart broke a little then. "Just . . . get out."

"But—"

"It is my wedding night. I do not want to spend it with you."

The door to the suite slammed shut so firmly the door rattled on the hinges. Olivia softly closed her own bedroom door. She had answers to questions she hadn't thought to ask.

Had she ruined everything from the moment she applied a little too much lip paint? And still, he'd returned. He'd never hollered at her the way he had at his friend. He'd never lifted a hand to her.

Olivia sank to her knees by her door.

But at the same time . . . that temper of his. It took her breath away to remember the flash of rage in his eyes and the barely contained fury as he paced about the room. As if to prove her point, the door slammed again. Had he left? She rushed to the window and peered out. After a moment she saw Phinn's brisk determined strides down Brook Street.

She knew her marriage would be a disaster.

She just hadn't expected the urge to fix it.

LATER THAT NIGHT, Olivia was sitting on the settee, waiting for Phinn. Far too many questions about him and their disastrous courtship kept her from sleeping. She had tried to distract herself with a perusal of the wicked books that had escaped his notice, but they only raised more questions. Common sense kept her from venturing out into the streets of London to search for him.

Thus, she anxiously waited up for her husband on their wedding night. Was he with another woman? She somehow doubted that. Was he at his club? Or wandering the streets?

It was long past midnight when he finally returned.

"You're still up," Phinn said when he saw her.

"It's our wedding night," Olivia said softly.

"Aye, a wedding night that you didn't want," he said. There was no point in protesting. But now that they were here, she saw things differently.

"I was scared," she explained. "And I didn't realize . . ."

"Olivia, it's late," Phinn said, exhaustion in his voice. "We're both out of sorts. This isn't how it should be."

This night wasn't the perfect, romantic, or lovely wedding night anyone would have hoped for. She had been so fixated upon wanting the perfect courtship that she'd ruined what might have been a good one. Understanding as much allowed her to comprehend that perhaps Phinn had his own ideas of romance that she continued to thwart. She had pushed him away; thus she had to bring him closer if she wanted the loving marriage she still dreamt of.

Chapter 15

"*Make your own rules.*"
—Olivia's Mysterious Midnight Rescuer

A few days later

At eleven o'clock in the morning Olivia found herself rummaging through her belongings in search of her embroidery basket. Even though she hated embroidery. But that was what she did at eleven o'clock in the mornings. She and her mother sat together, stitching and planning their visits for the day.

Olivia found her embroidery basket, sat down with it and started to sew.

It was soothing.

No, it was boring.

She looked around the drawing room. She was alone. Phinn had left at first light and gone off somewhere—to build the engine, she presumed. He returned late in the evening. This had been their routine for the past few days. He left, and she stuck to the schedule she'd been raised with because she didn't know what else to do. She couldn't exactly go out with this bruise upon her cheek either. She'd given the gossips enough fodder already.

But today she just couldn't muster enthusiasm for embroidery or staying in. Nor did she think she had to.

Phinn wouldn't know if she didn't do her embroidery. He probably wouldn't care. For if he cared about her, he probably wouldn't have essentially disappeared.

Her mother wouldn't know if she deviated from the schedule they had followed their entire life. Nevertheless, Olivia looked around furtively before taking the lot of her sewing and stuffing it under the settee.

Make your own rules, her Mysterious Midnight Rescuer had said. Following the rules hadn't worked. Breaking the rules hadn't worked. Perhaps there was merit to what he'd told her.

Perhaps she could go search for him.

She glanced at the clock. It was five after eleven. She was alone. Very much alone.

Thinking of the possibilities that afforded, a giggle escaped her. Why, she could board a ship and sail off to America if she wished it! She certainly didn't have to spend an hour on her watercolors, and there was no pianoforte to practice on even if she wanted to.

Given the scandalous circumstances before her wedding, the fact that she had actually married the Mad Baron, and her residence at a hotel, she did not expect many callers. And if they were to arrive, she would just declare herself not at home. Perhaps she'd say she was indisposed.

The point was, Olivia thought as she reclined on the settee, she could do whatever she wanted with this day. Phinn obviously wasn't concerned with how she passed the time, for if he cared he might have spent it with her. Or at least made inquiries. She avoided dwelling upon the strange sensation akin to sadness that she experienced at this thought. Almost as if she wished he were here to spend the day with her. There were so many questions she wished to ask him. What had happened to his hands? Why had he followed Rogan's advice? What exactly were those people doing in those books?

Why did he not wish to spend the day with her?

Why couldn't they talk, or try another picnic, or one of the wicked things from that book . . .

She had wanted Phinn to leave her—*before* they married when she might be able to find another match. It was more than a little vexing to have been left *after* the wedding. Why did he fight so hard to wed her if he were only going to ignore her?

Olivia decided she might enlist Emma and Prudence for a trip to the modiste rather than lounge around her hotel suite for another day.

She did just that. They traveled together in Emma's carriage to Madame Auteuil's on Bond Street.

"We thought you might have taken more of a

honeymoon," Emma said immediately, dispelling Olivia's hopes that it wouldn't come up. "With your new husband."

"Dare we even ask how things are faring?" Prudence asked nervously.

"What she really means is, tell us about the wedding night," Emma said with a mischievous grin that ordinarily would have made her laugh. Except their wedding night had been yet another disaster.

Olivia hesitated, recalling what she'd overheard during Phinn's conversation with Rogan. And by conversation she meant argumentative interchange of sentences delivered at top volume. Oddly, it felt like a betrayal to reveal what she had heard—she wasn't supposed to know the lengths he'd gone to court her. Even now she felt ashamed of her behavior and the desire to make it up to him.

"Well?" Prudence was impatient.

"Has it left you speechless? That's quite a good sign," Emma said.

"Nothing happened," Olivia said. She couldn't quite explain that the only *something* that happened was a fight she had eavesdropped on. What she had learned made her heartsick.

"Nothing?" Emma echoed.

"We toured our suite of rooms at the hotel. Then he went out," Olivia answered.

"Did you at some point walk into a doorway?" Prudence inquired.

Perplexed, Olivia replied, "No, why?"

"There is a bruise on your cheek," she said.

"Oh, that," Olivia said, lightly touching the faint bruise, which had faded considerably. She smiled at how she'd come about it. "We bumped our heads together."

Both Emma and Prudence were obviously and immensely skeptical. After all, she was married to the notoriously dangerous Mad Baron. But it had been a silly accident during a ridiculous encounter.

"Is everything all right, Olivia?" Emma asked, leveling her with a stern, inquisitive look.

"It's fine. I suppose," Olivia said, sighing. Thank goodness the carriage had rolled to a stop outside of Madame Auteuil's shop at that moment. "Now let's see about procuring me a new wardrobe."

Now that she was married—if only on paper and not in truth—she would no longer wear the white, ivory, and eggshell that made her seem like a washed-out angel or a virginal ghost. She selected the gowns she'd always wanted.

Emma and Prudence were excellent companions. They seriously debated the merits between a navy silk and a cerulean blue satin. Together, they earnestly considered whether a shade of ripe melon suited Olivia's completion when anyone could see it did not.

"Perhaps you might need some underthings, Olivia," Emma said discreetly.

"Why?" Olivia asked, but her mind wandered

to those images she had seen. The women, if they wore anything at all, wore delicate lacy things, the likes of which she had never actually seen.

"Because I'm sure the ones in your trousseau are . . . not quite right," Emma said, dropping her voice. "Mine weren't."

"She means plain, virginal, and not the sort of tawdry scraps of fabric that awaken a man's wanton side," Prudence explained, which begged the question of how she knew such things. Then again, Olivia suspected that no one led quite the sheltered life that she had.

"Do men have wanton sides?" she asked. "Or is that just women?"

"Are you avoiding the question, Olivia?"

"What question?"

Emma excused the seamstresses, and the three women found themselves ensconced in the small changing room. Prudence pulled the velvet drapes firmly shut.

"Have you—" Emma began.

"Become acquainted with your husband in the biblical sense?" Prudence finished.

"Made love to him?" Emma asked.

"Done the Act?" Prudence added.

"Had marital relations?" Emma inquired, with a lift of her brow.

"No, all right!" Olivia cried. She had not done the Biblical Act of Making Love or a variation. She'd spent her wedding night alone—not that she was quite ready to do otherwise. But given what she'd heard, it only drove home how, in her attempt to find love, she might have driven away her only chance for it. "He fought with Rogan, who apparently had been giving Phinn bad advice for wooing me. And then Phinn went for a walk. He's been getting up at first light and going off to build the Defense Engine—"

"Difference Engine," Emma corrected.

"It makes no difference to me," Olivia said dismissively. "The point is that he prefers machines to me."

"Is this the part where we point out she hasn't even been married a week?" Prudence asked.

Emma shook her head no and, a mischievous grin on her lips, asked, "Or is this the part where we tell her to seduce him?"

"After trying to run him out of town?" Prudence asked skeptically. Then, with a sigh, she added, "What will we do?"

We. That made Olivia smile. Phinn *had* ensured they could stay in London for a while. She was tremendously appreciative. How had he known, if he weren't sensitive to her? How much had she overlooked in her determination to cause a scandal?

"Well, what *are* we going to do?" Olivia asked. She wanted the same thing she'd always wanted: a chance at love. It seemed Phinn was her only chance now. Given what she had recently learned, perhaps he might not be as awful as she'd feared.

After all, it wasn't like she could find her Mysterious Midnight Rescuer man and convince him to live a life of sin with her. Marital vows were not rules she considered breaking.

Emma was the one to answer. "*We* are not going to allow opportunities for romance to pass us by when they are presented."

By *we*, she clearly meant Olivia.

Chapter 16

*A touch, a pressure of the hands, are the only external
signs a woman can give of entertaining a particular regard
for certain individuals.*

—THE MIRROR OF GRACES

PHINN COULDN'T AVOID his wife forever. Actually, he could if he tried hard enough. Why, he could leave her at Mivart's Hotel and ensure the bills were paid, while he returned to Yorkshire. It was possible. Absurd, cowardly, and ridiculous—yes. But it was possible.

However, he didn't *want* to leave Olivia. He just didn't know how to face her after their disastrous wedding night.

He'd lost his temper in front of her and had to leave because he couldn't stand to see the fear inevitably in her eyes. She had seen his bruised and swollen hands. She knew how dangerous he could be. What a bloody fool.

Every night when he returned—late—he considered knocking on her door. The bruises on his fists, which had only begun to fade, stopped him. He couldn't touch such lovely innocence with such violence on his hands. Every morning he considered lingering to see her. Instead he left at first light, fearing all the questions she wanted to ask him.

He lost himself in work instead, vaguely aware that this was just like his first marriage. But he'd married the opposite of Nadia—hadn't he? Even though Olivia caused scandals and had outbursts, there was a still a loveliness about her that he craved and that Nadia had never possessed. It didn't take a genius to determine that he was the common denominator in his disastrous marriages.

So when Ashbrooke asked, "How fares married life?" Phinn grumbled something noncommittal and instead broached the subject of the machine parts that still needed to be constructed. The duke fell for the distraction, debating different parts and strategies with Phinn for at least half an hour.

"So it's decided, than," Phinn concluded.

The duke nodded. "Also, the duchess and I would be obliged if you and your bride would join us at the opera this evening."

Ashbrooke said this in the sort of commanding ducal manner that left no room for disagreement. When Phinn broached the subject with Olivia later that day, he took care to avoid precisely that tone.

"Ashbrooke has invited us to attend the opera with him and Lady Emma this evening," he told her. "Would you like to go?"

"Did he, now?" Olivia replied, her lips quirking

into a smile. Made his heartbeat quicken, that.

"Aye," he said, holding his breath as he asked, "would you like to go?"

"Yes. Very much," she said softly, surprising him. She couldn't possibly have forgiven him for the series of disasters that occurred on their wedding night. What had happened that she should soften toward him?

At the opera

Somewhere between the dimming of the lights and the raising of the curtains, everything changed. It started with a simple brush of Phinn's hand against hers. Olivia's instinct was to jerk her hand away, but she overrode it and willed her hand back to linger near his.

Seize opportunities for romance.

And this, an affectionate caress in the dark, seemed to be a vastly preferable way of saying she was sorry and wished to try anew. She couldn't fathom saying the words to him, but she could manage this gentle affection.

They were just touching hands. In the opera house. They had gloves on. It was nothing. But it didn't feel like nothing.

There was the pleasure of it, to be sure. But it was tempered by the bittersweet knowledge that she had made it impossible to happen sooner. Her heart was still a tangled mess of rebellious longing for that man in the garden and slow dawning interest in her husband, who was turning out to be not the man she had originally thought.

His efforts to woo her had been misguided but genuine. With a flare of shame, she acknowledged that she hadn't made it easy for him. And yet . . . he was still here. Tenderly and tentatively caressing her hand. She wasn't sure which took her breath away—his dedication or his touch.

His hand brushed against hers again, a caress that she suspected was deliberate. So light, so fleeting, so delicate. Olivia slowly exhaled. It was nothing to be a ninny about. Hands. Just hands.

And it was then just fingers possibly interlocking then hesitantly letting go. The impermanence of the gesture was maddening, but not as much as the strange pleasure afforded from his touch and from the anticipation.

Will he hold her hand? Or will he not?
What did she want, anyway?

Olivia discovered that he would *not* hold her hand. Instead, she sat breathless as Phinn traced delicate circles around her palm. Softly, so softly, did he trace along her fingertips, venturing higher to her wrist, higher still to the madly sensitive skin of her inner elbow.

This . . . whatever this was . . . went on and on and on. Olivia's breath became short and shallow and she wondered whether *exquisite* or *agony* were a better term for what he was doing to her and how it made her feel.

It was nothing, nothing, nothing. They were in public—not that anyone could see what they did. The lights were dark. The audience's attention was focused on the opera singer. She and Phinn were discreet. But there was something slightly wicked about having these feelings—these smoldering, sparking, heated feelings—in public.

And yet, they were merely holding hands. Besides, she had gloves on. Had they done this prior to the wedding it would not have been grounds for marriage.

The gloves—those had to go. Phinn began to flip open the buttons of her gloves, one by one, with a masterful single-handed maneuver. How did he know to do that? Was he more of a rogue than she had thought? She'd never thought that he was an innocent, but she hadn't truly considered what he knew or what he could make her feel.

Next he tugged firmly at each fingertip, making his intentions clear. He wanted her bare skin. Olivia dared a glance at him and saw his gaze fixed ahead. No one would know. This was their secret.

Her glove fell silently to floor, followed swiftly by his.

The exquisite agony commenced anew, this time with bare skin upon bare skin. She had never truly experienced a man's bare skin against her own. This was new, and something she shared with Phinn alone.

Again, he slowly and softly teased the soft

skin of her palm with slow, deliberate circles of his fingertips. Because his touch was so light, she strained to be more aware of herself. Her every nerve was attuned to the light, fleeting connection of his skin upon hers.

Again, her breathing was affected. Again, he traced along her fingertips, his touch so light she held her breath to feel it fully.

And then he dared to trace his fingertips all along the sensitive and exposed skin along the inside of her arm from her wrist to the short tulle sleeves.

It was an arm. A hand. A simple touch. It was nothing that would lead to a special license, for instance. These were lies Olivia told herself. But each stroke sent shivers up and down her spine. She found herself forcing her legs tight together. Because of the heat, and the *desire*.

Her gaze was fixed upon the stage; she didn't see a thing. Her new corset was laced too tightly. That had to be why she was nearly overwhelmed with the urge to rip the stays. It was too hot in the box.

Phinn treated her to another long slow caress. She allowed another slow exhale, as if she might control her racing pulse. In an instant it became a sharp gasp.

If he could make her feel this just by holding hands, how would she survive anything more? She had seen the pictures. She had seen their expressions of ecstasy. She knew there was more than this. Truly, she feared it and craved it in equal measures.

Olivia tilted her head, curls brushing against her bare shoulders. She stole a glance at the man beside her. Husband. Stranger. He *was* handsome.

Phinn turned and caught her looking at him. Gazes locked. The song faded away. He offered a hesitant smile. Her heartbeat quickened. Olivia made the corners of her mouth turn up and discovered it didn't take much effort at all, really, to smile at her husband. Whom she knew almost nothing about. Except that with just his fingertips he could take her breath away. And if he was so tender and seductive, could he really be so violent?

She did not know this man. But now she wanted to.

Chapter 17

THE PREVIOUS EVENING, Phinn had taken advantage of the darkness afforded at the opera to hold Olivia's hand. Although that didn't quite describe the hours they had touched and she hadn't pulled away. For hours, he'd imagined *more*. The images from those illicit periodicals came to him, unbidden, and he couldn't resist imagining himself tangled up with Olivia. *Want* was not strong enough a word. That magnetic pull he felt toward her only increased in strength the closer he got to her.

Those hours had been passed in a tortured state of arousal, all the more enhanced by her willingness. By some miracle he had restrained himself from whisking her away to some dark corner of the opera house and burying himself deep inside. Not for their first time, at least.

He wanted to see her hair unbound, tumbling around her face, grazing her breasts. He wanted to sink his fingers in and pull her close for a long, deep, slow kiss. Nor did he want to stop there. He didn't want to stop until she was crying his name as she came and he felt her contracting around him. Then, maybe, he'd stop.

But Phinn held back, not trusting his ability to restrain himself from going all the way, immediately. Besides, to kiss her and to become intimate with her was to reveal secrets he didn't know how to share and wasn't sure he wanted to.

This morning he awoke even more frustrated.

He looked forward to a long day spent immersed in the construction of the Difference Engine. It absorbed his focus completely. He'd driven Nadia mad with his long hours devoted to his work. Would Olivia care? He didn't think she would.

He had thought Nadia would be satisfied with the attentions he gave her in the bedchamber—for all they didn't get along during the day, there was one place they were compatible. Combustible, more like it. He recalled nights and mornings, utterly spent. She'd been too tired to do anything but sleep peacefully.

He was thinking far too much of bedding. But Olivia was around and he was too aware of how badly he wanted her and how badly she hadn't wanted to marry him. He would not come on too strong. He would not scare her off.

He had to avoid temptation.

Phinn opened his bedroom door expecting to sneak out at first light, before his lovely wife awoke. Instead, he found her dressed and waiting.

"Good morning," she said a touch hesitantly. She offered him a shy smile. It did things to him, that smile.

"Good morning," he replied. She wore a pale yellow gown, and tendrils of her blond hair framed her face. Angelic, she was. Angel, he almost called her.

"I thought we might take the carriage together," Olivia said.

"Are you coming with me to work on the engine?" he asked.

"I could before I carry on to visit with Emma," she offered. Phinn recalled one of Nadia's visits to his workplace. She found it incredibly dull—and him by extension. But he wasn't too obtuse to realize that Olivia was making an effort.

It was just a carriage ride. He could endure a carriage ride without ravishing her. Especially at this hour. Because gentlemen did not ravish their innocent lady wives in carriages at ungodly hours of the morning. Especially gentlemen with dangerous pasts who terrified their virgin wives.

But God, he wanted to . . .

God made it so difficult not to.

Once in the carriage, Phinn was all too aware of Olivia. Her scent—like roses and woman—enticed him. Her face was bare, though her cheeks were faintly pink from either heat or a blush. Her eyes were blue and he couldn't look away. Her lips were pink and he wanted to make them red from his kiss.

And it seemed there was more of her to see. Something different about her.

He was used to seeing her in white. This gown was like a ray of sunshine, or a flame, or molten gold. It clung to the curves of her breasts. He wanted to touch them. Taste them. Love them. He'd admired her before and certainly hadn't found her wanting. But something was different.

"Is that a new dress?" he asked.

"Yes. I took the liberty of ordering a new wardrobe," Olivia replied, eyeing him nervously for his reaction. Of course—she knew what a devilish temper he had and didn't know what would set him off.

"I look forward to seeing it," he said, thinking that he really wanted to see all of her new gowns on the floor.

"Are you not going to question the expense?"

"Is it exorbitant?"

"Perhaps. I know not," she replied, again eyeing him. Was she testing him? They hadn't discussed her pin money, had they? They hadn't discussed much, and they were bound together for life.

Phinn just shrugged and smiled. "I'm sure it's fine."

That was the thing about having previously invented some of the more useful machinery of the day. She probably couldn't beggar him if she tried. She and the rest of London didn't seem to know that about him either. It wasn't as if he registered the patents under the Mad Baron.

Things that were not fine: what happened next.

Because the traffic at this hour was not the usually congested standstill disaster of later in the day, the horses progressed along at a steady clip. Given their speed, it would take them longer to stop should another vehicle, also progressing at a brisk pace, emerge in front of them.

When it happened, the driver maneuvered expertly, jerking hard on the reins and spurring the horses to make a quick turn to the left. As a result the carriage tilted on its wheels. As a result, both Phinn and Olivia found themselves tumbling together and landing in a very . . . suggestive, inappropriate, arousing position.

One that had been detailed in *Wicked Wanton Women*, though with far less clothing.

Phinn had managed to catch her in his arms and turn so he was the one to land on the floor of the carriage. There they were: a tangle of limbs and skirts and boots.

"Are you all right?" he rasped. He had hit his head hard, but all he could think about was the proximity of her luscious pink mouth and how very badly he wanted to kiss her.

"Yes," she gasped. "And you?"

Could she feel how badly he wanted her? Olivia wriggled her hips, brushing against his arousal and drawing a groan from his lips.

"I'm so sorry," she apologized.

"It's all right," he said. But really, he was dying. He closed his eyes. If only they were back at the hotel. In their suite. Preferably in a bed, but he'd take the drawing room floor over the carriage floor.

In the process of trying to disentangle herself, Olivia succeeded in reminding him just what he craved. He couldn't resist stealing a caress here and there. As if that would satisfy him. As if that didn't make him want her more. Perhaps the carriage floor wasn't the worst place.

She also succeeded in revealing her legs to him. Long, slender, shapely legs clad in delicate silk stockings. And what of the garters, and what of the rest? She returned to the upholstered seats and he finally dragged himself up beside her.

"Phinn, are you sure you're all right?"

She reached out and cupped his cheek with her hand. There was such concern in her gaze, as if she truly had no idea that it wasn't an injury that had left him speechless. It was desire. And if he wasn't mistaken, he might have detected some desire in her gaze, too.

No, things were not all right. But then things were about to be.

OLIVIA COULDN'T HELP herself. She reached out and cupped his cheek in her palm. She felt the firm line of his jaw and his slanting cheekbones. She had touched her Mysterious Midnight Rescuer like this. And like that night, her gaze dropped to his mouth. Only his mouth. Firm and sensual. Today she thought of kissing Phinn.

But then her thoughts took a strange turn. He just seemed so familiar in this moment. The feel of him under her palm. His mouth. It was a man's mouth. They were all the same, weren't they? She'd never given the matter much thought. No, she fixated on the hazy memory of her Mysterious Midnight Rescuer's mouth just after he had kissed her and before he kissed her again. It had been dark. She had been intoxicated.

She dropped her hand and looked away. It was all so familiar, that was all. Perhaps all men felt the same.

She didn't dare consider that Phinn and Mysterious Midnight Rescuer were one and the same. How absurd! She would have recognized him. A little laugh escaped her.

"What's so funny?" Phinn asked.

"Oh, nothing," she said dismissively. "Just a silly female thought."

"Hair ribbons?" Phinn guessed.

"No," Olivia said, smiling.

"Embroidery?"

"Definitely not," she replied.

"What to wear to Lady Penelope's Ball?"

"No. And how did you even know of that?"

"Miss Payton told me," he said, which she found strange.

"When have you spoken about that to Prudence?" she asked.

"Here or there," he said, seemingly uncomfortable. But she supposed they could have spoken at any one of the ton events they'd all attended. "What were you thinking of?"

"Kissing," she said softly. Because *young ladies do not think of kissing*. They especially do not compare the mouths and kisses of two different gentlemen, especially when one was not her husband.

"Kissing is not a silly female thought," Phinn said in a low voice.

"No?"

"You should do it more often," he said, his voice grave. "Even better than thinking about it . . ."

"Actually kissing?" Her voice was breathless. Her gaze dropped to his mouth. They hadn't kissed. Not yet.

"Exactly," he murmured, before lowering his mouth to hers for a light caress of his lips against hers. She felt a spark. *This.* Then he pulled back. A young lady would blush modestly and leave it at that. But Olivia was making her own rules now, and she wanted to know this man she had married. Having had a taste of a damn fine kiss, she wanted to know if she'd ever have a kiss like that again. She wanted to know now.

She lightly traced her finger along his jacket before holding on to a handful and pulling him closer. He didn't resist. Their mouths met again. Tentatively, she parted her lips, not caring if he found her wanton or forward. She wanted to kiss him deeply. This—the delicate caress of lips, a nibble here, tracing the seam of her lips there—was driving her mad in a wonderful way. This tease of a kiss made that initial spark turn into a smolder. Who knows what fire might have started had the carriage not rolled to a stop before Emma's residence at that moment?

Olivia looked at Phinn, dazed. He looked at her with darkened eyes.

Words weren't necessary. This was not over.

Chapter 18

Certain books are not suitable for ladies, for they might offend a woman's delicate sensibilities.

—COMMONLY HELD BELIEF, TO THE VEXATION OF
CURIOUS MAIDENS EVERYWHERE

OLIVIA CONSIDERED HAVING her caller informed that she was not at home. When alerted to the fact that it was her mother awaiting, she sighed and reluctantly closed one of the naughty books that Rogan had left—and that she may have kicked under the bed when Phinn was collecting them—that she'd been perusing, and absentmindedly set it aside. Then she ordered a tea tray to be set up and braced herself for the onslaught.

Her mother came bustling in, a small squall of ruffles and flounces, a large bonnet and a reticule that was undoubtedly stuffed with embroidered handkerchiefs and a bottle of Smythson's Smelling Salts. Only then did Olivia realize how calm her home with Phinn was and how much she liked it. There was never any bustling or fussing. With the exception of his outburst with Rogan, there hadn't been any raised voices either.

"Darling! I came to see how you were faring

in your marriage," her mother gushed, embracing her as if she had never forced her daughter to marry a man all of London knew as the Mad Baron.

"It's only been a few days, Mother," Olivia remarked. Was it too soon to declare the marriage a disaster? Or had those little kisses and delicate caresses indicated a flicker of hope?

"And already it's a scandal," Lady Archer said, and Olivia thought, Young ladies should not feel a frisson of excitement at the thought of being a scandal. But this one did. "Living in a hotel! Who would do such a thing?"

"I rather like it, actually," Olivia said truthfully. "There are no servants to manage, or menus to coordinate. I don't have to bother with the linens or ensuring that chandeliers are dusted."

These things were just magically done by a fleet of maids under the direction of the hotel manager. Just now, for example. One of the maids discreetly brought a tea tray, set it on the table, and left quietly.

She just happened to have placed the tray next to That Book. Olivia quickly looked away.

"But that is what you were raised to do!" her mother exclaimed. Olivia took a seat as well and poured the tea. The behavior of a proper hostess was ingrained in her. Even if the most improper reading material was just there, beside the tea tray. Fortunately, her mother was too involved in what she was saying to take any notice. "He is depriving you of your natural position in life and the purpose to which I have raised you."

"Well I find living in this hotel vastly preferable to rusticating in a remote and haunted country estate, fearing for my life."

Olivia wondered if she would have said the same had she come before the bruise below her eye had faded or if she'd seen the strange bruises on Phinn's knuckles, which had faded into an awful yellow color but were now barely visible. It struck her as tremendously unfair that her mother should stroll in with complaints about how she was handling the marriage she had been forced into.

Olivia sipped her tea. How long before her mother noticed the book, *50 Ways to Sin*? Should she remove it and preserve their modesty, or should she brazenly leave it out to perhaps give her mother a shock?

She considered it while her mother was busy with a critical review of her attire. "I see you have been to the modiste," she said. The disapproval of her choices was duly noted and dismissed. *I'm making my own rules.*

Olivia clung to that now, and the gravity of her Mysterious Midnight Rescuer's voice as he said it. But she felt herself wither, just a bit, under her mother's gaze. Was that disappointment? Her mother had never really been disappointed in her before.

"Yes, Emma, Prudence, and I paid a visit to

Madame Auteuil's," she said. She and her mother had always frequented a less fashionable modiste. "I thought I would update my wardrobe now that I am married."

"Well I hope you bought some new gloves. Rumors are flying that you and your husband had left your gloves in the duke's box at the opera. One of each! How on earth did that come about?"

"I'm sure I don't recall," Olivia murmured. Truthfully, she did not recall that part of the evening. But the sacrifice of a lone glove was completely worth the pleasure she had experienced.

"While your father has arranged for you to have a generous allowance—in case your husband spends all his money on that contraption he's building—you wouldn't want to spend it all on replacing gloves you've idly left all around town. After all, a lady must always maintain her modesty."

Olivia sipped her tea and thought about the glimpse of her legs she'd inadvertently given Phinn after their little tussle in the carriage. Had she been glad Emma talked her into the silk stockings! Lud, what would her mother say if she knew what she had bought?

"That is very kind of father," she said. Now if only her parents would have consulted or informed her of such kindness. She felt a flare of anger at being left out, again, of crucial matters about her own life.

She was a lady. Not a child.

"I suppose it's too soon to talk about grandchildren," her mother said, and Olivia nearly spit out her tea.

Phinn had been hoping to find Olivia alone. It went without saying that he was less than thrilled to find her with her mother. Worse, Lady Archer seemed to be in the midst of a lecture. He listened for a moment; it was something about her duty as a wife, suffering for a noble cause, and serving her husband and the legacy of the estate above all else.

Worst of all, he saw immediately that with her mother lecturing her, Olivia was not quite Olivia. Her spine was ramrod straight. The teacup was frozen in her hands. A polite half smile was frozen on her lips. And her eyes . . .

Her eyes kept darting anxiously to something on the table.

The tea tray? That didn't make sense. He took a step closer and saw the book. The incredibly illicit, possibly illegal book.

It was his panicked coughing that caught their attention.

"Lord Radcliffe!" Lady Archer exclaimed. She stood to greet him. Olivia took advantage to push the book off the table . . . where it fell open to a page featuring a woman pleasuring a very aroused man with her mouth and hands.

He forced himself to look away.

"Good day, Lady Archer. Olivia. I didn't realize we had a caller."

Lady Archer turned back to face her daughter. And that book. Open. He watched as Olivia discreetly tried to push it under the table with her slipper. He could see her sigh of relief when it slid out of sight.

"Mother has come to see how we are faring," Olivia replied. Dutiful, proper, and distant Olivia. She was not the vibrant girl he'd come to know—the one who painted her face to excess or danced wildly at balls or grabbed a fistful of his coat and pulled him in for a kiss. He was witnessing the Olivia he had thought he wanted at the beginning.

"I don't know what you mean by keeping my Olivia in a hotel," Lady Archer said. "It's a scandal. Everyone's talking about it. And it's a waste of her talents. I raised her to manage a household and to be the perfect wife. This arrangement does not do her justice."

"I had thought these temporary arrangements might suit until we found a residence in London that we found agreeable," Phinn said calmly. "But let's ask the lady herself. Olivia, what are your feelings on the matter?"

The smile she gave him . . . God, the smile she gave him was something else. It was genuine and happy. Like he had saved her just before she drowned.

"I rather like it here," Olivia replied. But he

didn't miss the nervous glance she gave her mother, as if seeking approval or fearing her response.

"Olivia," Lady Archer said in a my-patience-is-tried voice. "It's not a matter of what one likes, but what is proper."

"But is that more or less proper than disagreeing with my husband's wishes?"

Lady Archer narrowed her eyes and sipped her tea. It was a valid point and she knew it. Which was all well and good, but the words "my husband" on her lips gave him a deep feeling of pride. *Say it again.*

"People are talking," Lady Archer said.

Olivia opened her mouth and thought better of what she was about to say. He desperately wanted to know. Instead, she turned to him.

"Phinn, would you care for some tea?"

"Yes, thank you."

Their eyes met. Their gazes locked as she poured the tea. A little smile quirked at her lips. Was she also remembering the first time they'd met? She'd worn that awful paint and had taken every instance to flaunt the rules. He understood now. He didn't flatter himself that she was rebelling only against her parents—and not him. But they had all conspired to have her do their bidding, hadn't they?

This time, when she overpoured the tea, it was because they'd been making eyes at each other.

"Olivia!" her mother cried. "You're not attending!"

"Oh!" Olivia gasped. Startled, she dropped the teacup, which tumbled onto the table and onward to the floor.

Lady Archer bent to retrieve it. She was closest. But something else caught her eye.

"What is this?" she inquired, reaching for the book that Olivia had half shoved under the table. This time when Olivia's gaze met Phinn's, she was panicked.

All he could think about was Olivia, alone with the book, perusing those pictures . . . Did she find them horrifying? Or arousing?

"I must have an answer," Lady Archer demanded. "What is this rubbish?"

"It is something a friend left behind," Phinn answered.

"Your friend?" she asked, appalled. "Is that supposed to reassure me?"

"Yes, but I can see how it does not," Phinn admitted, stifling laughter. "At all."

"I cannot believe you have polluted Olivia's tender sensibilities with this . . ." Words failed Lady Archer.

"A young lady ought to be obliging to her husband," Olivia said demurely, which sent both him and her mother into a coughing fit. Lady Archer dug around in her reticule before removing a bottle of smelling salts. She held them to her nose and inhaled deeply. Phinn had half a mind to do so as well.

Olivia was . . . sometimes the perfect lady.

Sometimes the perfect minx, and occasionally the devil herself. He wanted her all of the times. Always.

"Olivia," her mother began patiently whilst holding the book between her thumb and forefinger. "Ladies do not do *this*."

Phinn tilted his head to see precisely what ladies did not do. It seemed they did not lift their skirts whilst bending over a settee while a gentleman takes her from behind while pleasuring her with his hands. God, he hoped Olivia was not a lady.

Phinn decided this scene had gone far enough. The less he considered that picture in front of his mother-in-law, the better. The sooner he attempted it with Olivia, the better. "I am terribly sorry to have upset you, Lady Archer."

"I am extremely overset," she said. "I have raised Olivia to be better than this tawdry den of sin to which you have absconded with her."

"Mivart's Hotel is a perfectly respectable establishment—" Phinn said, stopping when he saw that Lady Archer had something to stay and nothing would prevent her from delivering it.

"And you Olivia," she continued, fixing a strong Look on her daughter. "You have always been the perfect child. I don't know what has gotten into you of late, and it distresses me tremendously. I never thought I'd be disappointed in you. You may find all of this humorous and good fun, but I am mortified every time I show my face in society and have to answer the questions about your marriage—one which took you forever to make and has become the subject of scandal. You have a duty, and that is to be a good wife and provide heirs. That is all. I hope that you remember yourself, remember the woman I raised you to be. Good day."

OLIVIA SAT VERY still as she considered what was more humiliating: the dressing down from her mother or the fact that it was delivered in front of Phinn.

One moment she'd been enjoying asserting her newfound independence. The dresses, the lost gloves . . . really, that was the least of the trouble she had engaged in lately, which made it all the more frustrating that she should be chastised for it.

And the worst of it was—

She didn't want to be the Perfect Lady anymore. But she didn't want her mother's disapproval either—that was a *terrible* feeling. And she didn't quite know which rules to follow and which to break. She felt torn between pleasing her mother, pleasing her husband, and perhaps pleasing herself.

"You're not a disappointment," Phinn said softly. He understood. She didn't have to explain. Because of that, when he wrapped his arm around her, she leaned against him. *Like her Mysterious Midnight Rescuer.* Because it was comforting and familiar, she didn't move away. "You're not a disappointment to me. And I don't think you've done anything to disappoint her."

"But I have," Olivia confessed. "And I have done it purposely."

"Why?"

She was mad because she'd been forced into this marriage. Now that she was starting to find some measure of hope in it, her mother came along and informed her that she was doing it wrong. She wasn't measuring up to the exacting standards she'd been raised to, what with her wayward gloves and scandalous accommodations. She'd always been *perfect*. She'd never been a disappointment.

She'd only been trying to find happiness, and now . . .

"I was mad. You see, I always thought that if I was perfectly well-behaved I would be rewarded with . . . I don't know . . . true love and romance and happiness." His grip tightened. "And then I am constantly treated like a child. Always being told what to wear, whom to converse with, what to say, how to act, how to *be*. Decisions are made without consulting me."

"That's very disagreeable to you," he said. She felt so comforted and safe in his embrace—like her Mysterious Midnight Rescuer. And like that night she just couldn't hold back. It felt good to voice what was weighing on her mind rather than say "I'm fine" while seething inwardly. Like a lady would do.

"I find it tremendously vexing," she said, her voice rising. "I fear I might explode with the vexation of it. I cannot win. I cannot please everyone and still please myself. If I can, I do not know how."

What Phinn said next surprised her.

"Would you like to hit something?" he asked. "I find that soothes my temper."

Olivia gazed down at the discoloration that still remained on his bruised knuckles and then up at him, not a little bit alarmed. Honestly, just when she started to think that Phinn might share some very crucial traits with her Mysterious Midnight Rescuer—like the ability to console her and to understand her—he went and said things like *that*.

"Some unsolicited advice: you mustn't say such things when you are known as the Mad Baron," she ventured.

"That came out wrong," he said hastily. "I just meant that sometimes it feels good to release the pressure rather than try to hold it in."

"I don't think I want to hit anything," she said, considering the matter. "That seems painful and I shan't want bruised hands like yours. But I think I would like to break something."

She needed a release. The pressure of being the Perfect Lady and the Perfect Daughter and the Perfect Wife and trying to be herself was just too much.

And Phinn . . . he just grinned and gestured

to the drawing room at large. "Take your pick, Angel. Break whatever you want."

"You cannot be serious," Olivia said. "Whoever heard of deliberately breaking things?"

"I am perfectly serious," Phinn said gravely.

"What of the expense?"

"I can afford it," he told her. Olivia considered this. She probably wouldn't cause very much damage. Just a broken teacup or two. But then she thought of another problem.

"Will the manager or owner of the hotel be angry?"

"If so, they'll answer to me," Phinn vowed. For the first time, Olivia realized there might be benefits to having the Mad Baron in her corner. "Go on, Olivia."

Phinn handed her a china saucer. When he urged her in a low voice and smiled at her like that, she shouldn't quite remember why she ought to resist the urge to do what she wanted.

She took the dish and held it aloft.

"Are you saying that if I break this china saucer I will feel better?" She didn't quite believe him.

"Yes." He said this resolutely, as if he had experience breaking teacup saucers. Did she want to know about that? Perhaps later.

"You are encouraging me to be wicked," she said. She remembered admonishments as a young girl, when she'd still been clumsy. *Be careful. That's the good china! Olivia, take care!* She remembered the terror of breaking something. And now Phinn was encouraging her to do just that. "I'm quite certain that ladies do not willfully break the china."

Phinn just smiled and said, "Do as you wish."

"Close your eyes, then," she said. She herself shut her eyes tight before throwing the saucer down on the parquet floor. She winced as it shattered, and opened her eyes to see fragments of china scattered across the floor.

"That does feel good," she said, wonder in her voice. The sound was extraordinary.

Even better: she'd done something she always feared, only to look up and see Phinn smiling at her as he said, "I told you so."

Phinn gestured to the tea tray, where an assortment of china awaited her. He hoped she wouldn't ask how he knew that smashing things to bits, particularly china tea sets, had a wonderful mollifying effect on a woman's temper. Nadia had made him aware of that.

Nadia. Would he ever be free of her?

"Might I?" Olivia asked politely, after selecting the large plate that had, at one point, held an assortment of pastries.

"You may," he said. Nadia had never asked. She would just glance wildly about the room and grab the nearest thing at hand before launching it in the direction of his head. She had remarkably good aim. He had the scars to prove it.

"Even though my mother will be very disappointed in me?" Olivia asked, her voice wavering. *That* was why even though this scene had echoes of his past he didn't want to relive, ever, he said, "Even then."

The only thing that mattered was Olivia's happiness. He thought he might have understood her vexation. His father had wanted him to be like his elder, perfect brother George—who preferred sport instead of science, or a raucous night at the inn with ale and loose women to a quiet night with amiable company, intelligent conversation, and good wine. Nadia wanted him to be like George, too. But the only thing he'd had in common with his father and brother was the Radcliffe temper. It did them in every time.

Nadia wasn't the only one who'd expressed her frustration upon the china.

"What of this?" Olivia asked, selecting an empty teacup.

"Please, proceed," he said. She lifted it high above her head before sending it hurtling to the floor. He winced as it shattered—she did not. Olivia stood there, cheeks flushed, bosoms heaving, and hair advancing toward a state of disarray. She looked lovely.

"This is very wrong," she said with an apologetic expression that he supposed was what made it bearable.

"Completely wicked," he agreed.

"Just unconscionable," she added, now moving on to a porcelain shepherdess on the mantel.

"Appalling," he murmured, eyes fixed on Olivia. She was entrancing.

But whereas Nadia worked herself into such a temper that she exhausted herself in a flurry of tears and hurtful words, Olivia seemed to be having *fun*. Phinn released a deep breath he hadn't realized he'd been holding.

"I would be ruined if anyone knew about this," Olivia informed him seriously. But there was a mischievous gleam in her eye. "No one would receive me."

"To hell with them," he declared.

She laughed and said, "Exactly."

Then she smashed the shepherdess. He'd never been very fond of knickknacks, though now he saw their purpose.

"Breaking the rules wasn't enough," Olivia remarked lightly. "I have now resorted to breaking tea sets and porcelain figurines."

Her mood was improving. Happily, she strolled around the room, looking for things to break. There was a smile on her lips and a gleam in her eye. This was a version of Olivia he never imagined, but one he could quite possibly fall in love with. He would have to buy more tea sets in the event she ever again found herself vexed.

"Make your own rules, Angel," he murmured.

Olivia looked up at him suddenly. In an instant something changed. What, he didn't know. But had he been measuring the temperature and pressure in the room, he was sure there would have been a sudden drop.

"What did you say?" she asked slowly, softly.

His heart started to pound. What had he said? Shit.

"Make your own rules, Angel." He said the damning words softly. This wasn't how he wanted her to find out. He never wanted her to know.

Olivia started advancing toward him, carefully finding her way through all the remnants of china tea sets and porcelain figurines.

"How did you hurt your hands, Phinn?" This time when she asked, it was clear she already knew the answer.

He couldn't tell her. The last thing he wanted was secrets between them—he just wanted to love her. But because he wanted her to love him, he couldn't tell her.

"I can't tell you," he said. She was coming closer now. Her eyes were dark. He could see that she was thinking and putting two and two together and figuring out what he didn't want her to know. The minute she knew was the minute he lost her.

She reached out for his hands, smoothing over what remained of the bruises and cuts. It'd hurt like the devil—that bastard had a thick skull. But the pain was nothing compared to what she would have suffered if Miss Payton, ever attentive to her friend's well-being, hadn't alerted him to Olivia venturing out into the gardens with that stranger.

The pain of his hands would pale in comparison to losing her.

How did this happen? A moment ago they had been happy.

Olivia reached out slowly toward his face. He flinched. *Father. Nadia.* Phinn held his breath. He realized she wasn't about to strike him when her hand softened, holding him gently. She was gazing at his mouth.

Any second now Olivia was going to figure out that he had deceived her. That he was prone to acts of violence. That they didn't call him the Mad Baron for nothing.

Phinn couldn't move. He wanted to enjoy these last few seconds with her touch before she figured it all out and everything was over. He felt his chest tighten as she stood so close to him that their bodies were nearly touching.

He was achingly aware of wanting to touch her and achingly aware he might not. Ever. He should have known from the start that she was too good for the likes of him. He should stop her, really.

But he didn't. Because Olivia stood on her toes and pressed her mouth to his.

The minute he kissed her, really kissed her, she would know. So Phinn kept his lips firmly closed as she pressed her mouth to his. She was not dissuaded. Like a tempting minx, she licked the seam of his lips, urging him to open to her. It took everything—*everything*—in him to resist. Though he wanted to embrace her, he kept his hands clenched into fists at his sides. Though he wanted to give in . . .

He hardened as he felt Olivia's breasts brush against his chest. She had wrapped her arms around him, intent on wrenching this kiss—this confession—from his lips. He didn't want her to know how he'd followed her that night, or how he'd lied to her, or kept secrets from her.

"It's you," Olivia whispered. He felt her soft breath, and then her intake of breath. "You're the one who saved me at the Cyprian ball."

It was inevitable was it not? What goes up must come down. Phinn told her yes as he enfolded her in his embrace. He told her yes with his kiss. She wore him down—it didn't take much—and he kissed her back. For a moment they kissed deeply, tasting each other. Then it turned frantic, passionate. She sighed. He couldn't breathe.

For a moment he had a glimpse of what they might have. Then she broke the kiss.

"When were you going to tell me?" she asked, looking him in the eye. Phinn gazed deeply into her lovely blue eyes and bit back the word *never.*

He turned away from her then, lost in the recollection of that night.

PHINN REMEMBERED THE searing pain in his fists, which paled in comparison to the relentless pangs of his heart. Olivia had been in grave danger. If it hadn't been for Miss Payton keeping such a close watch upon her friend and alerting him . . .

He remembered exhaling. She was safe. They were alone.

And she had no idea who he was. He knew, because she didn't run or gaze at him fearfully. She sat down beside him and cried against his chest. When she began to confide in him, his temper didn't flare but his heart kind of broke. But his scientific training didn't fail him: he pushed aside his emotions and listened. Observed. Tried to learn.

When she was no longer afraid of him, she could open up.

When he was no longer busy trying to make her trust him, he could listen.

The kiss, then, was inevitable.

Tenderly, he had kissed her. He was ready for her to push him away. Sweetly, she followed his lead. He tasted the champagne she'd drunk earlier in the evening, and he remembered those first tastes of freedom and what a pleasure it had been. She sighed softly. It nearly undid him.

Phinn dared to hold her face in his hands, as if he couldn't let her go. But he needed to feel the softness of her skin and hair. He needed her innocence after his violence. Then he lost himself . . . this was all he ever wanted. Her sweet kiss, her tender touch . . .

Suddenly, she had stopped the kiss. Clasping his face in her hands, she gazed into his eyes and asked him to marry her. He'd fought a wry grin and told her, "Not tonight." But in the morning he would make her his wife. She just didn't know it.

"Phinn," Olivia's insistent voice pierced through. "When were you going to tell me?"

He gazed down at her, taking in everything: her blue eyes filled with questions he didn't want to answer; strands of her blond hair tumbling down. He couldn't lie to her now. So he told her the truth: "I wasn't going to tell you."

Chapter 19

*All of London eagerly awaits the commencement of the
Great Exhibition, which will showcase the greatest talent
and innovation of England. Many are working 'round the
clock to ensure their inventions are ready.*

—THE LONDON WEEKLY

OLIVIA WATCHED PHINN go. He apologized
and muttered something about needing to clear
his head. Ever attentive, he said he would send a
servant to clean up the mess she had made. She'd
felt glorious during that marvelous outburst he
had encouraged. Now she felt ridiculous as a
maid swept the floors around her.

"I'm terribly sorry," Olivia said. "Please let me
help."

"No ma'am, I couldn't possibly," the girl said.
After all, young ladies had young ladies for these
sorts of things.

There were things Olivia *knew*, like how to serve
tea, how to pair off dinner guests by the appropri-
ate rank, how to sew on a button. She had never
learned what to do when one learned one's husband was keeping secrets. Massive secrets. She
had accidentally fallen in love with him, thinking
him someone else!

She collapsed on the settee and dragged up the memories of what she had said that night.

I could never love him. She cringed. What an awful thing to say.

My parents are forcing me to marry a man I don't love. Her stomach began to ache. It was true, but she saw now that everything had been much more complicated than that.

I despise him. How must he have felt when she told him that? Her heart started to throb, as if it pained it to beat in such a cruel girl. Breaking the strict and stupid rules of society was one thing, being mean was another. She knew, too, how it felt to be the recipient of sharp words, thanks to Lady Katherine and everyone who called her Prissy Missy or London's Least Likely.

He is overbearing. She had told him that; perhaps it explained why he became so solicitous of her opinion? Staying in London, the hotel, asking her for her opinion today. She had made her wishes known, but she must have hurt him in the process.

And he says the worst lines. She had been stinging from the awkwardness of trying one of those lines and have it fall flat with Brendon (Brandon?).

Oh God. Phinn had seen her with him. Phinn had saved her from him. But he knew that she had been touched, tainted, almost utterly ruined, and married her anyway. Why, he could have left her and no one would have blamed him.

Utterly ashamed of herself, Olivia hugged a pillow to her chest, as if that might comfort her.

But it didn't compare to her Mysterious Midnight Rescuer's arms—or Phinn's, rather. It had felt so good to speak her mind. But it felt so wretched now to know whom she had confided in. While she felt foolish for having been deceived, could she honestly blame him? Had the positions been reversed, she might have kept silent, too.

As the afternoon light started to fade, Olivia ran through the scene over and over in her mind, to the best of her memory, feeling terrible each and every time. Embarrassment. Regret. Shame.

Quite a far cry from the bittersweet exhilaration she had felt after that first magical kiss. She'd fallen in love.

She asked him to marry her.

He'd said, *Not tonight.*

But the next day . . . She didn't deserve to feel this burbling excitement and anticipation. Phinn was not what he seemed. He was a man she'd fallen in love with.

And then he left, with no explanation as to his whereabouts.

What was the proper etiquette for such a situation? Was she to wait patiently at home, twiddling her thumbs, while he cooled his head? Did she dare go wander the streets of London alone in search of him? Did he belong to a club? Shouldn't she know if her husband belonged to a club?

Shouldn't she also know if he was in the habit of kissing girls like that? She should. She really, really should.

With that in mind, Olivia determined her course of action. She had thought she knew where he might be. And though traveling alone and dropping in uninvited was Not Done, she resolved to do it anyway.

Make your own rules, Angel.

The maid had finished sweeping up the remnants of a very fine tea set and adorable figurines.

"Is there anything else I can fetch for you, miss?"

"A carriage please," Olivia replied.

Devonshire Street

Olivia ordered a carriage to bring her to the warehouse where the engine was being constructed. She guessed it was most likely where he had gone.

As the carriage rolled through the streets, she wondered why she hadn't gone to see his workplace before. There was so much about him she didn't know. What was the source of the scar that slashed across his cheek? What had happened with his late wife? Why had he deceived her at the Cyprian ball?

Young ladies didn't pry into the sensitive matters of others. But Olivia was making her own rules now and she wanted to know, intimately and completely, the man she had married.

Upon arrival before a nondescript building, she gave her driver orders to wait. Then she strolled up to the door.

"I'm Lady Radcliffe," she told the workmen who were making their way out as she arrived. It was the first time she'd introduced herself as such. They shrugged, allowed her entry, and went home for the day.

Instead of a posh and exclusive haven with servants and ever-flowing spirits, her husband spent his hours in a large, sparsely furnished room. There were a few tall windows and large tables with sheets of paper spread out upon them. Looking closer, she discerned they must be plans and drawings for the engine. They were meticulously detailed and diagrammed, and while fascinating, could not compare to the machine itself.

The engine was not what she'd imagined. Very well, she hadn't given it much thought at all. But now that she set eyes on it, looking away was impossible.

It dominated the room. It stood at least eight feet tall and appeared to be almost as wide and three feet deep. It was a maze of shiny gold pipes attached to grooved cylinders engraved with numbers.

She circled the engine, riveted by its magnificence.

How did it work? How did all these metal pieces perform mathematical calculations? She couldn't fathom it. Yet not only did Phinn and Ashbrooke understand, they had invented it and built it. Olivia found herself in awe.

She wanted to understand how it worked and

see it in action. How did one give it an equation to calculate?

She circled the machine once more. Outside, daylight was fading and dusk settling in, the street sounds dwindling. Then she saw the lever. Of course! She'd just need to pull it and the machine would whirl to life and tell her everything she ever wanted to know about 16 times 327, or 11,000 divided by 34.

The lever wouldn't budge. She pulled harder, then pulled down with all her weight by grabbing onto it and lifting her feet from the floor. How ridiculous she must look! But she couldn't walk away from it without seeing it work.

It was then that she understood why Phinn was gone so long every day. She'd thought he'd been avoiding her, but now it seemed more likely that he was so passionately driven to see this machine in action that he couldn't stay away from it . . . and perhaps she was the only thing that captivated him more.

Finally, movement! The lever sank slowly toward the ground, kicking the machine to life.

It started to make an ungodly amount of noise—clacking, clanging, a waking-the-dead ruckus. The sound was so unfathomably loud she instinctively covered her ears.

Then—oh!—one of the cylinders flew off. She hurried to retrieve it, and a moment later another went crashing to the floor. She picked that one up too. They were quite heavy, she discovered.

Especially when there were three, then four, then five . . . Along with the cylinders there were pipes that had snapped off as well.

The machine kept rattling so loudly her voice would have been lost if she screamed, which she might have done anyway. One of the cylinders bent out toward her, as if it wanted to join all the pieces she'd collected in her arms. Olivia set them down gently and used all her weight to try to press that cylinder back into place.

Young ladies ensured that everything was in its place.

She wasn't quite sure when she gave up trying to fix the machine. After the cylinder had fallen off, perhaps, in the precious few seconds between that and the collapse of one after another. Soon the machine was reduced to a pile of metal parts on the floor.

With her beneath them.

Chapter 20

*Nothing mattered more than successfully completing the
Difference Engine in time for the Great Exhibition.*
  —PHINN'S INNERMOST THOUGHTS BEFORE . . .

PHINN LEFT OLIVIA in their rooms and set out
for a walk. He didn't know where he was going,
just that he had to go. He'd revealed the worst of
himself and the secret he'd sworn to keep. Knowing how she had feared him, how could he will-
ingly let her know about the violence of which he
was capable? And he had taken advantage of her
trust—in his mind, he was no different than the
soldier he'd found her with.

Of course, he hadn't intended to tell her.

Of course, she would be angry when she learned
of his deception and violence. Staying there and
watching her lose any affection she might have
had for him was a torture he couldn't bear. The
pain he'd felt led him to only one conclusion: he
must have fallen in love with her.

Love now made everything seem worse.

So he'd left.

He sought refuge in the streets of London,
losing himself in the crowds of pedestrians, the

hollers of street vendors and the warning shouts of carriage drivers. He replayed their afternoon scene in his head over and over again, trying to find the precise moment where everything had gone wrong. Was it before she smashed the shepherdess or after?

He had hoped to avoid this. He and Nadia would bicker. Things would fly and break. He would retreat to his workspace and she would lock herself in a bedchamber in an inconsolable sulk that might last for days. Phinn found himself treading familiar streets on the way to the Difference Engine. That's what he would do—go, work on the engine, lose himself in the machinery, where everything was what it was and just made logical sense all of the time.

Like Nadia, Olivia would—

No, they were nothing alike. One was dark and fiery, the other fair and sparky. One had loathed her lot in life—even though she'd brought it all on herself with a series of foolish decisions. The other was just trying to find her way. Nadia threw china plates at his head. Olivia scrunched up her face adorably and threw them on the floor after asking permission and telling him to close his eyes.

He had wanted something different. Craved it. With Olivia, he'd found what he wanted.

Why, then, was he falling into familiar habits? Nadia had been right about one thing—he left and lost himself in work rather than work through problems with her. Phinn looked up, aware that he was on his way to committing the same mistake he always did. The warehouse was just a block away.

If he wanted things to be different in this marriage, he couldn't just pick a different girl and hope for the best. He had to be different himself, and that meant facing up to things rather than running away and losing himself in his work.

He sucked in his breath. He should return to the hotel and apologize and promise to be better. The tightness in his chest eased; his heart felt lighter.

Until he heard the engine.

Phinn stopped. Turned. Cocked his head. Yes, that was the sound of the machine clanging loudly as it attempted a calculation. The only problem was that it shouldn't be running; it wasn't ready yet. The assistants he and Ashbrooke had hired knew better than to try to start it.

Phinn picked up his pace toward the warehouse. It was probably some shiftless person who'd sought shelter for the night and, seeing the machine, couldn't help but test it out. The machine did have a way of mesmerizing people, impelling them to touch it.

Then he heard the crash and broke into a run. He knew that crash—the damned thing had fallen apart and collapsed once before.

When he saw a carriage idling outside, his heart seemed to stop.

"Olivia!" Phinn shouted her name, but there was no answer. He shouted again, "Olivia!" and still no one answered. He ruined an eerie silence when he burst through the door. The force sent it slamming into the wall.

He could see her lying amidst the rubble.

No. Had he said it or just thought it or just felt it? *No.*

Not this. Not again. Not *her.*

But there was no mistaking the sight of Olivia, his wife, sprawled on the ground, a heap of engine parts covering her legs. Her arms were splayed and her hair in disarray. It seemed so wrong to see her lovely blond locks spread out on the dusty floor.

"Olivia," he said, his voice rough, as he approached slowly.

"Olivia," he said again, falling to his knees beside her.

Her eyes were closed and her expression was oddly peaceful, as if she had just decided to have a little late afternoon rest. Underneath a heap of heavy pipes and cylinders on the floor, in a desolate building in a remote part of town.

He felt her neck for a pulse and heaved a sigh of relief when he felt the faint but steady beat of her heart.

She was alive. This wasn't Nadia, all over again.

This could not happen to him again.

This could not happen to her.

Phinn started to clear the rubble, lifting one cylinder at a time and heaving it aside. "I'm sorry," he told her. One by one he steadily and methodically removed every piece of the damned engine between him and Olivia. "This was my fault. I'm sorry."

The pieces were heavy. After a while his muscles were burning from the exertion. But how did she feel, trapped underneath it all?

Feats of strength.

Another time, another place, he might have laughed. Perhaps if she lived he could impress her with details of this heroic rescue.

If she lived. If she spared him from being the man who lost not one wife but two.

But he wasn't heroic. He was a brooding, busy man who kept driving women to their own destruction. He loved her and had been so afraid she didn't love him back that he fled, like a coward. Now she was paying the price for it.

He couldn't breathe. His heart seemed to have lodged in his throat. And there was something in his eye. Something hot and wet, which a more sensitive person might have called tears. Phinn brushed them away with the back of his hand. Now was not the time. He heaved another cylinder away. It crashed into a table. He heaved another. It smashed into a chair, which collapsed under the weight and the force.

Hours and hours of work—careful calculations, intricately detailed drafts, hours spent drawing the designs, forging the metal, finishing each piece by hand until they were identical. He tossed it all to the side without a second thought.

Finally, she was free.

Phinn saw then that one of her ankles was badly injured—definitely broken.

"I'm so sorry," he muttered, in case she could hear him. Could he even say anything else? He tried. And if she could hear and assume the worst, he added, "I'm going to pick you up now and take you home."

She did not respond.

"We'll call a doctor. You'll be fine." That was another lie. Her ankle looked terrible.

She moved and murmured as he lifted her. A groan of pain escaped her lips. Really, he should have stayed in the hotel room and kissed her again and again. She might have left him anyway, but she wouldn't have been hurt like this.

Somehow he managed to get into the carriage with her, thankful she'd had the sense to tell the driver to wait. They set off at a canter. Phinn held her tightly in his arms until they reached the hotel.

"Call a doctor," he bellowed upon entering the busy lobby with the unconscious form of his wife in his arms, people staring. In the far recesses of his mind he was aware of how this would look. He could just see the newspaper headlines: *The Mad Baron Strikes Again.*

He deserved it. Olivia did not. If she lived.

He did not even want to contemplate how he would go on if she did not.

"Immediately," he demanded. A footman took off at a run.

Somehow, he managed to get her to their room, where he placed her gently on her bed. The doctor came and performed his examination, while Phinn supervised (or obstructed the process with his incessant questions and second guessing, according to the doctor) and paced frantically about the room.

"It's her ankle," Dr. Barkley said. "Broken. I'll set it. She should walk again, but I fear her waltzing days may be over."

Phinn thought of Olivia at the Cyprian ball, dancing with such grace and happiness. His gut knotted up and started to burn.

"Her head has suffered a hit, too," the doctor continued. "I'm sure she'll wake up. Let's hope she retains her memory!" he said with a friendly chuckle.

Phinn wasn't sure if that outcome would be good or bad. Would she remember how he'd lied to her? Would she remember how they'd been trapped into marriage? What if she didn't?

"Nothing to do but wait now," Dr. Barkley said. He left additional instructions with the maids before leaving.

Phinn clasped Olivia's hand in his as he sank to his knees by her bed. And waited.

AT FIRST OLIVIA only heard the voices. Everything seemed to be filtered through fog and cotton wool, so she could not understand the words. But oh, she could recognize her mother's anguished tone. Squawking, really. And her father was bellowing. Though she couldn't see, Olivia thought his face must be a shade of red wine, judging by the bluster of his voice.

All of which begged the question: where was she? Why were her parents in the throes of a hysterical fit?

Her weak efforts at movement were met with shooting pain. She thought twice before trying that again. As her awareness returned—she heard words now, though they were garbled and she didn't try to follow—she became aware that her hand felt warm and secure, as if Phinn were holding it.

Was that so, or merely wishful thinking? Was she thinking or dreaming? What on earth had happened to her? Curiosity impelled her to make an effort at opening her eyes.

Slowly, bit by bit, everything came into focus. She was lying in her bed at the hotel. The hour was late. The only light came from dusk outside and the candles scattered about the room. Her parents were having some sort of argument in the corner.

Phinn. He was here. Holding her hand.

"Olivia." He whispered her name. "I'm so sorry."

She blinked. He looked awful. Anguished, really. His mouth was set in a grim line. How long had it been since they were kissing? His eyes were reddened and his hair an utter mess. She knew that meant he'd been frustrated or vexed by something and pushed his fingers through it.

What had happened?

Olivia closed her eyes again. And listened. It was all she had strength for.

"Has she woken?" That was her mother, anxious. Olivia could just picture her clutching a handkerchief to her bosom.

"Just for a second." That was Phinn.

"If she dies—" That was her father, in the warning tone he used to threaten her. *If you don't cease leaving your dolls on the stairway . . .* But then his voice faltered. "I entrusted my daughter to you in spite of all those damned rumors about you. And it turns out you are just what they say."

"Worse!" her mother cried.

"You gave me your word as a gentleman," her father said. His voice rising now. "And you are a murderer and a liar."

Had she the strength, Olivia would have gasped at the accusation. As a man of honor, Phinn would have no choice but to call out her father for hurling such incendiary lies. They were lies, were they not?

"It was an accident," she heard Phinn say. He sounded desperate. "I swear to you, I never meant her any harm."

"As soon as she wakes we are taking her home," her father declared. She thought his face must have turned a shade of the lip paint she'd worn during her first disastrous meeting with Phinn.

"Where she will be safe," her mother huffed. And then she choked on a sob and cried, "There will be a divorce. Oh, what will people say?"

Divorce? Olivia considered summoning her strength to demand answers. But they always talked about her life as if her wishes didn't matter, so what was the point of rousing herself from this strange state of awake but not awake?

"People will say our daughter is safely delivered from the hands of an evil scoundrel," her father said harshly. Olivia imagined his face turning a shade the color of raspberry ice. Then she rather fancied a raspberry ice. But that would require waking up, an activity for which she presently lacked the strength and inclination. "I was a fool to trust you with something so precious as my daughter's life."

For a moment her heartbeat stopped. They cared. *Now* they cared.

"It was an accident," Phinn said, his voice rising. They were provoking him with the most cruel accusations. What if he lost his temper as he had done with Rogan or Brendon (Brandon?). She heard him inhale—he must be close!—and exhale slowly. When he spoke next, his voice was deep and rough. "Both. Accidents."

"Do you expect us to believe that?" her father bellowed. "Do you expect anyone to believe that?"

"You will not be received," her mother said

coldly. As if Phinn cared about that. She thought she might have learned enough about him by now to know that didn't matter to him. And then she was aware of her mother bustling toward her and sinking down on the mattress beside her.

"How has she not woken yet?" she cried.

"Did you call a doctor?" That was her father.

"Of course I bloody well called a doctor," Phinn replied.

"I think you should leave this to us. She needs her mother."

"You heard Lady Archer. Leave her with us. You should go."

Scarlet. His face had to be a shade of scarlet. Olivia cracked open one eye to see if she was right. She was.

She also saw that Phinn was turning to go. His hand was on the doorknob. Her mother was sobbing by her bedside. It was now time to summon her strength. He could *not* leave her. And above all, he could not leave her to the hysterical clutches of her parents. Not now. She liked the hotel and she wanted to be with Phinn.

"*Stay,*" she said. It was a whisper. She tried again. "Stay."

"Olivia!" Phinn turned quickly and rushed to her bedside. He fell to his knees beside her and she reached for his hand.

"She's awake! Archer, she's awake!" her mother squawked. Her father pushed Phinn aside, grabbed her hand and gave it a squeeze.

"It's all right, darling, we're going to take you home," her mother gushed. "You needn't stay here a moment longer."

"I'm so sorry, daughter, I had believed him to be an upstanding man in spite of his rumors. Otherwise I would have never contracted your betrothal. I should have allowed time for a courtship, as he wanted . . ."

This was too much for Olivia to take in now. But she understood enough. She'd been punishing Phinn for sins that weren't entirely his. All she could do was allow a weary sigh.

"Hush, husband," her mother said. "Can't you see she's overset?"

"We all can see it, wife," her father replied frostily.

Phinn stood behind them. Olivia found strength in his gaze.

"I know just the thing," her mother said, rummaging in her reticule. She could never find anything in her reticule in less than five minutes. Now was no exception. "Now wait . . . it's in here somewhere."

Finally, she was triumphant. She held aloft a bottle of Smythson's Smelling Salts. Then she popped off the lid and held the bottle under Olivia's nose.

Oh Lord, was that revitalizing stuff! Olivia took a deep, heaving breath, then coughed, then summoned all her strength to ignore the pain required in turning her head away from that curiously strong scent.

"It works! Every time!" her mother cried. "If you'd just bought the shares like I told you, we'd be rich and wouldn't have had to rely on Radcliffe's funds."

Olivia peered from her mother to her father to Phinn. Her gaze settled on him.

"Olivia. Please stay," he said. It wasn't a command, or a question, but a plea.

Somehow, in spite of all their protestations and accusations, Phinn managed to get her parents out of the room. The silence, oh God, the silence was heavenly. She closed her eyes to savor it but Phinn pleaded with her to wake up.

"What happened?" she asked once she finally managed it.

"The engine wasn't ready," he said, and she remembered the gleaming machine that she'd broken. Oh, he must be angry with her! "But you didn't know that because I didn't tell you. I stayed late each day and only returned after you'd gone to bed because . . . it's hard to explain."

He wasn't entirely making sense but she understood that he wasn't mad at her. If anything, he was angry with himself. It was clear by the anguish in his voice and the rough manner with which he pushed his fingers through his hair.

"I made a mistake, Olivia. It collapsed. It seems you have broken your ankle. The doctor thinks you'll walk again."

"Oh." Well that explained the wicked pain she felt whenever she tried to move.

"Olivia." He held her hand again. She remembered their night at the theater. She wanted that again. But one look in his eyes and she saw that he wasn't thinking of sweet little affections taking place in the dark. No, he was deathly serious. "We haven't consummated our marriage. I know you didn't have a choice in marrying me. It wasn't how I planned it, and my attempts to make things better only made everything worse. I thought it was the best thing for our reputations to go ahead with it. But you can leave now. We'll have it annulled. I'll go away. I'll take the blame for everything. You deserve better than this and better than me. And I will do *anything* to make you the happiest of women."

Olivia vaguely comprehended that one of those devastatingly romantic speeches she had always dreamed of hearing was finally, gloriously, being delivered to her. She wished that he would repeat it again and again so she could memorize it. It wouldn't do to paraphrase when she related this scene to Prudence and Emma. She had to get it *exactly*.

Phinn squeezed her hand. There was more.

"But, Angel, you'll make me the happiest of men if you stay."

"Oh." It was a heartfelt sigh. It was all she could manage. She was only aware of the slow beat of her heart, her hand warmed by his, and the genuine affection in his eyes. She had questions about this husband of hers. The only way to get answers was to stay.

There was a banging on the door. Did they not know how her head ached? Her parents burst in. There was more chatter of her leaving, of the marriage being annulled, of never seeing Phinn again. But she couldn't lose him now. There were too many unanswered questions, too many things she wanted to know, and too many kisses they hadn't shared.

"We are her parents. We should decide for our daughter."

That was it, wasn't it? They always decided for her. Everyone always decided for her. No one ever asked what she wanted. If she'd been able to, she would have pointed that out.

Instead, she sighed and waited for Phinn to reply that she was his wife, and thus he would make the decisions regarding her care.

Instead, he gave her every reason to stay when he said, "The choice is Olivia's."

Chapter 21

The Mad Baron Strikes Again
  *The notorious Lord Radcliffe was seen carrying the
unconscious form of his new wife through the lobby of
Mivart's Hotel, where they are residing. We fear the worst.*
  —THE LONDON WEEKLY

Olivia's bedchamber
Specifically, her bed

After the dramatic turn of events that left Olivia bedridden, she found herself . . . well, bedridden. And after the initial flurry of visits from the doctor (who declared her ankle broken), and her parents (who fussed excessively), and the wallflowers (who amused her with society gossip), she was left alone to rest.

This morning, Phinn had returned to his workplace to oversee the reconstruction of the Difference Engine, which she knew he would. It was important work he'd come to London to do. But he'd also come for a wife, who lay bedridden and alone. Who had broken the engine.

Olivia sighed. When he left earlier, she hadn't protested, as visitors surrounded her bedside. But they were long gone now and he hadn't returned. The light from her windows had faded from the bright yellow of midday to the violet of dusk.

She was so very bored and restless that she picked up the embroidery her mother had left within reach. For a moment she stared at the sampler in her hand. The blank fabric and needle and thread were everything she'd despised—the little woman who sat idly by and waited, kept busy by stitching biblical verses and decorative images onto a scrap of fabric that might, one day, be a pillow placed upon a settee that she might or might not be ravished upon by her husband.

Embroidery was useless work. Unlike Phinn's possibly revolutionary work.

Young ladies embroidered at home.

Men went out and sought adventures and did Great Things.

Rules, rules, rules! She knew them all too well. They took up too much space in her brain. They kept her all bound up, restrained, and squeezed into the mold of Proper Lady until she couldn't breathe. Thanks to her Mysterious Midnight Rescuer—Phinn!—there was only one rule she abided these days.

Make your own rules.

With a smile on her lips, Olivia picked up her needle and selected a vibrant pink thread. She started to stitch and kept at it until Phinn arrived.

"Right where I left you," he remarked, leaning

against the door frame before strolling into the room.

"Hello there," she said, smiling shyly. She was at once happy to see him, but all too aware that while she was properly dressed, she was laying on the covers of her bed and, because of her ankle, stuck there.

"My apologies for taking so long to return to you," he said. "The engine will need significant repairs."

Her smile faded.

"I'm so sorry," Olivia said. Truly, she felt horrid whenever she thought of what she'd done. All his work—gone in but a moment. "I didn't mean to break it. I only wanted to see if it worked."

She only wanted to see him and to know him. But those were words she couldn't quite bring herself to say yet.

"No, I'm sorry Olivia," Phinn said, sitting on a chair beside the bed and clasping her hand. He gazed at her earnestly. Apologetically. "I never should have walked out on you."

"Why did you?"

Phinn pushed his fingers through his hair. "You're so frightened of me, Olivia. You had seen the violence I am capable of. I thought if you knew that was me, you would be even more afraid and that you wouldn't let me touch you. So I couldn't kiss you, because then you would know."

Olivia regarded him seriously. She took in his green eyes, gazing at her with sorrow and a little bit of hope. Then her attention drifted to that scar, reminding her of his dangerous past, violent temper, and all the things she didn't know about him. She pushed his hair back, smoothing it with her touch.

"To be fair, you had come to my defense," she said. "I was being attacked. Phinn, if you hadn't been there, I shudder to think what I would have suffered."

As she spoke of that night, she watched his hands ball into fists. His jaw clenched. His eyes darkened from green to nearly black. For a moment Olivia felt a tremble of fear. Phinn's countenance had transformed from an attentive husband to a man who was not quite here, but swept up in his anger.

Bedridden and unable to walk, she was completely at his mercy. Though she didn't think he would attack her, it was quite unsettling to see the way the anger overtook him. She didn't forget that night either. His punches had been swift, sure, and relentless, until she'd cried for him to stop and Brendon (Brandon?) lay unconscious on the ground.

Not wanting to lose Phinn to this dark mood now, she rested her hands over his clenched fists and looked into his eyes. Gradually, she felt his grip soften and his fingers relax.

"I have a temper," he admitted.

"Really? I hadn't noticed," Olivia replied sweetly.

Phinn thought she must be daft. Then he realized she was jesting; to his surprise, he threw back his head and laughed. And like that, all the hot, stormy anger subsided. That was why he needed Olivia. No one else had the ability to soothe his temper or distract him from anger.

"What are you working on?" he asked, nodding at the fabric in her hands.

"Embroidery, actually," she said with a little laugh, glancing down.

"I thought you hated embroidery." Just when he thought he knew her . . .

"I do. But it was the only thing to do within reach," she said with a sheepish smile. His chest tightened. She was stuck in bed with embroidery all because of him—God, he'd be a beast if he were stuck in her position.

"I am so sorry, Olivia."

"I know," she replied. "Besides, I found a way to make it less tedious."

She turned the sampler she'd been working on to show him. He grinned as he read the words stitched in thick, upright letters with the occasional flourish: *Make your own rules.*

"What will your mother say when she sees that?" Phinn asked with a lift of one brow.

"She will say, 'Olivia, young ladies do not.' But I say that young ladies do."

"I hope so," Phinn murmured. Their gazes met. Locked. Once again he felt that force, drawing him to Olivia. Like gravity. Like magnetism. Like it was a law and there was no breaking it. Not that he wanted to; no, he wanted to be so close . . . he wanted to be inside her.

His gaze dropped to her lips, parted slightly. He wanted to kiss her. Then his gaze dropped lower, to the swells of her breasts straining against her bodice. He wanted to touch, taste, adore. He wanted his wife with an intensity usually reserved for one of his tempers.

Did she share his desire? The darkening of her blue eyes might suggest she did.

"And what are the rules according to Olivia?" Phinn asked, his voice rough.

"A young lady ought to voice her thoughts and opinions," she said. "I haven't been very good at it."

"You're doing all right now," he answered, encouraging her to speak her mind to him. If he knew her, he could please her. If she were happy, he would be happy. "What are some other rules of yours?"

"Only follow the rules that make sense," Olivia said, and his heart nearly burst with love for her. She smiled back at him. "For example, it is ridiculous that a lady ought to have a birdlike appetite and only pick at her food and be starving most of the time. One shouldn't put their happiness in the hands of anyone else. Some will treat it with disrespect," she added, and he could tell they were both thinking about the soldier. "Or very likely, no one will care about her happiness as much as she."

Phinn suspected she was speaking of her parents now. They meant well, but if they truly cared, they would have listened to their daughter and given her a choice in matters pertaining to her life.

"Any other rules?"

"A lady should discover what pleases her," Olivia answered softly.

"I like that rule," he murmured suggestively.

"I wasn't thinking what you are clearly thinking," she replied.

"Pity, that," he remarked. Truly.

"I am quite inexperienced in that regard," she confessed. Which he knew. Which he liked.

Phinn's heart started drumming harder and faster. "There's an easy remedy for that."

"But . . . but . . ." she stammered.

Phinn quirked one brow, encouraging her to continue but not wanting to seem so eager that he scared her off. They were becoming closer. She sighed.

"My leg. And I have seen the pictures, and while I find them intriguing, I am not quite sure about . . . all of those things. I confess, I am curious, however—"

"Olivia."

"Yes?"

"A lady should discover what pleases her," Phinn said. "And she should voice her opinion and make clear her wishes, be they 'Yes, I like that and want more' or 'Stop at once.'"

"A gentleman ought to obey a lady's wishes,"

she replied with a slight upturn at the corners of her mouth.

"Agreed," he said, voice rough, heart pounding.

Olivia let her embroidery fall to the floor.

Phinn pushed a wayward ringlet away from her face. He was going to kiss her now. She would know it was him and that would be all right. She might be nervous or afraid, but he'd demonstrate that she could trust him to keep her safe and happy. He'd help her discover what pleased her.

Though not lacking in experience, he felt nervous. Funny, that.

After this kiss there would be no turning back.

Phinn lowered his mouth to hers, determined to please his lady. It took all of his restraint, but he kept his kiss light and gentle at first. She'd seemed to like that before. But then, as if drunk from the taste of her, he couldn't hold back. He urged her lips apart so he could truly taste her.

Olivia seemed to like that, too. When he joined her on the bed, lying by her side, he felt her tense and then relax. She was innocent. He couldn't forget that. Nor could he forget what she thought she knew of his temper and his past. If he could only tear himself away from their kiss, he could explain.

Or he could just show her there was nothing to be afraid of. He just kissed her as if that were the only thing in the world.

Tentatively at first, she responded. And then she surrendered a bit more. Lightly, she pushed a lock of his hair away. As she did, her fingertips skimmed over the scar.

He felt her tense.

His breath caught.

Then she threaded her fingers through his hair, pulling him closer. He felt her breasts pressing against his chest. His hard arousal strained against his breeches. All he wanted was to bury himself inside her and thrust hard until he climaxed and shouted her name. Instead, he forced himself to go slow and discover her.

When he pressed hot, open-mouthed kisses along her neck, Olivia froze as if she weren't quite sure about it. Then she sighed and tilted her head back to give him more access. With her eyes closed, she didn't see his triumphant smile. He knew how to woo a woman until she was pliant and wanting in his arms. His breath caught, wanting and wishing to touch her bare skin.

Phinn skimmed his open hands along her side and caressed the delicate dip between her hip and her waist, and she pressed closer to him. He didn't stop there, or even when his palm closed around her breast. A perfect fit. Olivia gazed into his eyes. Then, smiling languorously, she closed them again. He pressed his mouth to the faint smile on her lips as he started to tug down her bodice, first exposing one beautifully pale, round shoulder. He had to press a light kiss there.

When he pushed aside all the fabric between them, she didn't protest. When he ducked his head and his mouth closed around one of the dusky centers of her breast, she sighed slightly.

As his tongue toyed with the sensitive peak, her sighs became moans.

When he moved against her, as if he were inside her, she tensed again. She either didn't like it or else didn't know what to do.

"Move with me," he said roughly. "Or tell me to stop."

YOUNG LADIES LET the gentleman have his way . . .

The rules still plagued Olivia. She found it harder and harder to hold back. Why was she so determined to resist him? She couldn't remember. Why couldn't she move with him? Instinctively, she wanted to. But she'd been told that ladies lie still, allowing the man his pleasure, and now he ordered her to move with him or to tell him to stop. Given the steady, spiraling heat and her feeling of deep desire and dissatisfaction at the moment, stopping was not an option. So she let down her defenses and allowed her hips to move with his. She felt the hard length of his arousal pressing to the vee of her thighs. She wanted only to feel more of him.

She had sworn to do *anything* to avoid marriage to this man, and now she was gasping for his touch. Somehow, Phinn managed to chase away the scary thoughts with the pleasure he gave her with his hands and mouth. He had pressed kisses along her neck, stimulating the sensitive skin there and making her forget how vulnerable she felt.

His hands, which might have hurt another

woman, roamed over her. Learning her. Pleasing her. Urging her legs apart. His fingertips traced light lines up her inner thighs where the skin was so sensitive.

"Tell me to stop," he said, voice rough.

"No," she whispered.

His hands moved higher and he started to stroke the bud of her sex with his fingertips. She bit her lip, biting back moans.

Young ladies should be seen and not heard.

"I want to hear you," he whispered.

So she sighed and didn't hold back as he traced delicate circles around her most sensitive place. The pressure increased, drawing a moan from her lips. She couldn't quite keep still. And she gasped when he slid one finger inside her. She'd never felt anything like it. The delicate, teasing strokes continued until she just felt vexed. It wasn't enough. Didn't he know it wasn't enough?

"Phinn," she rasped.

He kissed and slid another finger inside her, while pressing the bud of her sex with his thumb. This was all too much to process. She felt overheated—why the devil did she still have this dress on? Still, he moved his fingers in a wicked rhythm that was driving her mad. Tightness in her lungs made breathing hard. In fact, she felt tight and tense all over as if she might shatter at any second.

And then she did. The climax came hard and fast. Olivia cried out as she felt wave after wave of a pleasure she'd never imagined.

"Olivia," Phinn murmured, pressing more kisses against her neck.

"Mmm," she murmured as she wrapped her arms around him.

"There's more," he whispered. Or did he mean less? Her gown was thrown to the floor. His attire swiftly followed.

Olivia's eyes widened as she took in Phinn's broad shoulders, muscled chest. Her gaze lingered on his large arousal, jutting out. Then she looked away, back up to his darkened eyes.

"Olivia?" It was a question. There was only one answer. She smiled coyly and stretched her palms across his chest, feeling the warmth of his skin. His breath caught as her fingertips brushed over his nipples.

"Yes," she whispered. She wanted to feel that feeling again. She wanted to know him, too. He lowered himself above her, and for a second she tensed, feeling trapped. Then he kissed her and she was reminded of the pleasure to come. His embrace was warm. She discovered she didn't want to be anywhere else.

He claimed her mouth for another deep, passionate kiss—the kind that sent her wits fleeing and made her want more. She was aware of his arousal pressing against her. And as she drew her legs apart, she was aware of how much she wanted him.

Slowly, Phinn entered her. She was warm and wet for *him*. In spite of everything she'd done to get rid of him, there was no denying that she wanted him now. He pushed in; she gasped. He began to move with deep and slow thrusts. She wrapped her arms around him. Deeper. More. She caught his mouth for a kiss. Harder. Her hips moved with his. Then there was nothing but him and her, moving as one. Then there was nothing but pleasure as he hit his climax with a shout. Then there was nothing but the thudding of his heart and Olivia in his arms. It was everything.

Chapter 22

There is hope for Lord and Lady Radcliffe after all!
Lady Olivia was merely injured and will most certainly
live, though she might not see her husband for a while.
The Mad Baron will be busy attempting to rebuild the
Difference Engine before the Great Exhibition, which is
getting closer each day.

—THE LONDON WEEKLY

Olivia's bedchamber
Specifically, her bed
Still . . .

WHEN OLIVIA WOKE the following morning, everything had changed profoundly. They were now married in truth and there was no way out of it—save for an act of Parliament, which were as rare as acts of God. If she wanted love, romance, and happiness, she would have to make it happen—and make it happen with Phinn.

She woke up beside him. Safe. Adored. Some of her fears had been assuaged.

After breakfast he asked, "What would you like to do today?"

"I'd like to stroll in the park, visit the shops on Bond Street, dance a reel or run through a field while singing," Olivia said. Then, with a sigh, she added, "But I suppose I'll lie here instead."

"I'm so sorry, Olivia," he said, wincing. He felt guilty about her leg—as if it were his fault, when really it was her own. She oughtn't have tried to operate machinery she didn't understand.

She smiled and said, "You must stop apologizing, and make it up to me instead."

"Shall I bring your embroidery?"

"No, I finished my sampler," Olivia said. "And that might be all the embroidery I need to do for the rest of my life."

"Perhaps you'd like to paint?"

Or perhaps not, Olivia thought. She'd sworn off portraits of flowers and arrangements of decorative household items. But then her gaze settled on Phinn.

He sat in a chair beside her bed, wearing his breeches and a shirt that was unbuttoned, exposing the wide expanse of his muscled chest. His hair was a tussled mess—not because he'd been pushing his fingers through it in a state of frustration, but because she'd messed it up as she ran her fingers through it while they made love. Olivia smiled, wanting to capture this image of him forever and knowing that she could.

"Painting, Olivia?"

She grinned wickedly. "Yes. Though I may need your help with the subject of my painting."

"Anything," he said, obviously having no inkling what she was about to ask him.

HE HAD PROMISED her anything, which is how he came to be the subject of her portrait. Never mind that they had only a few days to rebuild the engine before the Great Exhibition. He was going to sit in this chair wearing naught but breeches and an open shirt and let his wife paint him.

Though not a religious man, he was also going to pray this watercolor of hers was never made public. It would be for her eyes only.

"I feel ridiculous," he remarked as she happily glanced from him to her painting, occasionally dabbling the brush in her paints and jar of water.

"But you look . . ." Olivia eyed him in a way that he found incredibly arousing. "You do not look ridiculous." She had a shy smile and faint blush. She couldn't quite say it, but she liked what she saw.

Phinn caught himself drumming his fingers on the arm of the chair, and she scowled at him. He thought of the engine . . . all those identical parts that had to be reassembled precisely and fit together perfectly. He exhaled sharply. The workers had assembled it once; they could manage to work without his overbearing supervision for an hour or two. Besides, he was busy. Sitting on a chair. Hardly clothed.

To distract himself from worrying about his work, he concentrated on watching Olivia as she painted. She bit her pink lower lip. She furrowed her brow as she stared at him, then looked down at her painting. He admired her hair, long, soft

golden ringlets that tumbled around her face—
subsequently pushed aside with paint-stained
fingertips. He smiled when he noticed a smudge
of red in her hair and a dab of white on her cheek.

Keeping her gaze fixed on the painting before
her, she asked, "How did you get your scar,
Phinn?"

"Why do you ask?" He resisted the urge to
touch the damned mark. It was a stark reminder
of one of the worst nights of his life—there were
two, and he could never decide which one was
worse, though one led to the other.

"Because I am curious about it as I paint it," she
replied. She stole a quick, hesitant glance at him.

"You could leave it off."

"Yes, but I want to do a portrait of *you*." He
tensed. Aye, he was the man with the mysterious scar and the man known as the Mad Baron.
He didn't like these things. But they were who he
was, and he wanted Olivia to love him as he was.

"I was in a fight," he said finally.

"With whom?"

Phinn hesitated. He couldn't say "my wife" because Olivia was his wife now. He didn't want to
say "my late wife," as that didn't exactly initiate
the most romantic conversations. He could say her
name, Nadia. But something held him back, as if
the moment he spoke her name aloud she would
become a third person in *this* marriage.

He shifted slightly in the chair before answer-
ing, "A woman."

"Over what?"

"Honestly, I can't even remember anymore."

Olivia glanced up at him, caught his eye. He knew all the questions running through her head. Which woman? Your first wife?

He didn't want to think about Nadia now. Nor did he want to think about his brother, the fight, and how everything had gone wrong—not when it was finally starting to go right.

"How much longer?"

"You must keep still," she admonished.

"I think I should see what you've done so far." Really, though, he wanted to make love again. If he was going to be delayed getting to the engine this morning, then he might as well indulge and make it completely worth it.

"Not until it's finished," she said in a kind but firm manner that gave him a glimpse of what she'd be like as a mother. He eagerly awaited the day. "Why," she asked. "Do you have somewhere to be?"

Phinn thought of the engine, the workers, the time required to rebuild the machine before the Great Exhibition, which would be happening soon. There was no room for mistakes now. He should be there, supervising and assisting.

This was why he had wanted a nice, docile wife who didn't make demands of him. But then he looked at Olivia, reclining on the bed, with paint on her cheek and her hair a tussled mess. She was beautiful and he wanted her more than anything else. She wore a pale blue silk robe and a dressing gown, both items that could be easily removed if he were so inclined.

He was so inclined.

"No," he said with a grin. "There's nowhere else for me to be. However, I think I shouldn't be the only one undressed."

"You're not," Olivia corrected. "I'm in my dressing gown. That hardly qualifies as dressed."

Phinn took off the shirt and dropped it on the floor.

"I'm not finished!" she protested.

He grinned again. "You're right. You have more clothing to remove."

She smiled coyly, tugging at the tie of the waist of her dressing gown.

Soon those lovely silk things were just a pile on the floor. Phinn took a moment to gaze upon her in the gentle morning light. Her breasts were round and full with stiff pink peaks that seemed to beg for his attentions. Olivia's soft curls tumbled down around her shoulders; he wanted to push them aside so he could admire the delicate arch of her neck and curve of her shoulders. Then he wanted to kiss his way down, across the gentle curve of her belly and lower. He wanted to show her another way he could bring her pleasure. And then he wanted to lose himself inside her.

Then he did all of these things, accompanied by the delicate sighs and moans of his wife. And then they did it again.

Olivia's bedchamber
Still on her bed!
Later that afternoon

Olivia had just enough time between when Phinn left and her friends arrived to have a bath and dress in a fresh gown. She was about to read the newspapers when Emma and Prudence burst in and immediately made themselves at home by ringing for tea and pulling chairs close to the bed.

"We came earlier but were told you were indisposed," Prudence said with a wicked smile.

"I suppose we needn't ask *why* you were indisposed," Emma added.

"Young ladies do not discuss marital relations," Olivia said, trying to sound prim.

"Don't tell me we are back to following all the rules of propriety," Prudence said dejectedly.

"Not at all," Olivia said, smiling. "All I shall say is that I have finally become better acquainted with Phinn." The warmth of her blushing cheeks should have been all her friends needed to see for them to know.

"Phinn?" Emma inquired curiously. "Not the Mad Baron?"

"Better acquainted?" Prudence echoed.

"Do you not mean intimately acquainted?" Prudence asked.

"Or acquainted in the biblical sense?" Emma added.

"I think she might mean exactly that," Prudence said, picking up Olivia's painting book and holding up the painting she'd done of Phinn, sprawled comfortably in the chair wearing naught but fitted breeches and a shirt carelessly thrown open. Olivia had spent a while staring at the broad expanse of his chest, considering how best to portray the contours of his muscles. She had labored over his expression, too, wanting to capture the desire in his green eyes.

She was more proud of this painting than she was of the still life of a basket of kittens that won her first prize at Lady Penelope's.

"See, I told you both you would be happily married before Lady Penelope's Ball," Emma said, smiling broadly.

Olivia and Prudence exchanged a glance and returned uneasy smiles. There was but a month before the anniversary ball and Prudence still had nary a suitor. And while Olivia was married and falling for her husband, there was still much she didn't know about him. He'd been vague when she asked about the scar, which was terrible because she imagined the worst. Then, they hadn't addressed how the Mad Baron rumors began. Or the fact that he'd been married before. When he touched her, she almost forgot. And when he kept touching her, he drove all thoughts from her head. But the questions always returned.

"I still don't know what happened in his past," she said. "I feel I still don't know him."

"Well, did you ask?" Prudence asked.

"I have tried. I think he was about to tell me that day in the gazebo," Olivia replied. "Before I succumbed to the effects of the poison. Or wine. Whichever."

"Just ask," Emma said. "What could possibly be holding you back at this point?"

It certainly wasn't some notion of keeping quiet or respecting the private matters of others.

"What if I don't like the answer?" Olivia said, anguished. "I am bound to him forever now. What if I have given myself to a murderer?"

"Then don't ask," Prudence said with a shrug.

"Instead, read *The Mad Baron: The Gruesome Story of an Innocent Maiden's Tragic Love and Untimely Death. A True Story*," Emma said. "I have brought a copy along with these other books from the circulating library."

"If he truly is a murderer, you could probably obtain a divorce," Prudence pointed out.

It was unrealistic, that. Olivia also noted the immediate *No* her heart issued.

"Or come live with Blake and me," Emma offered.

She could do that, she thought. Or she might live with Prudence in a cottage by the sea. Except for one maddening, confounding detail. She sighed and thought of Phinn making love to her and letting her paint him in a state of undress and asked, "But what if I don't want to?"

Emma and Prudence exchanged looks.

"Have you fallen in love with the Mad Baron?" Emma asked.

"I might have," Olivia muttered. How else to explain that she was inescapably drawn to him, even though she didn't completely know him? She was starting to trust him, even though there was still a chance that she shouldn't.

"Oooh, Olivia! I am so happy for you," Emma exclaimed, smiling broadly.

"Perhaps soon you shall have another full-fledged member in the nauseating newlywed club," Olivia replied. "I'm not quite there yet."

"Where is he now?" Prudence asked.

"Working on the engine," Olivia explained with a sigh. "He does that, a lot. Sometimes I catch him woolgathering and he is thinking of the engine."

"It'll be done soon," Emma explained. "They are scheduled to debut it at the Great Exhibition on the day after Lady Penelope's Ball, as a matter of fact."

Olivia pursed her lips. Was it wrong to be miffed that she was learning this critical information from her friend instead of her husband? See—he kept things from her, whether about the future or his past.

"As long as he makes it to the ball," Olivia said with only the slightest sulkiness. After all, half the reason she desperately needed a husband was to hold her hand at this torturous event.

"I am going to Bath," Prudence declared, apropos of nothing.

"That sounds lovely," said the bedridden Olivia. "When will you go?"

"Tomorrow," Prudence declared. Both Olivia and Emma's jaws dropped.

"What?" Olivia asked, shocked.

"Why?" Emma asked, equally shocked.

"This town is finished for me," Prudence said dramatically. "You are both married now. I have made the acquaintance of or am aware of every eligible man in London. They look at me and see Prude Prudence and nothing else. I have no prospects here."

"But . . . Bath?" Olivia asked.

"Lady Dare would like to take the waters," Prudence said, speaking of her aunt and guardian who often acted upon her every whim. "I shall accompany her. Perhaps I may meet someone in Bath."

"What if you must move there upon your marriage?" Emma asked, brow furrowing as she faced the possibility that her two friends might be whisked away to far off counties.

"It's closer than Yorkshire," Olivia said. She still did not wish to inhabit a vast, remote estate in Yorkshire.

"Indeed," Emma agreed. "But—"

"You will return in time for Lady Penelope's Ball, won't you?" Olivia asked.

Prudence hesitated, then said, "I shall try my best."

"Prue, you must go!" Emma exclaimed. "We must all go together."

Prudence just smiled sadly.

"You are both in love and I am truly happy for you both," Prudence said earnestly as she anxiously fisted her hands in the fabric of her skirts. "Truly I am. But you should enjoy this honeymoon time without fretting over your friend, the last wallflower."

Chapter 23

Booksellers are reporting extraordinary sales of The Mad
Baron: The Gruesome Story of an Innocent Maiden's
Tragic Love and Untimely Death. A True Story. *It
seems Lord and Lady Radcliffe's recent marriage and
subsequent accident have intrigued the ton.*

—THE LONDON WEEKLY

Still. On. Her. Bed.

Emma and Prudence left, leaving Olivia alone.
She lay back on the pillows, thinking of walking.
Or dancing. Or simply sitting upon the settee in
the other room. Ah, a girl could dream.

She wondered when Phinn would return. Dusk
was settling over the sky, casting her room in lav-
ender shadows. Awkwardly, she lit the candle on
the bedside table. Her gaze settled on the stack
of books Emma had left her. *The Mad Baron: The
Gruesome Story of an Innocent Maiden's Tragic Love
and Untimely Death. A True Story* was on the top.

Intrigued, and with nothing else to do, she ex-
amined the cover.

It featured a large, hulking man—with a scar
near his eye—with his fists wrapped tightly

around the long, slender neck of a slim yet exceedingly well-endowed maiden who had sunk to her knees before him. Olivia gulped, recalling the way she had exposed her neck for Phinn to caress with his fingers and press with kisses.

In the background a barn was on fire, flames reaching up to the sky. The candle on her bedside table flickered, as if there was a breeze. Olivia looked around, nervous. She was alone. The cover scene featured thick black clouds and a sliver of a moon. It certainly promised one terrifying story that she ought not read. Her heart thudded just looking at the ominous image.

She couldn't quite reconcile it with the Phinn she was starting to know. He'd been nothing but devoted and caring. His touch had been tender and gentle. Bedridden as she was, he'd have every opportunity to harm her. When they made love she opened herself to him completely and intimately. He didn't take advantage. She drifted off to sleep beside him and woke up each morning.

But there was so much about his past that she didn't know and he wasn't here to ask. Perhaps re-reading this would shed light upon all the secrets that still remained between them.

She really oughtn't read it, though. It felt like a betrayal. Yes she had read the story years ago at Lady Penelope's, but had only vague recollections. She'd just peruse it to refresh her memory.

She opened the book, but it felt *wrong* to read it. She knew Phinn now. While she didn't know what had happened, she didn't think he was a murderer. After all, she had spent the night with him alone and defenseless. If he were going to murder her, he had plenty of chances to do so—and have it look like an accident. Instead, he made her cry out with pleasure and slept peacefully beside her.

But what else would she do, if she did not read it?

At this moment she might have moved, accidentally brushing all the other books off the bedside table. The pages rustled as they fell to the floor, where they landed in a series of thuds.

"Oops," she said to no one.

Even if she wanted to pick up the fallen books or, say, embroider, she could not because her things were on the floor or in the other room. Olivia tried moving her ankle, which had been bound up tightly. Sparks of pain informed her that indeed she would be following the doctor's orders and remain abed.

For her health, Olivia turned to the first page and began to read.

The Mad Baron met his bride under secretive, scandalous, and highly questionable circumstances. Miss Nadine Prescott had been betrothed to the Mad Baron's brother, George.

"His brother!" Olivia gasped. She looked around the room for someone to share her shock. There was no one.

George ought to have been Baron Radcliffe were it not for his untimely demise at his brother's hand.

"Goodness," Olivia murmured, heart thudding. Phinn had murdered his brother, too? She couldn't quite believe it. One murder could be an accident. But two?

Then she continued to read.

'Twas love at first sight on the High Street one afternoon in Westlake Village when George first set eyes on Nadine. She was renowned for her beauty. Her eyes were perfectly almond-shaped and the color of chocolate. Her mouth was a perfect rosebud. Her hair was jet black and fell in silky strands to her waist. Her figure was perfectly slender, except for where it was perfectly voluptuous. There was no woman in possession of more beauty and charm in all of Yorkshire.

Olivia looked up from the page with a scowl on her face. Was it wrong for her to feel inadequate compared to a fictional yet dead woman? And lud, how was she ever to compare to her in Phinn's mind?

George was an accomplished sportsman and was popular with all the local gentry. There was no sport, feat of daring, or daunting endeavor that he did not succeed in. His father, the baron, was proud of his heir.

Olivia skimmed a full page listing all the sporting activities, feats of daring, and daunting endeavors that George excelled at. She was exhausted just reading about his jousting, boxing, fencing, fox hunting, running distances both long and short, climbing tall trees and then climbing down one-handed (for the other held a litter of squirming kittens). There was no mention of his younger brother, Phinn, and it was he that Olivia was curious about.

This Nadine and George had a passionate courtship. Olivia knew this because the book said, *Theirs was a passionate courtship*. Then she skimmed ahead of their perfect courtship. She wanted to get to the part about Phinn.

Their rosy romance came to an ABRUPT halt with the arrival of George's younger brother, newly returned from university where he had studied Strange and Dangerous Sciences. When he was not ensconced in a makeshift workshop in the barn on his brother's estate, he was committing his first grave sin: coveting the fiancée of his only brother, who had shown nothing but kindness to his unusual sibling.

Even worse, he schemed to win her for himself by fabricating horrendous lies about her which he told his besotted brother. Fictions, these were! There was no one more beautiful, charming, and perfect than Nadine. How DARE he cast aspersions upon his brother's intended, and for the sole purpose of seducing her himself?

"How dare you!" George accused his brother on a dark and stormy night.

His brother, already mad and bad but not yet a baron, said—

"Olivia."

She replied with a bloodcurdling scream.

When her heartbeat returned to normal and her wits returned, she saw that Phinn had returned. *She was alone with the Mad Baron!*

Olivia exhaled slowly. No, she was alone with her husband who had shown her nothing but devotion and tender care. Also, kisses that made her feel all the sparks and wonder and romance she'd ever wanted. Who was also known to everyone else as the Mad Baron who had coveted his brother's intended and possibly murdered them both.

She eyed him nervously.

"I'm terribly sorry," she said, collecting herself. "I was reading this awful piece of literature. It had consumed my imagination and I'd been quite immersed in the story. You gave me a fright."

Sheepishly, she held up the awful piece of literature.

Olivia watched Phinn stiffen. His jaw tightened and his mouth pressed into a firm line. Because she knew him now, she detected the signs that his mood was darkening and his temper on the verge of explosion.

She couldn't bear it if he hollered at her the way

he did at Rogan. Or if he hit her—no, he wouldn't. She knew that. In order to prevent a row, Olivia caught his eye, held his gaze and smiled.

"Really, it's awful," she said.

But the truth was, she had questions. He had secrets.

Phinn's eyes narrowed. He took a deep breath and exhaled it slowly, as one did when trying not to lose one's temper. She hadn't meant to anger him. She just wanted to know him, and he wasn't *here*, but off with his engine. And when he was here, they weren't exactly conversing.

"Phinn, look at me."

He looked at her. For a quick second she was taken aback by the darkness in his gaze. Oh, lud, he was angry. Which was ridiculous, really. Fortunately, she had enough sense not to say that to him. She just held his gaze and watched as he fought for control over whatever demon had possessed him.

PHINN KEPT HIS gaze focused on Olivia's lovely face. The cornflower blue of her eyes soothed him, especially when she peered up at him with such concern. He couldn't lose his temper now. He didn't *want* to lose his temper, for if he did then he wouldn't be able to idly spend the evening—and night—with her, which is what he truly wanted to do.

Phinn willed the anger to subside. He hated that book. It'd done more damage to him than

Nadia had, and that was saying something. Nadia had just tortured him, but that was in the past. That damned book had nearly cost him his future happiness. He hated that Olivia was reading it, but even through the hot flames of anger, he could see that he'd left her no choice when he hadn't told her the truth.

So, Phinn gave a short exhale and asked, "How bad is it?"

"It's dreadful," Olivia sent vehemently. "Listen to this. 'It was a dark and stormy, moonlit and wicked night when Miss Nadine Prescott's fate was altered forevermore.' I ask you, how can it be dark, stormy, and moonlit? And what is a wicked night?"

It had been a wicked night. That much he remembered. The rain had lashed at the windows. The candles were dwindling. The bottle nearly empty. It was the wrong time for George to ask what he thought of his future bride and the wrong time for him to tell his brother the truth. He had *meant* well, which was the most horrendous part of all.

"Her name wasn't Nadine," Phinn said finally. Olivia bit her lower lip, waiting for the truth. "It was Nadia."

"Was she really the most beautiful and charming woman in all of Yorkshire, with almond-shaped eyes the color of chocolate and a figure both slender *and* voluptuous?"

"Nadia was beautiful," Phinn admitted. He still

recalled his first glimpse of her after he'd returned home from university. She was laughing and taking tea and otherwise presenting herself as the most beautiful and charming woman in Yorkshire. She hadn't snared his brother yet and thus hadn't revealed her true nature. "She was also a nightmare—haughty, demanding, spoiled, jealous."

"Not the paragon of virtue this book claims her to be," Olivia murmured. Phinn pushed off the doorjamb he'd been leaning on and moved to the chair by her bed. "Was your brother the most accomplished sportsman and beloved member of the local community? Because if not, this author is quite a liar. For he goes on at length listing every sport your brother excelled at."

"Aye, everyone adored George," Phinn said. "Especially me. Especially our father, since George was everything I was not, and everything our father wanted in a son. Which was just as well—they left me to my scientific studies while they went off on sporting adventures. Mathematical equations and laws of physics don't try my temper the way my family had a knack of doing. And three Radcliffe tempers, plus my mother's flair for hysteria, add up to one thing: disaster."

Olivia nodded, drinking in every word. She continued to read the story.

"Everyone adored George. He thought about sport, Nadia, and ale. That was all."

"This book says you coveted Nadine—Nadia—for yourself and tried to dissuade your brother from marrying her," Olivia said softly. He glanced down at the book open on her lap. It was just an absurd fictional story to so many people. For Phinn, it was a hand reaching out from the past and dragging him back to scenes and memories he'd rather forget.

"Nadia didn't notice me," Phinn explained. "I was the quiet younger son with the peculiar interests in science. Nadia wanted George. She didn't bother trying to win me over and she never paid me much mind. She'd forget her pretty manners, thinking no one that mattered was looking. I saw her strike a maid for forgetting her gloves. And I saw her behind the Assembly rooms with John Huntford."

"I suppose these are the 'the horrendous' lies you told your brother about?"

"George didn't want to hear them. He said even if it were true, it was too late."

"Had he already proposed?" Olivia asked.

Phinn paused, considering how to answer that.

"He'd already made her his," he said, hoping that was sufficient.

"Oh." She seemed to understand. "Was it truly a dark and stormy night with violence in the air when this occurred?"

"My brother and I fought as only two Radcliffes can. He would not hear a word against her," Phinn said. He took another deep breath. He hated that night, hated the memory of it, hated having to relive it. But he also hated the fear he had seen in Olivia's eyes and the secrets that kept them apart and led to her getting hurt. "I have a temper, Olivia. I can't help it. I don't like it."

"I can see you counting back from ten and exhaling slowly," she said with a half smile.

"It's supposed to help," he said with a shrug.

"Does it?"

Phinn lifted his eyes to hers. "Not as much as looking at you."

Olivia reached out for his hand in a consoling gesture. But then she moved aside on the bed, making room, and beckoned him with her eyes and a half smile. Phinn joined her on the bed. Side by side they lay, reclining back on the pillows.

The damned book lay open on her lap. He glanced down at all the words just there, black on white, oblivious to the hurt they'd caused.

Fearing his strange, jealous brother, George rushed out headlong into the dark and stormy night with DANGER in the air. Only such TERROR would drive a man to venture forth in a driving downpour. He happened to encounter Huntford in town.

"George went to his house," Phinn said, pointing to the lies printed on the page. "George didn't want to believe me, but he knew I wouldn't lie to him. It wasn't an accidental meeting at all."

Olivia picked up the book and read aloud.

"'After hurling base accusations, Huntford

had no choice but to defend his honor. These two sporting men rained down violent blows upon each other, each one fighting for honor and dignity. But soon each man was only fighting for his life. For love.'"

"The long and short of it is that Huntford killed my brother," Phinn said. "He had no choice but to flee the country."

"So when it says that you took advantage of Nadine's utterly distraught, exceptionally emotional state of tragic grief and unrelenting bereavement to force her into marriage, I suppose it didn't happen quite like that," Olivia said. "One lover was dead and the other might as well have been. She would have been ruined. Marriage was her only salvation."

"Nadia begged me to marry her," Phinn said, recalling how in turns she begged and cajoled. There had been tears. Heaving bosoms. A damsel in distress on her knees before him, promising *anything* if he would just save her. He was tempted; Nadia was beautiful. She had a knack for bending a man to her will. But he didn't love her. "She said it was possible that she could be expecting," he said.

"Was there a baby?" Olivia asked, eyes widening. "*Is* there a baby?"

"No," Phinn said. He was never sure if he was saddened by the fact or glad because of the freedom it afforded him. Often he wondered how things would have fared if they had just waited to see if she were expecting. Or had she lied to him all along, eager to claim the title of baroness and the protection that would come with it? It seemed imperative that he marry her before the scandal broke.

"Why did you marry her?" Olivia asked. "Honor?"

"She would have been ruined otherwise. And I couldn't let my brother's child—should there be one—be raised in some outcast squalor," Phinn said. "And she was beautiful and had a way of manipulating a man with a terrifying combination of tears and seductive smiles."

"None of which were taught at Lady Penelope's Finishing School for Young Ladies," Olivia remarked wryly.

"Thank God for that," Phinn said. The last thing he wanted was another conniving and tempestuous wife.

Olivia rolled on her side to face him. He noticed her long blond hair falling in waves around her face and splayed across the pillow. He wanted to sink his fingers into it, pull her close and kiss her senseless. He never wanted to talk about his past again.

"Did you love her?" Olivia asked softly.

"I cared for her," Phinn said. And he did in time have an affection for Nadia. They were a bad match. He didn't give her the attention she craved, which drove her to act more outrageously, which drove him further away. But she was still his wife. He couldn't *not* care for her. "But I didn't love her."

"How did she die, Phinn?" Olivia's voice was

soft. She slipped her hand into his. "I assume you didn't strangle her in a fit of rage. Or, to quote the book . . ." She glanced down at the page. "'Enclose your massive fists around the pale, slender column of her innocent neck whilst she pleaded for you to spare her life.'"

"We settled into a routine in which we largely avoided each other save for fights at dinner and . . ." Here Phinn paused, remembering how their passionate outbursts became something else entirely in the bedroom. He remembered, too, how wretched and dishonorable he'd felt after each time. While Olivia was present, he didn't want to think of the way they made up after fights, let alone mention it to her, his lovely new bride. "And then we made up afterward," he said finally. "But she wanted more and more of my attention. She resorted to all sorts of dramatics and hysterics to get it. This only angered me, and with my temper, I thought it best if I just stayed away in my workshop and focused on my work."

"Which only angered her more," Olivia finished with a slight smile. "I can understand."

"I shut her out," Phinn said, pushing his fingers through his hair. "She hated it."

"Any woman would," Olivia said. She tugged his hand. He turned to face her.

This time, when their eyes met, hers weren't filled with fear. Phinn was aware of the soft rise and fall of her chest. Her lips . . . just there. But there would be no stopping this kiss once he started. He wanted to finish this story, leave it in the past and fully surrender to his future with Olivia, no longer haunted by secrets.

Reluctantly he kept talking.

"One night she went out to my workshop, in a fit of rage, of course. She never took an interest in my work. She felt competitive, I suppose. That night, she set fire to the workshop. I think she was trying to get my attention," Phinn said. And that was why he blamed himself. If he'd been better, tried harder, then she wouldn't have resorted to such foolish and drastic measures. That's why Olivia could never have scared him off with her antics. He was too determined to be devoted.

"A fire is one way to get your attention," Olivia remarked.

"She just couldn't get out in time . . ." Phinn said, his voice rough. In his mind, he was back there . . . the scent of smoking disturbing him as he sat down to dinner. He could still feel the way his heart lodged in his throat when he looked out the window and saw the flames—and then glanced at her empty space set at the far end of the dinner table.

He ran to save her. But he'd been too late.

"Something I was working on had fallen. She'd been trapped. And I hadn't gotten to her in time. So you see, I didn't really kill her. Not with my bare hands. But her death was my fault all the same."

Phinn held his breath, waiting for Olivia to

order him to leave. After confessing his entire, sordid family saga to her, he wouldn't blame her if she wanted nothing more to do with him.

But then she surprised him. Always, always, she surprised him.

"I'm so sorry, Phinn," she whispered. And then she somehow soothed the deep-seated fear he couldn't put into words but that weighed on him heavily. "And I'm so sorry for breaking the Difference Engine. I wasn't trying to break it or make you angry. I thought you might be there, which is why I went. Once I saw the engine, I couldn't look away."

There had been too many similarities between the day Olivia was injured and that awful night years ago. But this time she had been going to him, not running from him. This time, he'd saved her.

"But you really oughtn't lock yourself away with the engine," she said. "At least not while I am bedridden and desperate for amusement."

Phinn felt his breath catch.

"Amusement?"

"Just something to take my mind off the pain," Olivia said softly.

"Do you want laudanum?"

"No, just you," she said with the sweetest smile.

With his touch, Phinn distracted Olivia from the pain. He took it away, until there was nothing but pleasure.

Chapter 24

After a season of scandals and one of the rockier courtships this ton has ever observed, Lord and Lady Radcliffe seem to be quite in love. Is it too soon to celebrate their happily ever after?

—THE LONDON WEEKLY

A few weeks later

THEY HAD SETTLED into a comfortable routine. She and Phinn made love in the mornings and took breakfast together before he went off to work on the engine, and she spent the day hobbling around with Emma. They drank tea, read periodicals, shopped for the perfect dress to wear to Lady Penelope's Ball and wrote letters to Prudence, all of which troublingly remained unanswered. Then she and Phinn might attend a ball, or the opera, or just stay in. Once darkness fell, they made love and fell asleep beside each other.

Olivia started to know him in a way she'd never imagined. She learned his body so well that she could paint it from memory—though she occasionally still made him pose for her just because she liked to gaze wantonly at him. She could tell when he was distracted by thoughts of the engine by the far off look in his eye, which was different than how his eyes darkened and his body tensed when something sparked his temper.

She'd become adept at diffusing his anger before it turned into a fiery explosion of devastating and violent rage. But his temper had not sparked much. Things were good.

They were happy.

She was in love.

She had a can't stop thinking about him, lost in his kiss, counting the minutes until they met again, kind of love. Despite everyone's expectations including her own, she'd found herself happily married in time for Lady Penelope's anniversary ball.

She even had the perfect dress.

There was just one problem.

PHINN ARRIVED HOME later than expected. The construction of the engine had hit some snags. Some of the pieces were damaged during the collapse and had to be rebuilt, which slowed their progress considerably. The Great Exhibition was just days away. He and Ashbrooke had planned to debut the engine there, and hopefully catch the attention of a factory owner interested in producing more engines or a printer interested in partnering to publish a new set of ready reckoners.

If nothing came of this event, then all their work was for naught. Their machine was too good, too powerful, too revolutionary to gather dust in a warehouse.

When he walked into their hotel suite, he was plagued with worry, starving, and exhausted, and knew he would probably have to return to work later this evening.

He managed a faint smile for Olivia.

"You're home!" she said, hobbling from the settee and into his arms. He pressed a quick kiss upon her lips. Her ankle had healed marvelously; the doctor attributed it to all the time she had spent in bed, which prompted them to share a wicked smile thinking of the not-resting they did there.

"Have you rung for dinner?"

"How was your day?" she inquired, taking his coat.

"Fine. Long. Tired." Phinn strolled over to the sideboard and poured a whiskey. It was one of those days, and he faced another one tomorrow and the day after that. He probably wouldn't sleep for the rest of the week. "Dinner, Olivia? Did you ring for it?"

"I'll do that now," she murmured. He caught the annoyed glance she gave him. Phinn just sipped his whiskey and vowed to make it up to her later. She returned a moment later.

"Do you notice anything different?" she asked, gazing up at him eagerly.

Phinn studied her and tried, honestly, to discern what it was. He saw her blond hair and the color reminded him of the engine pieces to be remade. Her blue eyes reminded him of the ink with which he drew the plans—and the frantic calculations he'd spent the day poring over. These were not the right things to say. Any fool knew that.

"Tell me," he said, managing a slight smile, though hers became a frown. Damn.

"My dress. It's new. I ordered it for Lady Penelope's Ball." Olivia gave a little twirl so he could admire the dress.

"It's lovely," he said, appreciating the way the blue fabric flattered the flare of her hips and the swell of her breasts. Perhaps he wasn't so tired after all . . . He could lose himself in her curves, soft skin, and the mindless rhythm of making love. He set down the glass and went to embrace his wife.

Olivia flitted away from him.

"You mustn't wrinkle it!" she said, playfully swatting his hands away. But then she smiled coyly and said, "Though the ball isn't until Friday. I suppose it could be pressed."

"Friday?"

"Yes," Olivia replied. "I told you about this weeks ago."

Vaguely, he recalled something to that effect.

"This Friday?" Phinn asked, just to be sure.

"The very one."

Damn. He pushed his fingers through his hair. Sipped his whiskey. Then he broke the bad news.

"I'm afraid I won't be able to make it, Angel," he said regretfully. Of course, he wanted to be by her side constantly. But he *had* to have the engine completed in time. There would only be one opening day of the Great Exhibition and only one chance to make a stunning, spectacular first impression. Everything he had ever worked for was aimed at debuting the Difference Engine before the world.

"But I cannot miss it," she protested.

Phinn wracked his brain for a solution. "Can you go on your own?"

"That would be a fate worse than death," she declared dramatically. He fought to keep his brows from shooting up skeptically.

"Now you're exaggerating," he replied.

That was clearly the wrong thing to say, judging by the vivid flash of her eyes and ferocious expression.

"Why can you not attend?" she asked, and his heart began to thud unevenly.

"The Great Exhibition opens the next morning. I will be too busy finishing the assembly of the engine."

Olivia folded her arms across her chest and narrowed her eyes.

"I see," she said icily.

"Olivia—"

"Can't someone else do it?"

"I'm afraid not. It's too important. It must be done right," Phinn explained. Not only did the machine have to be built, it had to work. Otherwise it was just some rich men's folly, a collection of metal parts with no purpose.

"But this night means so much to me," she pleaded. Her blue eyes gazed up at him, and for a second he wavered.

"It's just a party for your finishing school," he said. He'd graduated from *Oxford,* and they didn't have anniversary balls that he felt compelled to attend. "We attend balls with the same people nearly every night of the week."

"Ashbrooke will be there," she challenged.

"Yes, but he doesn't understand the construction like I do," Phinn said.

"Are you truly picking a machine over your wife?" she asked incredulously. Somehow, this had become a choice between one or the other. Really, though, it was just prioritization. And he was *tired.* And *hungry.*

"It's not like that Olivia. It's my life's work."

"Well finding a husband has been my life's work—because that's all I'm allowed—and I'd like to celebrate that I succeeded."

Wearily, Phinn sighed and said, "If it means so much to you, I can try to be there. But I cannot promise."

Olivia's reply was the slamming of her bedchamber door, leaving Phinn utterly bewildered. It was just another ball, was it not?

"IT'S NOT JUST another ball," Ashbrooke explained a few days later. Phinn had spent nearly every waking moment at work on the engine; when he was in their suite, Olivia sulked and avoided him. He had obviously done something WRONG. Fortunately, Ashbrooke was on hand to translate.

"But it's the same people we see at every other ball, most of whom we don't even speak to. I can barely tolerate them on the best of nights. Usually, I count the minutes until Olivia and I can return home. I won't have the patience for a ton party when there is work to be done on the engine the night before the Great Exhibition."

"If I understand Emma correctly," Ashbrooke began, "this event is the equivalent of St. Peter at the gates. Apparently, no one in the one hundred year history of their finishing school has ever been unwed by their fourth season."

"Was Olivia on her fourth season?" Why didn't he know that? He should know that.

Ashbrooke nodded. "They resorted to desperate measures to wed. Well, Emma did."

"Then I suppose, despite her protestations, Olivia truly won't care if I don't go," Phinn said, "considering how much she tried to not marry me."

"That's what you deduce from four days of utter silence from your wife, save for the slamming of doors?" Ashbrooke asked incredulously. "You may understand physics, but you are clueless when it comes to women."

"I never said otherwise," Phinn muttered.

"I'm given to understand that it is a peculiar form of torture to attend this event while unwed, which Emma and Olivia can attest to, given that they've suffered through it three times."

"It's just a party," Phinn protested. "All they did was marry. It's not like, say, they built an engine that might transform every industry in England."

"First of all, while I might agree, I advise you to *never* utter that sentiment before one of our wives. At least not until after the engine is done. Can't have you murdered by a mob of angry ladies before it's finished. Secondly, who knows what they could accomplish if they were taught something practical during school? Thirdly, it matters to them—therefore it matters to us. If that is not a scientific law, it ought to be."

"But the engine—" Phinn wearily glanced around at the pieces strewn about the room and the half-built machine. Days. They had mere days to complete it.

"Will be done," Ashbrooke declared.

"How do you know?"

"I have confidence in you, Radcliffe," the duke said, clapping him on the back. "And a little jewelry wouldn't be remiss either."

Chapter 25

Just one more day before the Great Exhibition opens! The king will personally review the exhibits before an eager public is admitted.

—THE LONDON WEEKLY

The night before Lady Penelope's Ball

Olivia nervously knocked on the door of a town house on Curzon Street.

Young ladies do not pay calls upon gentlemen.

She smoothed out her skirts and adjusted the angle of her bonnet. She made her own rules now. Besides, Phinn would understand why she had to seek the assistance of another man. At night.

The butler answered the door and appeared surprised to find a proper lady on the front step.

"I'd like to have a word with Lord Rogan please."

She handed the butler her card: *Lady Radcliffe*. Her name was printed in black ink on heavy vellum.

Rogan saw her immediately, of course. He ushered her into the library and offered her brandy, which she declined. Not having much time to spare, Olivia launched into her scheme.

"I'm not sure how Phinn will feel about this," Rogan said nervously when she was finished.

"While I grant that he will put up a fuss initially, he'll eventually see that us joining together is for the best," Olivia said confidently.

"I do owe him . . ." Rogan murmured.

When Olivia and Rogan arrived at the Devonshire Street warehouse, they were not alone. Emma and Ashbrooke had come, too, along with an assortment of footmen and maids from the Ashbrooke residence. Some brought sustenance, wine and candles. Others had come merely to help build possibly the greatest machine the world had seen.

"Phinn?" Olivia called out into the darkness. She saw him bent over a desk, mulling over plans lit by a few paltry candles. As her eyes adjusted to the dim light, she saw pieces of the machine stacked on tables and the floor.

"Olivia? What are you doing here?" He stood and stepped toward her, pushing his fingers through his hair. "I'm sorry that I am not at home, and if this is about the ball tomorrow night—"

"Shhh. I am here to help," Olivia said.

"I as well," Rogan said, stepping forward. The maids and footmen proceeded to light candles, which illuminated the room—and all the others who had come.

"Are you *all* here to help?" Phinn asked, incredulous.

"We await your orders," Ashbrooke said, rolling up his sleeves.

"The pieces have all been constructed. All that remains is assembly," Phinn said.

"Let's lets begin," Olivia said. "Tell us what to do."

Phinn had always worked alone. His family had seen to it—giving him workspace far from the house that was quiet, out of the way, and too much of a bother to walk to. Work was something he did that kept him apart from those he loved and . . . life, really.

So it was a strange, warm, not altogether unpleasant feeling to see the enthusiastic faces of his friends, and his wife, ready to help. This was a gift. This was a generous gesture. This was help he desperately needed. So he grinned and started giving orders.

They worked through the night. The women organized and polished all of the pieces. The men put them into place, connecting them with each other, until the machine rose up before their very eyes.

The sun rose, too, and still the ragtag crew continued to build, because this machine was more important than anything, even much needed sleep. As the hours passed and the Difference Engine grew, Phinn realized he would have never managed this on his own. Perhaps there was more to life than work—as Nadia had so often told him. There were friends who helped a man in their hour of need, and generous and devoted wives who broke the rules concerning what women did or did not do, all in order to get the job done.

It was late afternoon on Friday, hours before

Lady Penelope's Ball, when the Difference Engine was finally completed.

"Now let's see if it works," Ashbrooke declared, rubbing his palms together enthusiastically.

"It has to work," Phinn said.

"If it doesn't, I have some ideas . . ." Rogan offered. Phinn paled. Rogan grinned.

"Someone else present the equation and pull the lever," Olivia said with a shudder.

She had overcome her fear of this great machine in order to help him. The realization brought a lump to Phinn's throat.

"Phinn, you do the honors."

He was one lucky bastard.

The machine worked.

They all cheered because, by God, it worked! Ashbrooke even had tears in his eyes. Phinn clasped Olivia's hand, needing to hold onto someone to remind him that this triumph was real. And it was all possible, he knew, thanks to his lovely and determined wife.

There was just enough time for everyone to return home, nap, and dress. A few hours later they all reconvened at Lady Penelope's Ball. Phinn had accomplished everything he had come to London to accomplish: find a wife and build the Difference Engine. There was only one thing he had left to do . . .

He pulled Olivia into an embrace in a darkened corner of the ballroom—because he could, and because his lovely wife wouldn't mind at all.

"I love you, Olivia, with your own rules," Phinn murmured. He had felt the words for so long, and it felt right to say them.

Olivia gave him that smile he always longed for, wrapped her arms around him and said, "I love you too."

At Lady Penelope's one hundredth anniversary ball, one of London's Least Likely broke the rules, scandalously and passionately kissing London's most notorious man in a secluded corner of the ballroom. It was perfect.

Except for one thing: Where was Prudence?

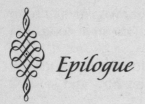

Epilogue

THE ESTATE IN Yorkshire was not the desolate, remote, and terrifying place that Olivia had feared. Radcliffe Manor was a lovely and rambling old stone house surrounded by beautiful gardens, vast lawns, and a forest. There was plenty of space for their four children to run, play, and have adventures.

There was no dungeon. She had checked.

That did not stop her from casually mentioning the possibility of a dungeon whenever one of her children misbehaved.

She and Phinn spent half of the year in London and the other half in Yorkshire. Life in the country was not the vast and lonely expanse of solitude she had feared. Guests came to stay frequently, the neighbors weren't that far and they came often for visits. Between her visiting friends, four rambunctious children, and husband, Olivia was so busy she had hardly any time for embroidery at all.

She did, however, find time to paint, although no one was ever permitted to see the portraits of Phinn she had composed.

Phinn had taken over the East Wing of the house as a workspace. His sons and daughters would tear though in the midst of games, disturbing his focus, but he didn't mind. Just as often, he put them to work polishing lenses or sorting through tools.

However, when his wife interrupted his work, he closed the door to his study. And locked it.

"What is keeping you busy now?" Olivia would ask, wandering through his workspace, looking like a vision, with her fair hair and luscious figure.

Sometimes Phinn told her about his latest project. More often than not he just smiled, pulled her into his arms and murmured, "You, dear wife."

Author's Note

THE DIFFERENCE ENGINE is widely considered to be the world's first computer. The inventor was the Englishman Charles Babbage, who had the idea *in 1821* while reviewing a set of mathematical tables riddled with errors. "I wish to God these calculations had been executed by steam," he is said to have exclaimed. This brilliant mathematician, inventor, philosopher, and charming man about town spent thousands of pounds of his own money as well as government funds to design and build a machine to reliably perform mathematical calculations.

While Babbage is considered a pioneer of computing, he's also known for failing to build the machines he designed—though not without making an incredible effort to do so. He teamed up with Joseph Clement, who was both a highly skilled toolmaker and a talented draftsman. They labored for years to build the machine before having a falling out.

Clement's role in building the machine was the inspiration for Radcliffe. I took the great liberty of imagining a different sort of relationship for Radcliffe and Ashbrooke (who is inspired by Babbage) and indulged in the even greater liberty of making my fictional heroes' efforts a success. One last liberty: the Great Exhibition did not actually take place until 1851, but I thought my heroes needed their own equivalent of Lady Penelope's Ball.

The Difference Engine wasn't built until 1991—just in time for the two hundredth anniversary of Babbage's birth—when a dedicated team from the Science Museum in London endeavored to build it once and for all from the original plans—and to finally discover if it would work. (It did! Brilliant!)

I am completely indebted to Doron Swade's book *The Difference Engine: The Quest to Build the First Computer.* It was a marvelous and riveting account of Babbage's life and the modern day quest to build the engine using Babbage's original plans.

As I embarked on a series of interconnected historical and contemporary romance novels (of which *Wallflower Gone Wild* is the second, after *The Wicked Wallflower*), I was deeply pleased to learn that the computer—of all things!—could be a link between Regency London and modern day New York City. The heroes of my Wallflower series will succeed where Babbage did not (because it's my fictional world and I said so). The hero of my contemporary series, The Bad Boy Billionaire, is a brilliant tech entrepreneur who, like so many men and women today, carry on the pioneering work of innovators like Babbage.

Discover the secret love story behind
Wallflower Gone Wild!

Meet Jane Sparks . . .
She's a modern-day girl trying to make it in the big city—while writing a novel shamelessly based on her own romantic misadventures.

Do become acquainted with Duke Austen. . .
He's a bad boy billionaire with the kind of smile most often found on rogues in romance novels.

Don't break the rules . . .
What began as a fake engagement quickly became something much more real and intense. Jane is falling for her bad boy billionaire but can't be sure if he wants her—or her good girl image. But Jane's shocking scandals conflict with Duke's attempts to be good . . . and the stakes have never been higher.

Keep reading for an exclusive excerpt from
The Bad Boy Billionaire's
Girl Gone Wild

The Bad Boy Billionaire's Girl Gone Wild

Duke and I slipped into one of the intimate red leather booths in the back. The restaurant was small, dimly lit, and decorated in the style of an old school steakhouse. Duke ordered a glass of Macallan 18, and I could tell I annoyed the waiter by ordering only water.

"So are you feeling faint?" Duke asked, apropos of nothing.

"What are you talking about?" That champagne and dancing from earlier had gone to my head.

"The Ashbrooke Effect," he explained. When I looked at him blankly, he explained: "As in the Duke of Ashbrooke. As in the hero of your novel. I'm assuming he's based on me. Vain, I know. But tell me, Sweater Set, am I making you weak in the knees?"

"I'm sitting down," I replied, as I started to get his references to my novel. *Oh dear God, he had obviously read my novel, which was based on us.* Suddenly, my knees did feel weak, even though I was sitting, because I had been counting on the fact that billionaire boys don't read romance novels. Of course, Duke had to be the exception to every rule.

"You look a bit flushed," Duke continued, and I could feel the blush of mortification flaming across my cheeks.

"I've been drinking," I said, and took another sip of water. Frantically, I tried to recall the things I wrote and—I closed my eyes.

"Feeling breathless?"

"I've been dancing," I replied. But really, how was I supposed to breathe when this guy had read the novel about us—that I had poured my heart into?

"Is your heart pounding with anticipation?" His voice was real low now because he had cuddled up next to me in the booth and wrapped his arm around my shoulders, pulling me even closer.

"Yes," I gasped. "Yes."

My heart was pounding, I was breathless, and a little bit dizzy.

"I'm surprised you read it," I said, taking another sip of water.

"I had to know what everyone was talking about," he replied. "And then I had to be able to converse intelligently about it with the author."

"I didn't think you'd read it," I muttered.

"So you never thought that I would find out that you described me as 'so handsome that he sucked all the attention in the room toward himself, as if he possessed his own personal force of gravity.'"

"No, of course not." *Otherwise I wouldn't have published it.*

"Or described yourself as a plain wallflower?"

"Nope. And this is embarrassing," I said.

"It's a good book, Jane," Duke said. "No matter what happens, know that. If it didn't . . .'"

"If it didn't what?" My brain snapped to focus.

"It complicates things," Duke said reluctantly, shifting so he wasn't holding me so close anymore.

"Because of Augustus?" I remembered the articles I read about their big—and overlooked—product launch because everyone was talking about my book and the anger of the big and overlooked investor.

"Yes," Duke said grimly. "But not just him. I'm a private person, Jane."

I couldn't help it—I burst out laughing.

"What's so funny about that?"

"You share everything about yourself online! You're in the papers, the blogs, on Twitter, Instagram, and on social networks I've never even heard of!"

"Yeah, but I notice I never tell them anything really personal or revelatory about me. It's all about Project-TK or the industry."

"It's true, isn't it? You don't tell anyone what you're thinking or feeling. No one really knows you, do they? Even me." I remembered being so frustrated knowing which articles he'd read, or having seen pictures of meals he ate, but having no idea how he felt about me.

"I told you things, Jane, that I never told anyone else. And now I see them published for everyone to read and make assumptions," Duke said.

I glanced up at him. His expression was inscrutable, but I saw the tension in his jaw. He took a sip of his whiskey.

"Ashbrooke . . . he's just made up," I said. It wasn't a total lie. Ashbrooke was fictional. He was just inspired by Duke.

"And Sam or Bennett or whoever?" Duke turned to face me.

"All right, so I used a bit from *my* personal life."

"Did I ruin your date the other night?"

My heart was pounding again as I whispered, "What if I said no?"

"Everyone thinks you're mine," he said. "And I'm starting to believe it, too."

"You say that as if it's a bad thing," I said.

There was something he was keeping from me. I could tell. It was there in the way he refused to meet my gaze and instead took a long sip of his expensive whiskey. It was in the way I had a sudden tremor of fear. All teasing aside, the success of my fictional book was causing real problems with Duke and me.

"Duke . . ." I rested my hand on his arm and tried to soothe away the tension I felt there. "I just wanted to write. I had something to prove to myself and to everyone. You understand that. I know you do."

He gruffly agreed.

"I could unpublish it, I guess." As soon as the words were out of my mouth, I regretted them. Because I *could* do it didn't mean I wanted to diminish my accomplishment in order to raise his.

"No, I wouldn't ask that of you," Duke said strongly. "It's just that Grey is pissed that all the media attention was focused on my fiancée's 'smutty bodice ripper'—his words not mine—instead of our new product launch."

I looked into his eyes and there was no denying the truth.

"He's not the only one pissed," I said softly. "You are, too."

Duke set down the now empty glass of whiskey hard on the table, making the cutlery clink and the candle flicker.

"I just worked so damned hard to build it. It was a huge risk and everyone was skeptical but I believed and I made my team believe, too. And now . . . for what? People aren't talking about it, which means they're not using it."

"I'm so sorry." I was. I positively ached with remorse. I just never thought anyone would actually read my book, let alone people in the tech industry. "If it weren't for that blogger overhearing Roxanna talk about it, this wouldn't be an issue. I didn't plan this. I wouldn't ever plan this. I am so sorry."

"It complicates things. The reason we're together is so that your good girl image can make me seem like an upstanding, responsible guy.

And now you wrote this book that has everyone thinking we're a sham. And then there are pictures of you dancing on a banquette."

"What?" I gasped. He grinned wryly and handed me his iPhone. The picture was dark, but light and clear enough: I was standing on a banquette with Roxanna beside me, we were both singing along to the song, waving our arms and sipping our glasses of champagne.

"That was from two hours ago!"

"I don't want to do this, Jane but—" There was a tense moment of silence when the waiter arrived with another glass of Macallan, which Duke immediately sipped from.

"You're going to pick your company over me," I said flatly. Why, why, why did my heart ache to say the words? I knew from the start that things between us were just pretend. Except somewhere along the line my feelings for him became all too real.

He gazed down at me, blue eyes full of sadness. That was what started to undo me—he did *care*. But I had fucked things up.

The champagne buzz was starting to wear off and a headache was taking its place.

"I want you both," he said softly. "But things can't go on like this. I can't ask you to give up your work for mine. But I can't slack off on Project-TK now. We're prepping for the IPO, Jane. Twenty billion dollars are on the line here. This is bigger than me and you."

"I get it," I murmured. And then, gazing into his eyes, I confessed: "I just don't like it."

This was the closest we'd come to talking about our feelings. What remained unspoken, but was finally understood, was that this was no longer just an act for either of us.

I could see it in his eyes. This guy liked me. Wanted me. Was tortured because of it. I could also see that his brilliant, billion dollar brain was coming up with an alternative course of action.

"Or . . ." he murmured, eyes lighting up. "We put the word out that we've broken up."

Telling people we had broken up wasn't the same as *actually* breaking up.

"Just thinking as a novelist here and not a jilted pretend girlfriend—do you think a breakup right now will really quiet all the rumors that we faked a relationship so you could score a hundred and fifty million dollar investment?"

"You wouldn't be a jilted girlfriend. We could still see each other in secret."

"A secret romance," I murmured. "I'm the one that's supposed to come up with that stuff."

"Fodder for your next book," he said with a grin. "What do you say, Jane? Want to be my secret lover?"